Dear Reader,

As a child, two things that gave me the most reading pleasure were cleverly crafted mystery novels and the heartwarming inspirational stories in *Guideposts* magazine. After reading them, I always came away with the conviction that I, too, wanted to write stories that entertain, puzzle, and uplift people. Many years later, when the editors at Guideposts Books asked me to write for their faith-based mystery series, Secrets of Mary's Bookshop, I couldn't say yes fast enough!

By the Book involves a mysteriously ignited fire at the bakery next to Mary's bookshop. As grace would have it, I happen to be married to a knowledgeable (and handsome) fire chief who generously supplied me with lots of helpful research and plot suggestions. (Thanks, honey!) And as the written pages piled up, it soon became apparent that secondary character Carol Bates and I share a common trait. As you read the story, see if you can figure out what that trait is.

Writing for Secrets of Mary's Bookshop brings together for me the best of both worlds—mystery and faith—a satisfying blend of elements that engage both the head and the heart. May God bless and keep you … throughout today, and throughout your life.

Love and grace,
Carolyn Greene

Secrets of Mary's Bookshop

A New Chapter by Kristin Eckhardt
Rewriting History by Vera Dodge
Reading the Clues by Charlotte Carter
The Writing on the Wall by Elizabeth Mattox
By Word of Mouth by Diane Noble
A Book by Its Cover by Elizabeth Adams
Poetry in Motion by Kristin Eckhardt
Missing Pages by Vera Dodge
Between the Lines by Elizabeth Adams

SECRETS *of* MARY'S
BOOKSHOP

By the Book

Carolyn Greene

Guideposts

New York

Published by Guideposts
16 E. 34th St.
New York, NY 10016
Guideposts.org

Acknowledgments

Every attempt has been made to credit the sources of copyrighted material used in this book. If any such acknowledgment has been inadvertently omitted or miscredited, receipt of such information would be appreciated.

"From the Guideposts Archives" originally appeared in *Daily Guideposts 2005*. Copyright © 2004 by Guideposts. All rights reserved.

Cover and interior design by Müllerhaus
Cover illustration by Ross Jones from Deborah Wolfe, Ltd.
Typeset by Aptara, Inc.

Printed and bound in the United States of America
10 9 8 7 6 5 4 3 2 1

To Floyd Greene, my resident fire chief.
After all these years, you still light my fire.

ACKNOWLEDGMENTS

Thanks to Madelyn Smith and GIG of Richmond for all you've taught me. I will use that knowledge for the rest of my life, and it pleases me to share some of it in this book.

Much gratitude to Tracy Dunham for the brainstorming sessions. I love how your mind works, and thanks especially for your friendship. Fondness and a heart full of appreciation go to Kristin Eckhardt for the encouragement, support, giggles, and the fun phone "visits" that make it seem like you're right around the corner instead of 1,300 miles away. Our DNA may not match, but I'm convinced we're twins who were separated at birth.

ONE

M ary Fisher led the way between the shelves to the back of the bookshop and started arranging chairs in rows for tomorrow's event. Twenty-something Nicole Hancock followed like an eager puppy. The younger woman, a mother of two small children, bounced excitedly on her toes while she watched Mary work. Mary smiled and found herself getting caught up in Nicole's enthusiasm.

"Mary, thank you so much for agreeing to host this learning annex. The people of Ivy Bay have been signing up in droves for your sister's workshop."

"You're very welcome. It's been fun working with you on this project." Mary pointed to the other side of the event space and suggested Nicole start a row of chairs there. "How many people did you say registered?"

Nicole hesitated and patted her pockets, apparently searching for her registration sheet, but she came up empty. "Um, I don't remember exactly, but it was a lot."

Mary nodded and then turned her attention to balancing a promotional sign on an easel. When the head waitress from the Black & White Diner across the street had come to her with the idea of hosting a learning annex for residents and tourists, it seemed like a great way to attract customers to the bookshop and give something back to the community.

As for Mary's sister Betty, whose passion was gardening, she just loved to talk about all aspects of one of her favorite hobbies, so she was happy to help out. If it weren't for the pain of her rheumatoid arthritis, she'd spend even more time working in their idyllic backyard. Unfortunately, Mary had noticed her stoic sister wincing in pain lately, and wished, as she often did, that there were something she could do to relieve Betty's discomfort.

Mary placed the easel at an angle to provide easy viewing from the chairs Nicole had helped to carefully arrange. Event planning was still new to Nicole, so instead of fretting, Mary had just taken a guess on the number of people signed up and had squeezed a few more chairs into the space facing the fieldstone hearth, which was on the back wall of the shop.

She stood back from the easel and admired the computer handiwork that her employee's seven-year-old daughter Ashley typed, cut, and pasted on the flip chart. "Pest-Free Gardening without Pesticides, featuring gardening enthusiast Betty Emerson. Tuesday, August 23, at 10:00 AM." A photograph of Betty graced the center of the poster.

Anyone who saw the photo would say the speaker was a young sixty-four years old. Mary smiled at the image. Petite like herself, with kind blue eyes and honey-blonde hair, her sister's expression gave no clue of the pain she was suffering from arthritis. Mary gave a sympathetic look to the photo as if to say, "Hang in there, Bets."

Nicole sidled up to her and thumbed the edge of the flip-chart sheets, then cast Mary a lopsided smile. "There are lots of extra pages here for us to fill with the workshops we'll be covering the rest of the year," she said, a note of excitement tingeing her voice. Before Mary could respond, she rushed on. "I've always loved social functions, and I have plenty of ideas to draw people in…."

The pretty blonde pushed her long hair behind her shoulder and practically quivered with anticipation as she talked about her ideas. Mary remembered being almost this excited when she opened her bookshop here in the small Cape Cod town of Ivy Bay not too long ago. When Nicole had come to her with the idea of presenting a series of workshops, Mary had considered it a great way to get to know more people in the community and welcome them into the bookshop.

Mary recalled their first conversation about the idea to team up. "I've always dreamed of becoming an event planner, and I'm looking forward to learning from you," Nicole had said, in a way that touched Mary's heart. The young woman had certainly done her homework, which had impressed Mary. The idea was for them to team up to present a learning annex focusing on a different subject by a local expert every other week or so, until the end of autumn. After a long talk and some sincere prayers, Mary had believed that the project "had wings," as Nicole had said in her description of the soaring success she anticipated. But Mary suggested they should start with just one annex and see how it went. And spurred on by her friend's enthusiasm, Mary had cautiously agreed to host the workshops in her bookstore and see where the Lord led them.

Mary sat on one of the chairs they'd just lined up and took in what Nicole was saying. Gus, Mary's cat, hopped up beside her as if sensing she might need something to do with her hands. He arched his back against her arm, and she automatically ran her fingers over his soft gray fur.

Nicole had a grand plan, but it was very ambitious, and they hadn't even presented their first workshop yet. "Let's see how tomorrow's event turns out before we start fussing over the next one," Mary said with a grin, trying to be supportive without being condescending.

Without missing a beat, Nicole scooted onto the seat beside Mary. Gus hopped down, apparently bored with the conversation, and strolled to a stack of books, his tail swaying as he walked. "We've already taken in a nice amount of money for Betty's gardening workshop," Nicole said. "With your help, I know the learning-annex series will continue to be a big success." She slowed down a moment, as if suddenly realizing she might have gotten a little too carried away. Then she said, somewhat hesitantly, "I really appreciate your help in moving forward with the program." Nicole turned to face her more directly, and their knees bumped. "We really do make a great team."

Mary liked Nicole. She was smart and earnest, and they got along very well together. But a sense of hesitation pulled at Mary's heart, urging her to slow down and not get too caught up in her friend's enthusiasm. Last month, when Nicole had suggested organizing the learning-annex series, she had happily accepted. She had no regrets and was glad to be involved. But, as a conscientious businesswoman, Mary had learned to carefully plan out all her business decisions and ask for God's blessing and guidance on seeing them through. And, as a woman of faith, she had learned to listen to that quiet voice inside that urged her to wait. Right now, something told her to go slowly.

"I really appreciate your trust in me," Mary said, grasping the young woman's hands in her own. "But, like I said, let's get through this first workshop, and maybe one or two more after that, before we plan too far out. And in the meantime, let's both pray and ask God to show us His will as we do these projects together."

Mary had already been praying for tomorrow's event to go smoothly, especially since her sister was the guest instructor, and she wanted it to be a success for her sake. More than that, she prayed Betty's arthritis wouldn't prevent her from sharing her gardening knowledge. On good days, you'd hardly know Betty had a health concern. On not-so-good days, she needed to stay home and get extra rest. Betty rarely complained, but Mary almost always knew when she was going through a rough time.

"Yes, of course. Praying is a good idea." The young woman squeezed her hand, then leaned forward to glance at Mary's watch. "Oh my! It's almost time for my shift to start. I have to get ready for the lunch crowd before they start clamoring for the daily specials. We're serving seafood quiche today."

She leaned over and gave Mary a quick hug before dashing out the door. The bell over the shop door jangled to announce her departure. A moment later, it jangled again when Nicole popped her head back in.

"I'll see you tomorrow morning at Betty's talk," she called. Then she was gone again.

At the front of the shop, pigtailed Ashley sat behind the cash register on a swivel stool, watching Nicole dart across Main Street to the diner.

Looking out the shop's big front window, Ashley watched her enter the diner, then gave herself a twirl on the stool. The little girl's joyous approach to the little pleasures in life was infectious. And her giggle reminded Mary how important it is to enjoy all of life's little moments.

Ashley's mother, Rebecca, and Mary exchanged glances and tried to stifle their smiles. Rebecca Mason was the official employee of the shop, but whenever young Ashley was around, she served as the "filler-inner." The precocious child with the pale blonde hair had spent many days in the shop this summer, ringing up sales on the old-fashioned cash register, tidying up, and reading books that she later recommended to customers. Her least favorite thing was to be treated like a little kid, so Mary tried not to show her grandmotherly amusement at the cute things she said and did.

Ashley picked up the pencil cup and upended it, sending pencils of varying lengths rolling across the counter. She removed the short ones and set them aside for Mary to take to church, where they would be placed on the backs of pews for use by parishioners. Then she gathered up the longer pencils and turned to Mary. "I'll sharpen some pencils for the students to use tomorrow."

"Thank you. Before you do that, would you like to be my assistant gofer girl? I'm going next door to pick up some iced sugar cookies for tomorrow's workshop participants, and I could use some help."

Sweet Susan's Bakery provided a constant source of temptation for Mary and was the cause of a couple of extra pounds—especially since Susan had started offering this season's special of cinnamon rolls shaped like little lobsters.

Tourists loved the edible souvenirs that gave a nod to New England, and Mary loved their melt-in-your-mouth goodness.

"Do you want me to be the conscience that sits on your shoulder?" Ashley grinned and shook her finger. "*Noooo* cinna-lobsters for *youuuu*."

Rebecca made an amused choking sound and turned away.

"I don't think that will be necessary," Mary said, suppressing a grin. "But I would be most charmed if you would be my assistant cookie carrier."

Ashley returned the longer pencils to the cup and stepped out from behind the counter to join Mary with a salute. "At your service."

Mary and Ashley were greeted with a tantalizing array of smells when they walked into Sweet Susan's Bakery. Cinnamon, blueberry, yeast, and sweet frosting, to name a few. And... burned chocolate?

The owner, a plump, dark-haired woman in her forties, bustled behind the counter in a yellow apron tied around her ample waist, filling orders for a couple of customers. As sweet as the treats she sold, she smiled at the people in line, her eyes almost disappearing into happy crescents. The expression made people feel as welcome as if she were inviting them into her parlor and offering tea and crumpets.

Nearby, a display featured an ever-changing selection of delectable offerings. Flaky croissants, hearty scones, crumbly blueberry muffins (her specialty), loaves of crusty bread, and glistening fruit pies were all strategically placed to tempt buyers into adding "just one more" to their purchases. On any given day, there were at least a half dozen varieties of cookies. Mary hoped there were plenty of cookies left for her to take back for attendees at tomorrow's learning annex.

Standing in line in front of them, a woman in her forties with shoulder-length blonde curls tried to engage Susan in conversation. Susan, being the professional that she was, leaned an ear in the woman's direction while she filled a wax-paper bag with muffins for the two at the counter.

Behind the order counter, a large pass-through window allowed customers a peek at the prep table and, beyond that, a glimpse of the antiquated oven that produced the goodies Susan sold every day. Mary especially loved to watch Susan assemble and decorate her fabulous wedding and special-occasion cakes. Today, the prep table held two large pans of something an unfortunate shade of black. In the far back, Susan's husband slammed the oven door with more force than necessary, then took off his baseball cap and smacked the dials with it. He muttered something unintelligible. Considering his mood, Mary was glad the words hadn't carried to her and her young charge.

She and Ashley must have come in on the tail end of a rush. To the left of the shop, several customers holding telltale Sweet Susan's Bakery bags milled about the round, tiered display table, obviously in no hurry to leave, and several more sat at the three tables by the picture window looking out onto Main Street.

The chatty blonde customer ahead of them in line shifted from one foot to the other in front of the daily specials board.

Mary quickly clapped a hand over Ashley's eyes, and they both pivoted away from the sign on the counter announcing today's specials.

Ashley started their little game of trying to determine, by smell alone, the specials of the day. "I guess your yummy cinna-lobsters and blueberry muffins."

"And I guess iced raisin bread and"—Mary sniffed but the burned chocolate odor was throwing her off—"coffee-mocha cookies."

They turned on their heels and waited for the customer to step away from the dry-erase board that advertised the daily specials. The woman seemed in no hurry, nor did she notice that Susan was preoccupied with activities going on in the kitchen.

"When you first opened the bakery, how did you decide how many of each item to bake? Didn't you worry you'd run out? And weren't you concerned about waste if you baked too much?"

An exasperated sigh emanated from the kitchen area, and Susan stole a worried glance at her husband before turning her attention back to her customer. "I made a guess and hoped for the best. After a while, you start to develop a sense of what sells well and which days tend to be busier." She gave the woman a patient smile. "What can I get for you, Carol?"

The woman positioned her cheetah-print glasses on her nose and took her time studying the goodies in the glass display case. "How about a whole-wheat spiced-applesauce cupcake? I'm trying to eat healthier lately."

After she moved to the cash register to pay for her cupcake, Ashley pointed to the specials board. "Cinna-lobsters and blueberry muffins!" she declared. She fisted a tiny hand and pulled it to her chest in a gesture of victory.

"There's iced raisin bread." Mary paused. "And New England brownies. You win, so we'll ask Susan to decorate one of those sugar cookies especially for you."

They stepped up to the counter, where Mary noticed keys lying beside the cash register. The first time Mary had spotted keys there, she assumed they'd been left by a customer. Since that time, she had come to see the keys as a sign that a crowd of early-morning customers had swarmed the shop as soon as Susan opened up and unlocked the cash register. She gave a little prayer of thanks for her neighbor that business was flourishing today.

Carol stepped away from the register, peeled away the cupcake liner, and sank her teeth into the treat.

Susan shut the cash-register drawer and plopped two orange meringue candy kisses on a bit of wax paper. She turned her full attention to Mary and Ashley and slid the candies across the counter to them. "So nice to see my favorite bookstore owner and her trusty sidekick."

Ashley's eyes widened at the unexpected gift. She thanked Susan heartily and acted out her bliss as the sweet confection melted on her tongue.

"What can I get for you today?" Susan asked Mary.

Before Mary could order, Susan's husband, Ryan, came to the front and declared they needed a new oven.

Susan's easy smile suddenly went south. "If wishes were horses..."

Ashley bounced on her toes. "I know that nursery rhyme! 'And if "ifs" and "ands" were pots and pans, there'd be no work for tinkers!'" She pulled a thoughtful frown. "Whatever that means."

Ryan seemed lost in his own thoughts and spoke more to himself than to his wife. Even so, his deep voice reverberated throughout the tiny shop, probably more than he would have wanted. "If I replace one of the wires, tweak the gas intake, and hold my tongue just right, I might be able to keep it limping along until we can afford a new one." He lifted his New York Yankees ball cap and ran anxious fingers through his thinning hair. The gesture left a greasy stripe across his forehead. As an afterthought, he noticed Mary and Ashley and nodded in their direction.

Susan nodded. "As long as you can keep it from burning more brownies like it did this morning, I'll be happy."

Ah, so that was the burned-chocolate smell. And it explained the blackened pans on the prep table.

The reminder that more baked goods had been sacrificed to the vintage oven provoked a disgruntled response from Ryan. He shook a fist in the direction of the kitchen and grumbled something about an eye for an eye and putting the decrepit machine out of its misery. After he was done with his momentary rant, he mentioned that he needed to pick up a part from Jimmy's Hardware.

Susan gave her husband a quick once-over. Covered in grease and grime, he needed a power washing before he was fit to be seen in public, much less touch anything between here and the hardware store, which was only two doors down. "I'll go get it for you," she offered. "Just let me take Mary's order first."

Mary made a shooing motion. "You go ahead now, while there's a lull in activity. Ashley and I can wait. In fact, we're still deciding what color icing we want on our cookies."

Ryan wrote down the part he needed and said Jimmy would help her if she had any questions. "This ought to cover it," he said, pulling a twenty out of his wallet. He frowned at the now-empty bill section, then folded the wallet and stuck it back in his hip pocket.

"Thanks. I'll be right back."

While his wife hurried out of the shop, Ryan turned to Mary and splayed his work-darkened hands. "I'd take your order, but I don't think you'd like this flavor." He shrugged and gave her a wry smile. Mary wisely declined.

He disappeared back into the kitchen, and Ashley wandered through the store, straightening jars of wild beach plum jam and stacking souvenir recipe postcards so they were easier for customers to see.

The woman whom Susan had called Carol made a sour face at the cupcake in her hand and mumbled something about liking her own frosting recipe better.

At first, Mary wasn't sure whether she was talking to her, so she didn't reply. The woman belched delicately. Her blue eyes widened with embarrassment behind her cheetah-print glasses, and she hastily put a hand to her mouth.

"Pardon me!" She held the half-eaten cupcake at arm's length and glared at it with suspicion. Then she turned to Mary and met her gaze directly. "That kind of rudeness isn't like me. I'm beginning to wonder if the cream cheese in the frosting might have turned."

If that were the case, Mary thought it odd that she would have symptoms after taking only a couple of bites. She darted a glance through the tiny shop to see if anyone had overheard the comment. It wouldn't do to start rumors about Susan's baking. Fortunately, the few people remaining in the shop continued going about their activities, including Ashley, who was straightening a jacket on the wall hook opposite the cash register.

"I'm sure the frosting is fine," Mary said, knowing she sounded a bit defensive on her friend's behalf. "Susan is very particular about all the ingredients she uses."

Carol tossed the remainder of the cupcake into the trash can. Then she fished in her purse, pulled out a ratty roll of antacids, and peeled back the blue-and-white paper. She popped a white tablet into her mouth and continued on as if she hadn't interrupted herself. There were obviously issues she wanted to discuss.

"You know, this is a nice shop, but you'd think there would be more than one bakery in Ivy Bay. Customers like to have choices about where they buy their cupcakes."

Mary didn't know what to say to that. She was spared a response when a sharp bang rang out from the kitchen. A glance in that direction showed Ryan preparing to deliver another kick to the cantankerous oven, but the bell over the door signaled Susan's return, and he restrained himself.

The woman who'd ditched her spiced-applesauce cupcake grimaced and trotted briskly past the checkout counter to the back of the shop. Ryan passed her on his way to the front and shot Mary a quizzical look.

"What's wrong with her?" he asked.

She shrugged. "Indigestion, I suppose."

Susan handed Ryan the bag from Jimmy's Hardware, and he disappeared back into the kitchen. Although her husband hadn't noticed anything amiss, Susan's tight-lipped expression told Mary something was wrong.

"Susan? What's the matter?"

Her friend moved behind the counter, as if being in that familiar place made her feel a little better. "Oh, it's nothing," she said, waving a hand. "Just a weird little altercation with Jimmy's nephew."

"The boy who's helping out this summer?" Mary had seen the teen a couple of times and found him to be somewhat aloof. Like he had a chip on his shoulder.

"Yeah. Tyson. I gave him a twenty for a seven-dollar purchase, and he handed back a couple of ones and some coins. No ten. When I politely pointed it out, he got all huffy." Susan's cheeks reddened at the memory. "Jimmy overheard, and he stepped in to straighten it out."

"Good. You got the ten back."

"Yes, but the boy flung the money on the counter and said, 'I might not be Goody Two-shoes, but I never steal.'" She looked as though she might cry. "Mary, I just assumed it was an innocent mistake. I never accused him of stealing."

"I'm sure you didn't." Mary reached across the counter and patted Susan's arm. "He probably has some issues of his own that he's dealing with, and you just happened to be a handy target for him to lash out at."

Susan sniffed and busied herself with straightening the counter. "You're probably right."

She frowned and patted the counter near the cash register. "Have you seen my keys? I could have sworn I left them right here."

Mary had just seen them a moment ago, so they couldn't have gone far. "Maybe Ryan put them away."

Carol returned from the bathroom, her ruddy complexion now a sickly gray, and paused at the cash register. "Just so you know...your cupcake gave me food poisoning. You might want to check the expiration date on your cream cheese so no one else gets sick."

She was gone before Susan could say a word in response. Baffled and clearly overwhelmed by all the problems that had presented themselves in the short time Mary had stood in line, Susan blinked hard, and a small tear glistened in her lashes.

Mary reached across the counter and squeezed her hand. "It's just not your day, is it?" Mary knew she would worry over Carol's troubling comment. Susan wanted all her customers to be happy.

She shook her head. "No one in the food business wants to hear something like that, but I'm glad she told me so I can fix matters."

Mary seriously doubted there was anything wrong with the cupcake, but she knew her friend would take the comment seriously and do whatever it took to keep her customers safe.

Ashley danced back to Mary. "I know exactly what decorations we should ask Miss Susan to put on our cookies. Bugs! Because that's what Miss Betty is going to talk about tomorrow." She clapped her hands, obviously proud of herself for having thought of that. "Flies and beetles and spiders...

Well, maybe not spiders, because they're good bugs for your garden, but maybe aphids. Do you want me to go back to the bookshop and find a picture of an aphid?"

Mary twisted her lips and gave her a thoughtful look. "I wonder how some of our guests might feel about eating bugs?"

The grimace that crossed Ashley's pretty features almost made Mary laugh.

"Good point," Ashley conceded. She turned to Susan. "Maybe we should decorate the cookies with flowers instead."

As good fortune would have it, Susan had already baked an ample supply of sugar cookies but had not gotten around to icing them yet. This meant Mary could take them back to the bookshop today instead of having to order them now and pick them up tomorrow. One more item checked off the to-do list.

"Flowers are an excellent idea." Susan counted out cookies from the display case and squeezed icing on them to form a variety of flowers common to New England. She chewed the inside of her cheek as she worked.

Her culinary artwork may have been cheerful, but Mary could tell Susan's mind had wandered somewhere else.

———

Because of the extra work preparing for Nicole's learning annex, Mary found herself working later than usual to finish her daily bookshop responsibilities. She checked her watch. Barely after nine o'clock. She'd just finished entering the day's receipts. Another half hour stocking new books on the shelves and she'd be ready to go home and have a few minutes of sister time with Betty before hitting the pillow.

She opened a box of books and on top sat *Cape Cod* by Henry David Thoreau, one of her many favorites; it was a small but steady seller among the tourists ever since she'd opened the shop. Despite the work that needed to be finished, Mary opened the book to a random page and found herself drawn into one of its many descriptive passages.

The breakers looked like droves of a thousand wild horses of Neptune, rushing to the shore, with their white manes streaming far behind; and when at length the sun shone for a moment, their manes were rainbow-tinted. Also, the long kelp-weed was tossed up from time to time, like the tails of sea-cows sporting in the brine.

Mary sighed with pleasure and might have lost herself in the beautiful words if not for the ringing of the phone. Who could be calling at this time of evening? She would have let the answering machine pick it up, but on the off chance it might be Betty calling the shop number instead of her cell, she set the book aside and answered.

It was Susan, and she sounded groggy. An early riser, she told Mary she'd already been asleep for a short while but had been awakened by a concern that, in her haste to leave the bakery, she may have left containers of milk on the prep table.

"Ever since Carol Bates got sick after eating one of my cupcakes, I've been questioning myself," Susan said. "Wondering if the cream cheese had turned as she said, but I'm always so careful about using fresh ingredients and keeping them at the proper temperature."

"If no one else got sick, it was probably just a summer virus she picked up."

"No one else got sick because I threw out the rest of the whole-wheat and spiced-applesauce cupcakes and made a new batch of cream cheese frosting." She sighed into the phone. "I tried to call Carol to check on her before I went to bed, but there was no answer."

"Good! Maybe she's feeling better now and is running errands or spending time with friends. Besides, Carol seems rather"—Mary paused in an effort to come up with just the right word to describe the woman's odd behavior—"high-strung, so it's very possible she just overreacted." Mary liked Susan's good-hearted nature. If she had a flaw, it might be that she sometimes cared too much about people.

"That could be, but I hope she's feeling better. Even so, I'm still worried the milk may be going bad on the prep table as we speak. Would you do me a huge favor and go over to double-check?"

When it came to cleanliness and food safety, Susan was a total by-the-book kind of baker. She followed and surpassed all the rules and regulations of her business and had never had any complaints. Not until Carol, that is.

A while back, Mary and Susan had exchanged shop keys in case of emergency, so she'd have no problem letting herself in. "I'll take care of the butter for you, Susan. By the way, did you ever find your keys?"

A short silence ensued while Susan apparently ran the question through her sleep-groggy brain. "No, but I'm sure they'll turn up eventually."

"Go back to sleep, and don't worry about the bakery."

A few minutes later, Mary walked the short distance to the shop next door. Main Street looked different at night. No visitors strolled the tree-lined streets, laughing and enjoying the salt air and historic sights. The shops were closed, the streets bare, and only an occasional car passed by, its headlights cutting through the charcoal dusk.

Mary let herself into the bakery and switched on the light. Passing the front counter, she walked down the hall to the kitchen on the right and flipped on the fluorescents.

Susan must have indeed been in a hurry to leave today. The prep table had been rolled in front of the oven, and both surfaces were piled high with cake boxes, paper bags, and kitchen towels. Mary could only assume her normally tidy friend had been in the middle of assembling boxes and taking inventory before leaving for the day.

Although the prep table lay cluttered with packaging materials, not a single block of butter was included in the mess. She walked to the refrigerator and pulled open the oversize stainless-steel door. To one side of the top shelf, several one-pound bricks of yellow butter sat neatly stacked in preparation for tomorrow's baking.

The sound of the refrigerator door closing seemed louder at night than it would have during the day. But it wasn't just the rubber gaskets sealing in cool air that Mary heard. She could have sworn there had been a simultaneous *clack* from outside the kitchen.

Following the sound, she leaned into the L-shaped storage room and flicked on the light. Nothing out of order on this side of the storeroom, but she didn't go inside to check out the far corner. Everything was now eerily quiet.

An unsettling sensation sent cold, clammy chills down her spine.

Too many mystery novels. Having read hundreds—maybe thousands—of sleuth and detective stories since her youth, those memories and the nighttime stillness combined to create prickles of awareness in her imagination.

Feeling strangely uneasy about being alone in the neighbor's shop so late, Mary went to the back door, stepped into the yard, and looked out into the night. She took a centering deep breath. The businesses on this side of Main Street had their own private backyards, each separated by low fences.

Something darted through the yard, and Mary instinctively backed up the steps to the relative safety of the doorway and watched the movement of the small creature through the well-tended yard.

A cat. Mary released the breath she hadn't realized she'd been holding. The fluffy orange creature had been hanging around the shops a lot lately. Probably a stray searching for a meal. Sympathy for the cat's plight surged through her, and she decided she would try to catch the animal to find out if it wore a collar and tags. But not now. A case of the willies came over her, and all she wanted to do was get out of here.

A movement beyond the gate in the second enclosure to the left caught her attention. Curious, and slightly freaked out, Mary stood on the high stoop and squinted into the semidarkness.

A motion-activated light had already switched on behind the hardware store, and Jimmy's teenage nephew Tyson crossed to the shed at the back of the property, carrying a can of something she couldn't quite make out. If it wasn't from the cat investigating the trash bin, then the opening of the hardware store's back door must have made the noise she heard from inside the kitchen. Like her, Tyson must have been putting in some overtime hours tonight.

Feeling a little silly for having been unnerved by the normal activity of a neighboring business, Mary laughed and stepped back inside. Even so, she had no desire to linger, so she quickly shut off the lights and returned to the bookshop to finish her work.

A short while later, an acrid odor distracted her from her task of breaking down cardboard boxes to reuse. It smelled like a dirty ashtray, but that couldn't be, because Mary didn't allow smoking in the store. Her eyes burned, and her nose started to run.

She walked to the front of the shop and looked out the window, but saw nothing out of the ordinary. Well, maybe a haze around the streetlight, but she couldn't be sure. She peered closer, and that's when she saw it. Smoke, coming from the direction of Sweet Susan's Bakery.

Mary grabbed her keys, unlocked the front door, and rushed outside. Her keys still in her hand, she ran to the bakery and shaded her face to peer in through the picture window. In the back of the shop, beyond the pass-through window, flames leaped and licked and belched thick, black smoke.

Panic swept over her, and she shoved the key in the lock. Just as quickly, she stopped herself. If she opened the front door, the rush of fresh oxygen would feed the fire. She pulled her cell phone out of her sweater pocket and dialed 911.

From behind her, a car came around the corner and moved up Main Street. Mary turned and flagged them down to help, even if all they could do was wait with her until the fire department arrived. The black car moved up the street, its headlights off, and made no effort to stop.

Mary stepped off the sidewalk and into the street and peered after the retreating car. It was too dark to make out the license plate, but there were definitely two people in the car: a male driver and a female passenger with long blonde hair.

"Ivy Bay Police, Fire, and Rescue," the voice on the phone said. "What is the nature of your emergency?"

TWO

◆◆◆

Susan Crosby was among the first after the fire department to show up. The rest were either curious passersby or friends who had heard about the fire and had come to offer support. Susan wore navy slacks and backless sneakers, and an orange knee-length nightie peeked out from under her Windbreaker jacket. Sleep wrinkles creased her cheek. Strangely, her husband, Ryan, was nowhere to be seen.

Susan stepped over a fire hose and clutched Mary's arm as if she were a fatigued swimmer clinging to a life preserver. "Thanks for calling me," she said, her voice small and tight. "And thank God you were here to notice the fire before it got too far out of control."

Mary hugged her, and they held on, each drawing comfort from the other. She hated to think what might have happened if she'd gone home even a few minutes sooner. The fire could have spread to her bookshop, and to Sophie Mershon's tea shop on the other side of the bakery. As it was, the kitchen was fully involved, and the fire had started to move to the front of the shop by the time the fire crew arrived.

"Has anyone told Roger?" At Susan's negative response, Mary pulled out her cell phone and handed it to her.

When she returned the phone, Mary asked, "What did he say?"

"He's on his way."

If you didn't count the fact that he had put off making all but code-enforced repairs to the building, easygoing Roger Cline was a mostly decent landlord. The rent was reasonable, most likely due to the building's state of perpetual disrepair, with its ancient wiring and plumbing, and woodwork that had seen better days. He stayed out of Susan's hair, and she made whatever surface improvements she could, such as painting the chipped plaster walls a cheerful yellow and covering up small eyesores with frilly curtains and eye-catching posters.

By now, a small crowd had started to form. Benjamin McArthur, chief of police, directed his officers on maintaining a safe boundary around the fire scene, and Ivy Bay firefighters swarmed between the noisy fire engine and the bakery, which blasted heat and smoke out of its open door.

A firefighter in sooty yellow turnout gear made his way over to where Susan and Mary stood watching. When he lifted his face shield, Mary felt a surge of relief to see this young man's familiar face. He reached up and twisted what appeared to be the beginning of a handlebar mustache.

A new firefighter, freshly graduated from recruit school, Wyatt Heath had recently gone door-to-door through the business district, offering free fire-safety inspections and advice on where to install smoke detectors. When he came to Mary's Mystery Bookshop, she had happily accepted his offer. And after he'd found a worn extension cord under a rug, she'd been so relieved and grateful that she'd suggested Susan have him check out her shop as well.

"Sorry about your bakery, Mrs. Crosby." Wyatt removed his helmet and wiped sweat from his face. "The fire is mostly under control now, but there's quite a bit of damage to the kitchen, storeroom, and counter area."

Susan trembled, probably from nerves rather than the cool night air. "Do you have any idea how the fire started?"

"The fire investigator will come tomorrow and make the final determination, but from what I can tell, it looks like it started with an electrical short near the oven."

Susan gasped and put a hand to her mouth. "That outlet you pointed out. I put in a call to my landlord like you suggested, but I had to use the oven until he could make arrangements to fix it." She slowly shook her head, apparently going through a littany of what-if's in her mind. "I always do everything by the book. Food safety. Workplace safety. This shouldn't have happened to me."

Considering how long it had taken laid-back Roger to fix the other problems in the building, Mary suspected Susan's lease might have run out long before the electrical outlet got any attention.

Wyatt shrugged off her self-blame. "It might have held out for another couple of years. You never know about these things."

A moment after Wyatt went back to the pumper truck to help pack hose, Ryan showed up, dressed in jeans and a button-front shirt. His gaze flitted distractedly over the scene, and he clenched his hands in what appeared to be futile frustration. Mary spotted her friend Henry Woodrow in the crowd and waved to him. He appeared to have been searching for her, and when his gaze fell on her, relief seemed to melt the tension from his face. As she moved away from the Crosby couple, she heard Susan ask her husband, "Where have you been?"

In a departure from his usual cable-knit sweaters, flannel shirts, and henleys—many bought for him by his late wife— Henry sported a blue polo shirt in deference to the warmer summer temperatures. He made his way to Mary and laid a big hand on her shoulder.

"You had me worried for a moment there. When I didn't find you…"

He didn't need to say the rest. Since she'd mentioned to him earlier today that she'd be working late tonight, she knew, even without his saying so, that as soon as he'd heard about the fire on Main Street, his thoughts had gone straight to her. Her childhood friend had always been very protective of those close to him. It was one of the many positive qualities that she appreciated about him.

"I'm fine, and so is Susan," she assured him. She gestured toward the soot-streaked building. "Unfortunately, we can't say the same for the bakery."

He nodded, taking in the destruction. "Where's Betty?"

"At the house. I called her right after I called Susan. There didn't seem to be any point in her coming, so I suggested she stay at home."

"It's all your fault! You and your cheapskate ways." Ryan's booming voice reached an octave Mary had never heard before.

All heads, including Mary's, turned toward the commotion. Ryan jabbed his finger accusingly at the sheepish landlord whose red face almost matched the pale burgundy henley shirt he wore.

"If you had kept up repairs on the building like you were supposed to, this never would have happened."

Susan closed her hand around Ryan's pointed finger and gently pushed it down to his side. "What's done is done," she said. "Getting your blood pressure up is not going to make it better."

Ryan shook his head and turned to her. "It's bad enough you have to work so hard, using shabby equipment that only functions right part of the time. You don't need *this*"—he waved a hand through the air—"unnecessary catastrophe making matters worse."

"We'll get by," Susan said. "God will see us through."

Despite her brave words, Mary could tell she had her doubts.

By now, Roger had recovered his composure after the verbal attack. "Don't you worry, Miz Crosby. We'll get the repairs started as soon as everything's cleaned up, and you'll be selling cupcakes again in no time."

He stood there beside Henry, arms folded over his chest as they silently watched the firefighters do their work. After a moment, Henry cordially said to the other man, "Looks like you've been fishing recently."

It was something Mary's now-departed husband, John, used to do. In a stressful situation, he would strike up a conversation about some ordinary, everyday activity that seemed to put people at ease. Quite frankly, Mary welcomed the change of subject. Henry's casual tone and the subject of fishing seemed to soothe the frazzled nerves of her and others who listened in on their conversation.

A professional fisherman himself, Henry must have noticed the landlord's red face had come from the sun rather than from embarrassment. Henry loved to talk fishing with anyone and everyone.

Roger blinked at the unexpected change of subject. "Uh, yeah." He rubbed his arm and fidgeted with the knit cuff at his wrist. "Went out on the *Bonnie Sarah* today. Had a really nice time."

Henry was launching into a story about the time his boat *Misty Horizon* got caught in a sudden squall, when Mary caught sight of Chief McArthur. She excused herself to go over and talk to him.

"You're just the woman I wanted to see," the police chief told her. He'd already been going through the crowd, asking who had seen what. Now he opened a notepad and turned his attention to Mary. "I understand you were the first to notice the fire."

"Yes. I smelled the smoke first."

"Can you tell me where you were just before then? What you were doing?" Though professional in every way, he seemed almost embarrassed about the line of questioning. His expression was soft, as if he wanted to give her every opportunity to explain herself.

"Am I a…a suspect?" Mary was stunned. For a brief, irrational moment, Mary's mind flashed back to what she'd said at the diner the day before: That, even as much as she loved Susan, she sometimes wished there weren't a bakery right next door. At the time, she had pinched her own middle and joked about the couple of extra pounds she carried as a result of eating Susan's cinna-lobsters. She didn't see how anyone could take the comment seriously, but you never knew how people might misinterpret the most innocent remarks.

Chief McArthur shook his head. "Not really, Mary. It's just standard procedure. Since you were the one who called in the fire, I just need you to tell me exactly what happened."

Mary gave herself a mental shake. It was silly to be paranoid. She took a deep breath to calm her nerves. Chief McArthur knew she had no motive for wanting to burn her neighbor's place. Mary's Mystery Bookshop was doing well, and there was no way she'd risk damaging her own shop.

She answered his questions as thoroughly and carefully as she could and included the black car she saw driving past with its lights off.

"They may have forgotten to turn them on," he said, but jotted a note about it on his pad. "The streetlights sometimes fool people into thinking they already have their lights on."

When he was done, Mary said good-bye to Susan and Henry and went to her silver Impala, where Gus waited in his carrying case on the front passenger seat. After calling 911, she had rushed back to the bookstore and cornered the frightened cat behind the carpeted claw-foot bathtub in the children's reading nook. He hadn't been happy about the smells and commotion, and now he made a low grumbling noise as if to express his displeasure at having been inconvenienced.

"I'm with you, buddy. Let's go home."

———

Back at the two-story Federal-style house she shared with Betty, Mary let Gus out of his carrier and offered him some of his favorite canned salmon, which he rejected before light-footing his way to the living room where he curled up on the blue-and-white-striped damask sofa. After she switched off the lamp, his eyes gleamed in the mostly darkened room, but Mary wouldn't be joining him for a cuddle in his favorite spot. Not tonight. Tonight she needed to read, even if only for a few minutes, to calm the nervous energy buzzing inside her body before she drifted off to a much-needed sleep.

She turned to tiptoe upstairs to her room, when a soft voice called to her from the bedroom on the main floor. "Mar?"

Mary changed direction and made her way through the dark to Betty's room before her sister found the switch on her nightstand lamp and scooted up in the bed, her back against two fluffy pillows. This used to be the office of her husband, Edward, but after he died, Betty turned it into a bedroom so she wouldn't have to trudge her aching joints up and down the stairs every day.

"I saw a cluster of homeless honeybees today," Betty said without preamble. "They were swarming down in that wooded area at the end of the block. Too bad we don't know any beekeepers so they can round them up and add them to their hives."

Mary knew her sister well enough to realize Betty was delaying the moment when Mary would give her the unfortunate details about Susan's bakery. She was bracing herself, preparing for the bad news. More than that, she was giving Mary a chance to calm her nerves before rehashing the drama she had witnessed over the previous couple of hours.

Mary nodded and followed Betty's lead. "I'm sure someone at the garden center will be able to put us in touch with a beekeeper. If you'd like, I'll drive us over to Tanaka's in the next day or two."

"That's a good idea," Betty said. "I need to buy some grass seed while we're there."

Mary moved to the opposite side of the bed and slid in beside her sister. Betty slipped a hand into hers, and Mary gently kissed the gnarled fingers. Those fingers had dressed dolls with her when they were young children, helped Mary apply her first strokes of mascara, and later fastened the buttons on Mary's wedding dress. Now they patted her hand. The simple touch comforted her, and Mary felt her tense muscles relax like melting cheese.

"How's Susan?" her sister asked, finally broaching the subject.

Mary had been about to ask how Betty was feeling, but her sister didn't have much patience with listing her own aches and pains. As always, Betty focused on others. "Upset. And worried about lost income until the damage is repaired."

"Susan is a smart lady and a hard worker. She'll find a way to work things out. And I'm sure the people of Ivy Bay will pitch in to help in whatever way they can."

Mary nodded. The sense of community that the inhabitants shared had been a big factor in her decision to return to the town where she was born. Though her family had moved away to Boston when she was three, many happy childhood summers had been spent here. It was only after Mary's husband, John, died that she realized how much she needed to be near not only her sister but also the salt air, the charming and welcoming old-fashioned buildings, and the people of Ivy Bay, whom she'd come to think of as her extended family.

"We can cancel your pest talk tomorrow, if you want."

Betty smiled. "Only if that's what *you* want. As for me, I've found that, in troubling times, it's best to act as normal as possible."

Mary shook her head. Betty had certainly seen her share of troubling times and had plenty of practice trying to keep her days as normal as possible. "We'll need to be well rested for our learning gig tomorrow."

She started to scoot off the bed, but Betty tightened her frail grip on Mary's hand. "Susan needs our prayers."

Mary returned to her sister's side, and together they asked God to comfort Susan and give her the strength to put her shop back together and get her business operating again.

THREE

The next morning, Mary moved the learning annex to the bookshop's lovely backyard since the store still smelled of smoke. She propped the front and back doors open and placed a large box fan at the back to draw out the odor. Ever the optimist, Betty had declared the yard a better venue for a gardening talk than indoors anyway. Not to mention, Betty had argued, it was where her gardening skills were already on display in the shrubs and flowers she had already planted there.

All told, about twenty residents and tourists either milled about the backyard or sat in the rows of folding chairs Mary had moved outside, chatting as they waited for the workshop to begin. Even Tess Bailey, the owner of Bailey's Ice Cream Shop across the street, had taken time off from work to attend. Mary gave thanks for the beautiful seventy-two degree weather. She had taken care to set up a couple of patio umbrellas, and one of the attendees—a pale young woman with a bandanna wrapped around her short hair—claimed a chair in the shade. The fluffy orange cat, which had just started showing up recently, arched his back against the woman's leg, and she reached down to pet it.

Mary grabbed the plate of Susan's exquisitely decorated cookies, introduced herself, and offered the treats to the grateful attendees.

"So you're *the* Mary of Mary's Mystery Bookshop," the girl in the bandanna said as she selected a cookie with a daisy on it. She couldn't have been more than nineteen or twenty.

"Perhaps I should have called it Mary's Mystery Bookshop and Miscellaneous Events," Mary joked, with a wave toward the coffee table behind her.

Beside the seating area, under the shade of a red maple tree, the antique coffee table had been brought out from the bookshop and loaded with an assortment of books and magazines on gardening, canning, and Cape Cod wild flowers that she'd ordered specifically for this event, in hopes of coaxing a few sales. Mary noted the scarred finish on the coffee table. She hadn't realized until just now, with the midmorning sun illuminating its flaws, that it really did need a new finish.

"I love the selection of mysteries you have in your shop," the young woman said. "I've been doing a lot of reading lately, and a cute little blonde-haired girl in your shop suggested a couple of Agatha Christie novels."

"Yes, she's one of my favorite authors. I hope you enjoyed the books."

"Sure did. I'm Melody, by the way," she said, wiping cookie crumbs off her fingers before reaching to shake Mary's hand. "I'll be coming back for more books, at least for the next few weeks."

The girl's statement and pale complexion suggested to Mary that she was either in Ivy Bay on an extended vacation or she was recovering from an illness. Mary suspected the latter.

"Excellent. Be sure to look for me and say hello when you pop in. Any of us in the shop will be glad to help you find some good stories."

Though Mary didn't know the exact nature of the girl's ailment, God did, so she said a silent prayer and asked for healing.

While the attendees browsed through the books, talk turned to last night's fire.

"It's a miracle the fire didn't spread to any other buildings on this block. That would have been a shame."

"I heard it was set by a gang member as an initiation rite."

"Nah, there aren't any gangs in Ivy Bay. Somebody probably left the doughnut fryer on, and the grease caught fire."

It was no surprise that the fire had captured their attention. Yellow tape stretched across the front of the bakery, and a Cape Cod fire investigation vehicle remained parked out front while officials finished poking through the burned mess.

Mary would have set them straight, but a glance at her watch told her it was time to introduce the featured speaker. Betty finished arranging the natural pest-control samples on the umbrella table in preparation for her talk. She showed no sign of nerves or any fatigue from their late bedtime. And after Mary's glowing introduction, she delivered her information like a pro, fielding questions with an ease that came from decades of identifying various pests and saving her plants from their voracious mandibles and destructive nesting practices.

Neem oil, food-grade diatomaceous earth, and even diluted dish liquid were among her environment-friendly solutions to the ongoing battle between humans and insects. Attendees hastily scribbled notes on the pads Mary had provided, and toward the end, Betty led them around the yard, searching for signs of insect damage to show them on the shrubs and flowers that lined the perimeter. When the hour was up, the participants applauded Betty, and several clustered around her to ask some final questions. Mary couldn't have been prouder of her sister at that moment.

Nicole had arrived a bit late but in plenty of time to see just how much of a success the workshop had been.

"*Yessss!*" she said, holding her fists up like a world-wrestling champion. "That was fabulous. Congratulations on a fantastic event. Betty, you were pitch-perfect." She snitched a cookie from the plate on the coffee table and nibbled around the pansy decoration. "And, Mary, all the darling little touches you thought of made everything extra special."

Mary smiled, more than a little pleased herself. It always made her feel good to offer products and services that made her customers happy.

Obviously flush with the excitement of having produced such a successful event, Nicole said, "I overheard that older gentleman over there ask you what the next workshop will be about. I told him to check back with us, so it looks like we already have a customer for our next workshop."

Mary followed her gaze across the yard to the older man who sipped some punch and spoke to a fellow attendee. Nearby, Tess spoke to Betty, then made her way through the stragglers toward her and Nicole. The pleasantly plump woman wasn't wearing her white bib apron this morning, and her pale yellow shirt seemed to intensify the glints of auburn in her hair. Tess thanked Mary for hosting such an informative and interesting workshop, and the warmth and praise in her voice made Mary feel as if she'd just conquered Mount Everest.

"Betty's talk makes me think rose-petal ice cream might just have to be a future offering in my shop," Tess said.

At that, Nicole swiveled to face her and tilted her head. Hopefulness lacing her voice, she asked if Mary would be willing to host another workshop. "I was thinking that, before the weather turns cool, it would be nice to offer a learning annex on how to make your own ice cream. Perhaps you and Tess could be coinstructors?"

"I'd love to," Tess said, without a moment's hesitation. "That is, if Mary is so inclined."

Taken aback by the suggestion, Mary hesitated. Honored and humbled to be asked to teach a class alongside an ice-cream pro, she didn't think Nicole would need her when they had Tess.

"Come on, Mary," Nicole urged. "Everyone in Ivy Bay knows you're the mastermind behind some of those quirky flavors Tess features at Bailey's."

In her usually gracious manner, Tess embraced the idea. "Do say yes. Teaching a workshop together would be a wonderful opportunity to get to know each other even better."

Despite a couple of minor hitches, Betty's pest-free gardening session had gone quite well, so Mary agreed and found herself looking forward to rolling up her sleeves and experimenting with new ice-cream flavors. Nicole practically danced with delight, and Tess beamed with pleasure.

If all continued to go well, she and Nicole might be teamed up on this learning-annex project for the rest of the season. Or longer.

———

The remainder of the morning flew by in a blur. Just as Mary had hoped, many of the workshop attendees perused the shelves on their way out and left with an assortment of carefully chosen books. Additional book sales had been one of Nicole's selling points when she had first pitched the learning-annex idea to Mary. That hadn't been the reason Mary had agreed to help, but it sure turned out to be a nice little bonus.

Shortly before lunch, Susan entered the bookshop and found Mary working at the back, near the pair of overstuffed chairs. Exhausted from the events of the previous night, Susan said she had slept in this morning. She certainly looked the worse for wear, but Mary wasn't about to tell her that.

"The fire investigators are almost finished checking the place out." Susan flopped into the reading chair as if her muscles had just melted, and she wiped a hand across her puffy eyes. "They won't let me inside the bakery. Do you mind if I wait here until they're done?"

"Of course not." Mary perched on the edge of the matching chair. "Did they say anything more about how the fire started?"

"They won't release a statement until they're finished with the investigation." She sighed, the sound long and defeated. Gus seemed to sense her despair and jumped up on the arm of the chair where he offered his back for a stroke. Mindlessly, she tunneled her fingers into his soft gray fur. "I don't know how we're going to get through this. Ryan and I depend on my income from the bakery."

Mary thought about what she said. Her first urge was to assure her that all would be well. But neither of them knew what the future would bring, and she didn't want to offer meaningless platitudes. Instead, she reminded her friend of the one thing she could control.

"All you can do is focus on today. If you get ahead of yourself and start worrying about tomorrow, you'll certainly feel overwhelmed."

"I know," said Susan. "God is in control, and He will provide."

Mary nodded in affirmation.

"And I'm praying a lot."

"As are all your friends."

Susan met Mary's gaze and held it for a long moment. "I had an awful thought, and it pains me that I even considered the possibility," she said at last. She pulled herself upright in the chair and leaned her elbows on her knees.

With the back massage over, Gus hopped down from the chair.

At Mary's nod of encouragement, Susan continued.

"My keys went missing shortly after Carol Bates was in the shop," she began with hesitation, "and the thought crossed my mind that Carol might have used the keys to let herself into the bakery and start the fire in retaliation for having 'poisoned' her." She sniffed and pulled a battered tissue from her pants pocket. "I know it's silly of me to think such thoughts, but Carol was so sick, and she seemed convinced it was my fault."

While she dabbed her nose, Mary reminded her of their conversation with the young firefighter last night. "Wyatt told us it looked like the fire started because of old wiring."

And Mary wanted to believe that was the case. But the black car with the darkened headlights kept nagging at the back of her mind.

"I know," Susan said and tucked the tissue back in her pocket. "The keys will probably turn up soon. It's just that I hate thinking mean thoughts about *anybody*. I'm not that kind of person."

Mary got up from her chair and bent to hug her sweet friend. "Of course you're not. Don't beat yourself up. It's understandable for a person's mind to leap to conclusions when under stress."

That explained Susan's suspicion. But Mary couldn't as easily explain away her own misgivings about the cause of the fire.

FOUR

·◆◆·

After the fire investigators removed the yellow tape and gave Susan the all clear to enter the bakery and examine the damage, Mary accompanied her for moral support. Chief McArthur and a couple of fire investigators stood near the sooty display table, speaking in low tones.

It seemed that not even an inch of the front of the shop had been left untouched by smoke. The once-frilly curtains around the pass-through window behind the cash register hung in black tatters, and nearly all the menus, posters, and gift baskets on and around the counter were scorched. The kitchen was worse. The piles of boxes, bags, and towels Mary had seen on top of the prep table and oven last night had been reduced to ashes. The stainless-steel appliances hadn't burned, but the oven's plastic knobs and handles drooped like Salvador Dali clocks, and the refrigerator door hung agape as if it were gasping for air that had been consumed by the fire. The contents had been transformed into a blackened, melted mess. It was impossible to tell from this vantage point how far the flames had spread through the back of the shop.

"State Fire Marshal Jerry Spradlin," the white-shirted man said, and extended a hand in greeting to both women.

Chief McArthur nodded, his expression serious.

Spradlin pushed his wire-rimmed glasses up on his nose. He met Susan's gaze and got straight to the point. "It appears the fire in your bakery was deliberately set."

Susan put a hand to her chest. "How can that be? Last night a firefighter—Wyatt Heath—told us the fire started because of old wiring. Sparks from an outlet near the oven."

"Unfortunately, Firefighter Heath is not a certified fire investigator," Chief McArthur said, his voice gentle. "He was just offering his personal opinion."

Wyatt's very inexperienced opinion, apparently. Mary took a slow breath, trying to absorb this latest development. "How do you know it wasn't accidental?"

Spradlin rubbed a palm over the stubble of his close-cropped hair. "The string mop that had been left propped against the outlet was supposed to make it look accidental… as if the cotton strings had caught a spark and spread the fire to debris piled on the table."

"Debris?" Susan glanced at each of the men, her gaze finally resting on Mary. "There was no debris on the table. We always take the trash out every night before closing up. And the mop always stays in the storeroom when we're not using it." She clutched the tiny silver cross that hung from her neck. "In fact, the prep table always stays on the other side of the kitchen, under the pass-through."

Mary spoke up. "You weren't folding cake boxes on the table before you left yesterday? That's what it looked like when I came over last night."

She described what she'd seen, and the fire marshal made a note of it.

"No," said Susan. "I always start and end the day with everything in its place. If I didn't, I'd never be able to get all my baking done before opening time."

A queasy feeling hit Mary in the pit of her stomach. Someone had stacked the table with paper and fabric to fuel the blaze. And whoever had placed them there had been in the shop before—and possibly during—the time Mary entered the bakery last night.

Spradlin glanced back at his clipboard. "We found evidence of an accelerant that had been used to ignite the materials on the table. Possibly gasoline, considering how fast the fire progressed."

Susan made a noise that sounded like something between a cry and a groan. Her gaze landed on Mary, and she tilted her head ever so slightly. She frowned, as if a disturbing thought had occurred to her. "Mary, did you …?" Almost immediately after she spoke the words, Susan vigorously shook her head in answer to her own question. "Forget that. It's ridiculous to even imagine such a thing. I'm just stressed out beyond belief."

As far as Mary was concerned, the near accusation was already as good as forgotten. She knew Susan didn't believe she had set the fire. The stress and confusion of the moment had the bakery shop owner stretching for an answer—any answer— to resolve who had perpetrated the hateful act and why.

Now that Mary had been excluded as a suspect, Chief McArthur quizzed Susan on who might have reason to set the fire.

After a long pause and another apologetic glance at Mary, Susan reluctantly mentioned her fleeting concern about Carol

Bates. "I don't have any proof that she took the keys, and I don't want to say that she would do such a thing. It was just a crazy thought that crossed my mind."

Crazy? Or had Carol, perhaps, been the blonde passenger in the black car Mary saw last night? Supposing, of course, the black car had been a getaway vehicle.

Spradlin nodded. "That's okay. We're not accusing anyone at this point. Just considering possibilities." Deep in thought, he smoothed his mustache. "The situation with the missing keys would be consistent with the fact that there was no sign of forced entry."

No sign of forced entry. Could she have—? Mary quickly did a mental playback of her visit to the bakery last night. There was no question she'd locked the front door after her departure, because she'd had to use her key to reopen it for the firefighters. But what about the back door? She had opened it to look outside for the source of the noise she'd heard. Had she remembered to relock the door when she went back inside?

But, no, the arsonist had already been in the building, as evidenced by the boxes and ignitable materials piled on the table. So he—or she—had already found a way in. But how?

"It's easy to prove that a crime of arson has been committed," Spradlin said. "The hard part will be proving who did it." He went on to explain that, according to the Federal Bureau of Investigation Uniform Crime Report, typically less than 10 percent of all arsons result in an arrest.

Mary frowned. It sounded like a warning for Susan not to get her hopes up. Chief McArthur met her gaze and seemed to know what she was thinking. He furrowed his brow and nodded almost imperceptibly, as if to assure her that this case would not be brushed off. She knew him to be a conscientious public servant, but were the odds so stacked against them that Susan would slide into that ever-wondering 90 percent? A thousand thoughts flashed through her mind. Remembering Chief McArthur's detailed questioning last night, she wondered if he'd had a suspicion then that the fire had been intentionally set.

"I can't imagine why someone would do this, Susan," Mary said with a sweep of her arm to indicate the damage. "To *you*, of all people. You're one of the sweetest people in Ivy Bay."

Susan shook her head in defeat. "Tell that to the arsonist."

———

Mary placed calls to those in her prayer chain, and by that afternoon, the bakery overflowed with willing workers, proving that prayer and action work together to create miracles. She glanced around at the blackened remains of the once-homey shop and shook her head. It would certainly take a miracle to get the place customer-ready again.

Thank goodness for Rebecca, who was taking care of the bookstore. It meant a lot to be able to leave the shop in her capable hands. Hers and Ashley's, as was the case today.

The fire had caused some structural damage in the kitchen and made a mess of the appliances. In addition, the dividing wall behind the cash register had incurred major burn damage and needed to be replaced, and the pass-through window rebuilt. The landlord had promised to get the repairs started as soon as possible, but in the meantime, Susan and her helpers worked to salvage what they could from the burned and blackened shop.

It would be pointless to do a deep cleaning at this stage, so the primary focus was on clearing out the ruined items and swabbing up the surface filth.

Earlier this afternoon, Susan had taken inventory of all that had been lost to the fire and smoke. Other than the oven and refrigerator, which sustained damage from the direct flames and heat, much of the other equipment and certain canned goods could be salvaged. But the bulk containers of flour and sugar came in heavy paper packaging that had been permeated by smoke and had to be tossed. The dollar figure Susan mentioned had staggered Mary. Understandably, Susan's normally cheerful mood had disappeared right along with her inventory.

Wearing rubber work gloves that Jimmy had donated from the hardware store, Mary focused her efforts on the back of the shop, paying special attention to the scorched papers in a metal in-tray on top of the filing cabinet, which had apparently been stacked there to be sorted and handled later. She took the tray into the L portion of the storeroom that served as a tiny office. The left corner of an envelope from Bingle Property Rentals sported a wooden doorknob as its logo, an interesting variation on the hospitality pineapple. It wouldn't do to misplace Susan's rental information, so Mary tucked the papers in the top desk drawer for safekeeping during the cleanup efforts.

Although sooty, the office nook and back half of the storeroom had been spared severe damage, as most of the fire had been concentrated around the areas of the kitchen and storeroom closest to the hallway doors. Mary concluded that the arsonist must have walked through the hall, sloshing gasoline into the rooms on either side, and slipped out the back door after igniting it. If he—or she—had left through the front, Mary most certainly would have noticed any unusual pedestrian activity near her shop at that time of night.

She was turning to leave the area when her gaze fell on a smudge, or more like a faint rectangular ring, of liquid on the floor. That was odd. Susan was meticulous about "a place for everything, and everything in its place," so there was no reason for any baking oils to have been in the office area. Mary knelt and touched a gloved finger to the partially evaporated liquid and sniffed. The sharp, pungent odor drifted to her. Gasoline, or something very similar. This must be the accelerant that the investigator said started the fire. She wiped her glove on a cleaning rag and performed a closer inspection of the office area.

Someone had set a can of flammable fluid here, even if only for a moment. A memory from last night returned to her, of leaning into the storeroom and peeking inside to see what might have caused the noise she'd heard. Had the arsonist hidden in the office area, gasoline can at the ready, just out of her line of sight? When the reality of it hit her, a creepy sensation crawled over her skin and raised goose bumps all the way up to her scalp.

After a moment, the creepy, slightly fearful feeling gave way to anger. How dare anyone slither uninvited into dear, sweet Susan's place of business and purposely attempt to destroy all that she had worked so hard to build. Righteous indignation tore at Mary, clenching her jaw muscles, and knotting her hands into fists. Rage over the unfairness of what this person had done fueled her desire to see justice done.

She would continue to help with the cleaning, but her efforts were now spurred by a need to learn more. To see what other telltale signs the perpetrator may have inadvertently left behind.

Moving with a purpose that surpassed her former goal of merely helping to clear out the burned debris, Mary moved from the office nook through the rear of the sooty storeroom in search of any other overlooked hints that the intruder had passed this way. She was about to leave the storeroom when, on a shelf stacked with bags of flour and sugar as well as canisters of baking soda and cocoa, a blue-and-white scrap of paper caught her eye. Amazed that the bit of trash had managed to escape the flames, she picked it up and held it over a large black plastic bag.

She paused, her mouth pursed as a thought scampered through her mind. Blue-and-white paper. Something seemed so familiar. She turned it over and studied it. Although the torn scrap revealed only a couple of letter fragments, she recognized it as the bottom portion of a now-empty roll of antacids. The crumpled wrapper directed her thoughts to Carol, the customer who had already triggered suspicion in the normally easygoing Susan. Carol had no business in the storage room. So, if the wrapper belonged to her, what was it doing in here? More important, what had Carol been doing in here?

Mary slid the paper into her pocket and moved to the kitchen where the ignitable items and string mop had been staged to look like an accident. Prayer group members and best friends Lynn Teagarden and Amy Stebble had already cleared away most of the rubble around the oven and taken it outside to be hauled away. On the other side of the pass-through window, yet another prayer group member, Dorothy Johnson, was taking down the blackened curtains. Mary smiled to think of the ever-present pearls that Dorothy always wore and hoped she had remembered to leave them at home today.

Lynn attacked the floor with a broom, sweeping the trash into a pile. Tall and slim, the forty-something wasted no time returning order to the kitchen. In her zeal as she whisked her way across the floor and under the oven, something metal clanged against the oven leg and skittered farther back under it.

"What was that?" Amy asked. Upon receiving Mary's call, she had immediately left work and come to help. Fortunately, the new school session hadn't begun yet, which afforded her some flexibility in her schedule. Being an elementary-school principal accustomed to listening for sounds of mischief from her tiny charges, Amy had alerted to the noise like a bird dog to a quail scuttling through underbrush. Placing her hands on her plump hips, she bent and stared as if trying to decide the best tactic for retrieving the errant item. Even if she weren't too short to reach under the oven for it, groping through all that muck would have her covered in black soot within seconds.

Lynn shrugged. "I don't know what it used to be, but it's worthless now."

Curious, Mary grabbed a large cookie sheet and used it to drag the item out from under the oven. Out came a small, palm-sized object that showed glimpses of silver under all the black.

Mary turned it over in her hand, and the two women gathered around to peer over her shoulder. Using the cleaning rag, she wiped away enough of the soot to discern a faint, embossed emblem: I ♥ New York.

Amy gasped. "I'll bet that was used to start the fire."

Mary flipped the hinged top of the Zippo lighter and spun the thumbwheel. On the second flick, a yellow-and-blue flame leaped from the device.

Though it hadn't burned her, she flinched, and the lighter dropped to the floor. The three women stood there and stared at it, contemplating the implications.

With a sense of impending doom, Mary considered the possibilities. Although it was a fairly common souvenir item from the Big Apple, she knew only one person who owned a lighter like this one. Someone who was known to enjoy a cigar on special occasions. Someone who relished the simple ceremony of lighting his stogie and drawing in the first puff of apple-scented tobacco.

She retrieved the lighter and noticed the varied dents on the ancient oven as she straightened. Were they the result of normal wear and tear, she wondered, or had they all been put there by Ryan in a fit of anger over its unreliability? Had he been angry enough to follow through on his threat to deliver "an eye for an eye" after it had burned yet another batch of brownies?

"Maybe," Mary said in response to Amy's comment. But in an effort to maintain perspective, she added, "Or it could have been accidentally dropped by someone who had a legitimate reason to be in the kitchen." Perhaps it had merely fallen out of Ryan's pocket while he worked on the oven earlier that day. She prayed that was the case.

Then again, Ryan had been mysteriously absent when the blaze started. Even his own wife had questioned his whereabouts.

The prayer group friends went back to work, and Mary ambled toward the front of the shop where Dorothy had progressed from taking down the scorched curtains to removing all the formerly lovely pies and decorated cakes from the display cases and tossing them into a large plastic trash can. Although they hadn't been burned, the heat from the fire had melted them into lopsided atrocities, and pale-gray smoke particles clung to the white frosting.

It was a sad sight to watch those luscious goodies hit the can with an unceremonious *plop*. For the most part, Susan tried to make only what she believed she could sell each day, but custom orders such as birthday cakes, wedding cakes, and themed cupcakes were often made the day before the event. Not only did those customers lose their specialty cakes to the fire, but Susan had no way of replacing them in time for their planned events.

Dorothy paused in her chore and cast Mary a curious look.

Mary contemplated the ongoing repercussions of the fire. "I was just thinking what a shame it is to throw away all that delicious food. Even worse, the people who ordered the cakes must be frantic to get replacements."

She and Dorothy got along well enough, but sometimes Mary detected a bit of prickly tension in her fellow church member, especially when their mutual friend Henry Woodrow was around. Today, Dorothy seemed pleasant enough, but Henry wasn't due to show up until later.

"Would you believe," Dorothy said, "that after midnight, when Susan finally left here, she got on the phone to a baker in Falmouth, roused him out of bed, and gave him all the orders that were supposed to be picked up today?"

Mary moved behind the counter and reached for the trash can to adjust the plastic liner that had slipped off the rim. "That is so like Susan to be thinking of others even when she's in the midst of her own crisis."

Dorothy nodded and continued tossing the confections. "And her husband is such a dear. He's been out all day, first picking up cakes from Falmouth and then delivering them all over creation. The Crosbys are actually losing money on the orders, but those two refuse to leave their customers high and dry."

With the trash can full, Mary helped Dorothy push it from behind the counter. Quick as lightning, Dorothy bent to pick up something out of a pile of burned debris that had been swept into a pile in the corner. She wiped off oily soot with her gloved hand, studied it for a moment, then tossed it into a basket on the counter before continuing with her task. The basket contained hair barrettes, a faux-leather cell-phone case, an earring, and a clear plastic coupon pouch, all of which were dirty but still salvageable. The latest addition turned out to be a thin black metal case. Maybe an iPod?

"Lost and found," Dorothy said. "A customer must have dropped it."

Mary helped wheel the trash can outside along with the rest of the debris and piled it in a pickup truck provided by a church member. Seagulls' cries could be heard in the distance, but Mary doubted even they would be interested in the contents of this truck. Well, maybe the cakes. She climbed into the bed of the truck and tightened the red plastic tie on the trash bag to make sure it stayed secure.

Shorts-clad shoppers and tourists strolled past the yellow-fronted shop, enjoying the warm August sun. They swung wide of the bakery's front door where busy workers scurried in and out. A small snaggletoothed boy clung to his mother's hand. He appeared to be unaware of the bustling activity, his focus riveted to the shop sign. "Bakery, mama. Let's get a cupcake!"

The little rascal reminded her of her grandson, Luke—so enthusiastic and happy to enjoy the small pleasures of life.

"Sorry, sweetie, not today," his mother said, taking in the commotion in and around the shop. She added something else that Mary didn't hear, and the boy seemed appeased by whatever she had suggested.

Back inside, Mary's thoughts returned to the latest addition to the lost-and-found basket. Since it had been found behind the checkout counter, it likely belonged to Susan, Ryan, or their two part-time employees. But when she lifted the item out of the basket to take to Susan, she was surprised to discover it was much too light and too thin to be an iPod.

Mary frowned and turned the flat case over in her hand. If it had been smaller, she would have assumed it to be a business-card case. On one side, the words *Ribbie Collectibles* curved around an image of the tip end of a baseball bat.

She opened the metal cover. Nestled inside was a baseball card in a clear Lucite display holder. Ever so carefully, she shook the acrylic-protected card from the metal container. The faded black-and-white image of a handsome young ballplayer at bat stared back at her. She flipped it over and read the stats: #92, Ted Williams. Birthplace, birth date, height, and weight. And the fact that he bats left and throws right. The text noted that Williams "has a great future."

Clearly, this old card held either sentimental or monetary value for someone. Maybe both. Why else would they have gone to such trouble to put it in two protective cases? It wouldn't do to leave it out here on the counter where it could get misplaced or, worse, accidentally damaged or thrown away. She took it to the office and tucked it in the drawer where she'd left Susan's important papers. Her friend had walked over to the hardware store for more cleaning supplies, so Mary would mention it to her later.

She returned to the front of the shop and found that a few of the workers had left and, after word got around, a few new volunteers showed up to take their places. Among the new crew, Roger Cline worked at the front of the shop, pushing a broom around the corners of the room and the round display table. A slim, rather average-looking man, he wore a ball cap atop his limp brown hair, presumably to distract from vaguely awkward facial features that gave him an unfortunate appearance. Mary's husband, John, had taught their son to remove his hat whenever he entered a building, but nowadays people seldom adhered to that rule of social etiquette.

"Where's Bruce?" Dorothy called to him from where she scrubbed a display case.

His stern concentration broken, he paused in his sweeping and a grin flashed over his face. Whoever Bruce was, Roger obviously cared about him. "At the house. Didn't want him getting hurt or carrying all this soot back home with us."

For Mary's benefit, Dorothy added, "Bruce is his hound. That dog goes everywhere with Roger. I wouldn't be surprised if Bruce thinks he's human."

Roger cut a playful glance at her. "You mean he isn't?"

The landlord continued dragging the broom through the room toward the counter area, his actions ineffectually pushing the sooty clutter back and forth rather than piling it into a heap. Even so, Mary thought what a nice gesture it was for him to come and help with the cleanup. Then again, the building belonged to him, so it was certainly to his benefit to get the bakery back up and running as swiftly as possible.

Mary leaned back and stretched her aching muscles, then finger-combed her sweat-dampened hair. She'd been going at it for a couple of hours without a break, and even her curls were starting to droop. What she needed was a few minutes of rest and some fresh air. And she knew just the place.

After letting the others know where they could find her if they needed her, she opened the back door, stepped out into the New England sunshine and inhaled the fresh air that carried a scent of salt from the nearby bay. Her sudden appearance startled the orange cat, which was loitering again, and it slipped between the fence slats into the adjoining yard. Mary sighed and realized she'd missed an opportunity to get closer to the cat and discover whether it was a stray or a lost pet whose family was searching for it. She should start carrying kitty kibble in her pocket. Maybe food would help it overcome its skittishness.

Her gaze automatically veered to the shed behind Jimmy's Hardware where she had seen Tyson last night. The only movement she saw at the moment was a gray squirrel scampering across the roof of the shed. Tyson had been carrying a can about the size of the marks she'd found on the floor of the office area. Could he have…?

Mary pulled the door shut behind her and shook her head to clear it of that troubling thought. Just because he was a teenager and had acted surly with Susan yesterday didn't mean he was guilty of anything. It could have been pure coincidence that he had been carrying a similar size can around the same time she'd heard that strange noise from Susan's bakery.

She wasn't naive, but she refused to be cynical either. Whatever the young man had been up to, she prayed it had been with good intentions.

A padded rattan bench beside the flagstone path beckoned her to relax and release her cares into the lush green garden. She and Susan had sat here a couple of times and enjoyed tea from the Tea Shoppe next door. Unable to resist its lure, Mary sank onto the comfy furniture and lifted her face to the sun's warm rays. She wouldn't sit here long enough to burn, but a few minutes of natural vitamin D were sure to replenish her energy.

She opened her eyes and watched a brown creeper slowly spiral its way up the trunk of a beech tree in its quest for insects. It always amazed her how people constantly worried about what might happen tomorrow, yet all along, God's creatures knew that all they had to do was look for it, and their needs would be provided for. Just the other night, her Bible reading had led her to Deuteronomy 11:15: "I will provide grass in the fields for your cattle, and you will eat and be satisfied." No life was perfect. If hers were perfect, John would still be here with her. Despite that, Mary loved her life here in Ivy Bay. What more did she need than her sister and friends who loved her, good books to read, and plenty to eat to keep her satisfied? But she had to admit she was really going to miss those cinna-lobsters until Susan eventually reopened the bakery.

After the tiny bird had circled the tree to the top of the trunk, it fluttered down to the ground to begin its search anew at the base of yet another tree.

Mary continued to watch for the next few minutes, the bird's actions mesmerizing her as it made its methodic ascent. Finally, the little brown bird moved to the base of the white wooden gatepost to begin its search there. Unable to suppress a laugh, Mary thought how like humans it was—herself included—to sometimes go searching in the wrong places to get needs met.

The tree creeper made it about halfway up the post when something dangling from the gate moved in the breeze and startled the tiny creature into taking flight.

Mary rose from the wicker bench and walked to the gate at the back of the yard. Perhaps a vine had twined up the fence and frightened the feathered visitor. If so, she would dispatch the unwanted hitchhiker. Betty's constant efforts at pulling weeds and vines to maintain a beautiful garden had taught her to tackle life's little problems early and often to keep them from gaining a choke hold.

On closer inspection, the "vine" actually turned out to be several strands of hair that had been snagged by the gate latch.

Mary froze where she stood, her gaze fixed to the unexpected sight.

Long blonde hairs moved once again in the afternoon breeze and waved a taunting hello at her.

FIVE

---◆◆◆---

The next morning, Mary went to prayer group at Grace Church of Ivy Bay. It was early, and Jill Sanderson had not yet arrived. The group of eight—Mary, Dorothy, Jill, Lynn, Bernice, Trisha, Millie, and Amy—seemed to be just the right size for an intimate session of prayer and discussion, but they always welcomed anyone who wanted to pop in and pray with them.

While Dorothy—pearls embracing her slim neck—put the prayer room in order the way she liked it, Lynn Teagarden brought them up to date on the prayer needs of those in the community. Bea Winslow, a sprightly seventy-something-year-old, was preparing for a 5K race to be held on Labor Day weekend and wanted their prayers for her and all the other walkers and runners. A local building contractor had seen a slight downturn in business lately and could use more work. And librarian Victoria Pickerton wanted to share her joy of reading with children and asked the group to pray for an enthusiastic turnout for the upcoming Children's Reading Adventure.

"Don't forget Gino Azzara," Amy said. "His daughter Bibi brought a barnacle to school for show-and-tell and shared that her daddy's boat had to be taken out of the harbor for scraping and repainting."

She didn't have to say the rest. Anyone who lived around Ivy Bay knew that time spent out of the water impacted the livelihood of the waterman who owned the boat. It was especially bad for it to happen at the peak of the tourist season. Most fishermen and tour-boat operators scheduled their boat repairs for the off-season when people weren't clamoring to be taken out on the water for fishing and touring excursions.

"Not only that," Amy continued, "but they found a small leak in the hull, so that's going to prolong the repair time."

Jill Sanderson chose that moment to poke her blonde head into the room. "Have you started yet?"

"No," Mary said. "We're still going over the prayer list."

"Good, then I'm not late." The young woman glided into the room as gracefully as if she were wearing a silk ball gown instead of a blue oxford shirt. "Luman and Benjamin insisted on playing paparazzi, and I had to be Taylor Swift at the mall." She fluffed her hair and joked, "Do you see the resemblance?"

The eight- and ten-year-old boys were quite a handful, but they never failed to entertain the church members.

Before anyone could comment, Jill diverted the conversation back to the prayer list. "Did you tell them about Amelia Shepard's request?" she asked Amy.

"She's next on the list."

Jill slid into an empty chair and plunged in with an update on the hardware-store owner's wife. "Amelia wants us to pray for her nephew who's staying with them for the summer."

Mary swung her attention to the pretty blonde. "Tyson? The boy who's working at the store?"

"Same one. He's been having some trouble over the past year or so, and his parents thought that a change of venue for the summer, along with Jimmy and Amelia's positive influence, would help steer him in the right direction."

Dorothy finished buzzing around the room and settled into the prayer circle with the others. "Amelia told me he's been coming home late, usually with flimsy excuses. Why, a couple of nights ago, he claimed the car broke down, and he came home reeking to high heaven."

An uninformed passerby might think the women were gossiping, but that kind of attitude couldn't be further from their hearts. Any personal details that were shared remained in this room and in the friends' daily prayers. Although they knew that God heard and understood all prayers—even those with the most vaguely defined concerns—several of the members liked to channel their prayers like laser lights. "Specific is terrific," Amy always said, quoting one of the English teachers from her elementary school.

"Does Amelia think he was doing drugs?" Lynn asked. "If he'd been smoking something, the odor could have been clinging to his clothes."

Jill slowly shook her head. "She isn't sure, because she doesn't have any experience with that kind of thing. All she knows is that he was acting very secretive."

An uncomfortable possibility occurred to Mary. The bakery fire had been set a couple of nights ago, while Tyson's car was supposedly broken down on the side of the road. His black car, perhaps? "What kind of vehicle was he driving?"

Jill tilted her head, obviously curious about Mary's odd question. "It was Amelia's car. Why do you ask?"

She shook her head in dismissal. There was no point in raising suspicion about the boy until or unless some solid evidence came up to connect him with the arson. Until then, she would keep her eyes and ears open. And pay attention to what kind of car Amelia owned.

"Anyway, to make matters worse," Jill continued, "his older sister, whom he adores, is undergoing chemotherapy. I wouldn't be surprised if that's playing a part in his troubling behavior."

They all agreed. Heartsick for the entire family, Mary started off praying for Tyson, his sister, their aunt and uncle, and, of course, Susan.

She couldn't help feeling like she should have listened to her instincts and called the police immediately after hearing the strange noise at the bakery the other night. Most of all, she was concerned for her friend Susan, the innocent victim of a very troubled person. An overwhelming need gripped Mary's heart, compelling her to find the culprit so justice would be served and Susan could have peace of mind.

But first, Mary would have to find out who set fire to Sweet Susan's Bakery. And why.

———

Late that afternoon, at the Tanaka Florist and Garden Center, Mary and Betty were browsing the aisles for grass seed in preparation for fall reseeding in their backyard. One real reason they came here together was to find a gift for Susan, in hopes that a pretty plant, or maybe a wind chime or sun catcher, might cheer her up. While she and Betty were here, it was a bonus to enjoy some sister time and check out new garden items to make the yard as inviting as possible, for both wildlife and humans. Today, Betty had an added mission— to find a local beekeeper to advise her on what to do about the swarm of homeless honeybees she had spotted in the neighborhood.

The thirty-something florist wore a green apron with leafy vines embroidered up the left side that culminated in a beautiful white morning-glory blossom over her heart. Pinned inside the flower, her name tag read Leslie Sadowski. The last time they were here, Leslie had delightedly shared that she had just learned the meanings of her first name and surname from a genealogy Web site. *Leslie* was derived from a Gaelic name meaning "garden of holly," and *Sadowski* was derived from a Polish word for "orchard." Blown away by the odds that both of her names, as well as her occupation, had a garden connection, she had taken it as confirmation that this was the job she'd been divinely called to perform.

Leslie handed Betty a scrap of paper with the name of a beekeeper who lived on the outskirts of town. "If Deborah can't help you, she can put you in touch with her beekeepers' club."

They chatted for a bit, and Mary and Betty soon discovered that the buzz around the gardening shop wasn't just coming from bees. Leslie lived next door to the Crosbys, so she was naturally concerned about her neighbors. Mary filled her in on the progress that had been made cleaning up the bakery, and the young woman shared some of the speculation she had heard regarding the fire.

"One theory is that Sophie Mershon set the fire to chase Susan out so she could expand her tea shop."

A bit of amused eye rolling ensued among the three, for anyone who knew Sophie knew that the former ballet dancer was more interested in beauty, ambiance, and enjoying the company of her customers than in ruthlessly expanding her business.

"And then there's the boy who works at the hardware store."

Tyson. Mary had confided to Betty what she had seen the night of the fire, but she hadn't said anything about it to anyone else to avoid sullying his name any further if his actions had, indeed, been innocent. Now her sister met her surprised gaze.

"According to someone who knows someone who knows his aunt," Leslie said, making it clear that the information wasn't 100 percent reliable, "the boy came home the night of the fire smelling of gasoline."

This morning, the prayer group had assumed the "reeking" odor on the boy indicated he'd been smoking something. But a gasoline smell pointed a finger at something else altogether.

Betty sat on a stack of fescue grass-seed bags, a sign that she was tiring and they needed to head home soon. "Are you sure about that?"

"As sure as hearsay can be. I'm only mentioning it because the bookshop is three doors down from the hardware store. It would be wise to stay extra alert to his comings and goings. You know, pay attention if he's lurking somewhere he's not supposed to be."

Despite the fact that Mary had seen Tyson carrying a can of liquid out of the hardware store, she didn't want to believe the teen could be behind the fire at the bakery. Her heart hopeful, she reminded herself that his car had supposedly been broken down on the side of the road that night.

"Maybe his car ran out of gas," she said, more to herself than to the others. "And some could have sloshed on him when he carried it back to the car."

Betty nodded, and Mary could tell she also wanted to believe the best about the situation, but neither of them was fully convinced.

Betty rose from her perch, and Mary reached to pull a bag from the stack of grass-seed bags, but Leslie seemed lost in thought and totally ignored their subtle hint that they were ready to make their purchase.

After an uncomfortably quiet pause, the young woman finally said, "You're friends of Susan's, so I know this won't go beyond you."

Mary and Betty exchanged glances.

"Two nights ago, Susan asked me if I had seen Ryan. He hadn't come home for dinner, and she couldn't reach him on his cell phone. She tried to play it off as if there was a miscommunication regarding their schedules, but I could tell she was really worried. He didn't come home until much later." She paused significantly. "Not until *after* the fire."

The snippet of an overheard conversation clanged in the back of Mary's memory. *"Where have you been?"* Susan had asked her husband when he finally showed up at the fire. His absence merely indicated he hadn't been at home that evening. It didn't necessarily mean he had started the fire.

"Are you saying—?"

"I'm just saying he didn't show up until after the fire trucks had been called. Whatever is going on, I'm sure Susan could use a little extra support from her friends."

There was no question that Susan had their support. But right now, Ryan had their curiosity.

———

After Mary dropped Betty and the grass seed off at the house along with the wind chime that Betty had offered to wrap, she headed back downtown to Bailey's to talk to Tess about their upcoming ice-cream-making workshop. She had just passed in front of the Black & White Diner when the door swung open and Nicole stepped out onto the sidewalk. Judging from the droop of her normally perky ponytail and what looked like a close encounter with blueberry syrup on her uniform, she must be nearing the end of her shift.

"Oh good. I was just headed your way," Nicole said. "Do you have a minute?"

Mary cast a quick glance at her watch. Her meeting with Tess wasn't for another ten minutes. She stepped out of the way of the door. "Sure. What's up?"

"I have a workshop opportunity for next weekend," she said, watching for Mary's reaction. When there was no resistance, she hurried on. "After what happened at the bakery, now would be a good time to squeeze in a fire-safety session. Wyatt Heath has already agreed to teach it."

The original plan had been to conduct one workshop every two or three weeks, which would give them plenty of time to set up and publicize the events. But this one was a mere ten days away.

"Wyatt and I will handle all the logistics," Nicole assured her. "We've already reserved a site on the beach and requested a permit for a bonfire. Seems appropriate to go along with a talk about fire, don't you think? All you need to do is type up a flyer and post copies around town to promote the event."

The original deal had called for Mary to host the workshops in her bookstore. After Ashley had taken it upon herself to print flyers to announce Betty's talk, Nicole had raved over how good they looked. Now it appeared that Nicole expected Mary not only to provide flyers for their workshops, but for Mary to distribute them and promote the events as well.

Nicole glanced inside the diner and seemed anxious to get back to her customers.

That was okay because Mary was anxious to move on to her meeting with Tess. Nicole was right; the best time to get a fire-safety message across to citizens was right after a highly publicized incident like the bakery fire. Although Mary's confidence in Wyatt's knowledge had taken a nosedive after his inexperience had led him to declare the fire an accident started by a short in the electrical wiring, she supposed he'd do fine with basic fire-safety advice. Since Nicole and Wyatt were taking care of the learning-annex site, her own part would certainly be doable. Especially if Ashley helped out by formatting the flyer.

With just a hint of reluctance, Mary agreed to help with the event. "I'll have Ashley do the flyers, and we'll post them in the shops on our block, but you'll need to distribute the rest."

Ashley wouldn't mind creating another flyer. In fact, she relished the task, so Mary didn't mind asking her to make one for this next event. However, she didn't have time to run all over town, posting them in shops and taking them to bulletin boards. She felt certain Nicole would understand that her own work had to come first. At least she hoped so.

"Thank you so much! You're a doll." Nicole pulled the door open to return to her waitressing duties, then called over her shoulder, "By the way, since this is sort of a public-service affair, there won't be any charge to attendees. So naturally there won't be any profits for us to split on this one. I hope that's okay with you."

Not that it would have mattered, for Nicole ducked back inside before Mary could answer yea or nay. Oh well, the busiest part of the tourist season would be behind them after the ice-cream-making session, which was scheduled to take place the Saturday after Labor Day. After that, most of their learning sessions would be geared toward year-round residents, with a sprinkling of die-hard tourists who lingered on to enjoy the chilly fall weather.

Inside Bailey's Ice Cream Shop, business had slowed during the predinner period. Customers were still out enjoying the sites and attractions of Ivy Bay, at home preparing their meals, or getting ready to go out and have dinner at one of the many nice restaurants in the area. Mary knew from personal experience that the ice-cream shop would be deluged a little later, after the main feature at the movie theater let out.

"Thanks for agreeing to meet here," she said as she slid into the chair opposite Tess. "The bookstore still has a faint smell of smoke. A sooty overtone on the flavors would put a damper on our brainstorming new recipes."

"Thank *you* for agreeing to do this workshop with me. It'll be fun teaming up to teach folks how to make their own ice cream, and it's a good opportunity to lure people into the shop."

Tess pushed back her short auburn hair and straightened the large silver hoops that hung from her ears. Though the rest of her was slightly heavy, her face was slim and attractive. Her best feature, though, was her smile, which she used frequently. And this late afternoon, Mary enjoyed basking in the glow.

"You've already shared so many creative recipes with us," Tess said, "so I tried to come up with a list of flavors we haven't used yet."

Shortly after Mary had returned to Ivy Bay to live, Tess had learned of her talent for making ice cream and invited her to create a new flavor for Bailey's to feature each month. Her concoctions were an instant hit among the locals, who often made a point of visiting the shop just to try out the latest offering.

The two women brainstormed for a while, then moved behind the counter to create sample-sized combinations of flavors. Every so often, Tess's daughter Paige reached over, snatched a taste, and offered her opinion. Before long, they had narrowed the ideas to three possibilities, all of which needed major editing. To keep things simple, they decided to choose one flavor to perfect and spotlight at the workshop, then offer advice for workshop goers who wanted to experiment further at home.

Mary gathered up the notes and slid them into a folder. "I'm sure I've ruined my appetite for dinner," she said with a laugh. "Fortunately, Betty asked me to pick up the meat-loaf special of the day from the Black & White Diner, so I'm sure their delicious aromas will bring back my appetite."

The bell over the shop door rang, and Wyatt Heath entered, wearing a navy T-shirt with "Ivy Bay Fire Department" printed over the breast pocket. "Aha, two birds, one stone," he said when he noticed them together. "You're just the ladies I need to see."

He started by thanking Mary for agreeing to help publicize next weekend's fire-safety workshop, and for offering to help set up for the event.

"Nicole will be working at the diner Saturday. If she can't cut out of work early, she may not be able to come until the first half of the talk, but she suggested you and I show up about thirty minutes early to set up a few folding chairs and arrange the bonfire."

Really? Whatever happened to just typing up a flyer and posting a few of them on her block? She shrugged her shoulders as if the action would also help her shrug off the mild irritation at having the workshop duties change and grow without her consent. The important thing to keep in mind was that they were providing a beneficial service to the community.

Besides, a bonfire on the beach at the end of the day would be a nice opportunity to spend some sister time with Betty. Maybe Henry would come along too. She made a mental note to bring a blanket and some chairs for them to sit on and marshmallows to roast over the fire.

"No problem," Mary told the young firefighter. "I'm happy to help you set up. It's very kind of you to volunteer your time to share your knowledge."

Wyatt straightened his wispy mustache and gave her an aw-shucks expression, then turned his attention to Tess. "I thought we'd start your fire inspection by checking out the operability of your smoke detectors."

Tess clapped a hand to her mouth. "Oh my goodness!" she said with a laugh. "With all the commotion going on around here, our appointment totally slipped my mind." She caught Mary's elbow to keep her from hustling away. "Wyatt and his family are dear friends of ours. Blake and I couldn't be prouder of him if he were our own flesh-and-blood nephew."

She went on to explain that Wyatt had recently finished his firefighter training and had 100 percent attendance at all the fire calls since he was certified two months ago.

"You'd be amazed how many emergency calls there are in a small community like Ivy Bay," Wyatt added, in what seemed to be an effort to take the attention off himself. In addition to fighting fires, he also responded in a paramedic capacity, but it was clear that the fire aspect of his job was his primary interest. "And the number of calls really shot up in the second quarter of this year. Most of our calls are 'smell of smoke' calls. But recently, there was a deck fire where someone left cleaning rags to self-ignite, a yard fire where someone started their car over a pile of dry leaves," he said, ticking them off on his fingers, "and several brush fires started by cigarettes thrown from cars." With a nod to Mary, he added, "And, of course, the bakery fire. That was the biggie."

His face glowed. At first, Mary had attributed his pink hue to embarrassment under Tess's gushing praise. But after hearing him talk about his job, she began to wonder if the rosy hue came from excitement about the fires he had attended.

He stretched out his chest and absentmindedly pulled at the elastic band on his wristwatch. "My goal is to increase fire-safety awareness by inspecting places of business and by giving a talk down at the beach next weekend." He went on to tell Tess about the workshop he was planning with Nicole and Mary and invited her to attend.

"I wish I could go," Tess said, "but I'll be serving ice cream and milk shakes to overheated vacationers on Saturday. I hope you have a great turnout."

Mary hoped so too. Seeing Wyatt's enthusiasm to help others, she imagined he'd be crushed if no one showed up.

SIX

Thursday proved to be an unusually slow day at the store, so Mary popped over to the bakery to see how Susan was coming along. On occasion, customers stopped in at Mary's Mystery Bookshop on their way to the bakery, but today, the hungry shoppers seemed to be congregating on the other side of Main Street.

With the burned and sooty trash removed from the bakery and the walls and floors scrubbed clean, the smoky smell had almost disappeared from Mary's store. Unfortunately, Susan had no idea how long it would be before restoration work would begin on the building. The only date she'd been given was "soon."

She found Susan in the office area and handed her a gift wrapped with yellow paper and an even deeper yellow ribbon—yellow was Susan's favorite color.

"It's from Betty and me. We wanted to give you something to cheer you up."

Unfortunately, the unexpected gift had the opposite effect. Tears welled up in Susan's pretty eyes and overflowed down her round cheeks. "This is so sweet," she said as she untied the bow. "You shouldn't have."

"It's not much," Mary said demurely. "We just want you to know you're loved. We wish we could do a lot more."

Susan stopped unwrapping and rested her palm on Mary's hand. "You've already done so much. I feel blessed to have such good friends." She lifted the wind chime from the box. Colorful metal butterflies swayed with the movement, and the weights jangled merrily.

Just as Mary and Betty had hoped, the wind chime turned Susan's sad expression into a smile.

"My bakery is an ugly caterpillar right now," Susan said, taking in the disorder around her, "but I'd like to think it'll soon be a butterfly. Thank you. I really appreciate it."

That was just like Susan, to look on the positive side. What a great role model for how to endure with grace the inevitable times of trouble that come into one's life.

To make sure her friend didn't overlook the papers she'd stashed away, Mary pulled open the desk drawer in the bakery's tiny office nook and showed Susan where she had stashed the documents that had been found the day after the fire.

"Oh, and in that small metal case is a baseball card that Dorothy found behind the counter. I thought it might belong to Ryan since he's such a baseball fan."

Susan opened the case and examined it closely. She shook her head. "No, it's not Ryan's. He loves baseball, as anyone in Ivy Bay can attest, but he's not a collector. He always enjoys participating in the game or watching it, but any baseball stuff he buys has to be useful. Like that Yankees cap he always wears, or the Red Sox apron he uses whenever he cooks out on the barbecue." She gave Mary a halfhearted grin. "He believes in giving equal time to both rival teams."

Something in Susan's demeanor told Mary that more was going on with Ryan than she let on. Something that clearly troubled her.

Mary reached for the card and took another look. Ted Williams, the player featured on the card, had been with the Boston Red Sox back in his rookie year, 1939. And the lighter she'd found in the kitchen sported the NY logo. For the New York Yankees, perhaps?

"If it's not Ryan's, do you have any idea who this card might belong to? One of your employees, perhaps?"

One of the part-timers was a seventy-something retired woman who often worked the morning shift, and the other a girly-girl teenager who came to work after school with her hair carefully spiked, eyes loaded with makeup, fingernails painted green, blue, or whatever other color caught her fancy, and wearing enough jangly jewelry to fill in for a tambourine player in a folk band. Therefore, neither seemed to be the type to collect sports memorabilia.

Susan shrugged. "No, it's definitely not theirs. Maybe a customer dropped it by accident."

Behind the counter? Mary didn't think so. If it hadn't been dropped there by Susan, Ryan, or one of the employees, that left only the arsonist. And, quite frankly, Mary had a funny feeling Ryan wasn't entirely innocent.

"Do you mind if I hang on to this for a while?" Maybe it was a clue. Or maybe it was just an innocently dropped item that had nothing to do with the fire. But it wouldn't hurt to see what she could find out about it. At the very least, maybe she'd be able to reunite the card with its rightful owner.

Susan slanted a wry smile in Mary's direction. "I know what's going on here," she said, her tone direct yet soft, "and you've taken this on as another one of your mysteries to solve." Her teasing smile faded, and a quiet pause hung between them. "Thank you, Mary," she said in all sincerity. "I know Chief McArthur is on the case, but it's nice to know you're keeping an eye out too."

Mary nodded. "I just want to help." Mary had learned in recent years that God had gifted her with a curious mind and an ability to notice details that other people sometimes overlooked. So it pleased her to honor Him by making use of that gift.

"Sure, Mary. I'll let you know if anyone comes in asking for the baseball card."

When Mary returned to the bookshop, Chief McArthur was waiting for her. Seven-year-old Ashley had kept him entertained with her cat's cradle demonstrations, and now his big fingers were hopelessly trapped in the tangled spiderweb the child had woven around them. If he had to reach for his gun in a hurry, he'd certainly be in a fine pickle, as Mary's mother used to say.

"Oh, Mary," he said, disengaging himself from the unintentional trap Ashley had put him in. "Just the person I came to see." He smiled at Ashley. "Besides my young friend here, of course."

Once he had freed himself, Ashley went off to untangle the yarn, and the chief quickly got to the matter he had come to see her about.

"Any suspects yet? Made any arrests in the bakery-fire case?" he asked with a teasing grin.

During the time she had known him, Mary always tried not to interfere with police investigations, even when she was certain she had sleuthed out prospects that police officials may not have considered. In return, Chief McArthur mostly respected her thoughts and opinions, and sometimes even bounced ideas back and forth with her. They occasionally butted heads, but most of the time, the chief appreciated Mary's interest in local mysteries. Today turned out to be one of those days.

"No. I was hoping you were coming to tell me you'd found the culprit," she said.

He shook his head. "We're still gathering information. Do you have any possibilities?"

"One or two," she said with hesitation.

"Weak evidence, or someone you're hoping didn't do it?"

"Both." She considered telling him about Tyson coming home late the night of the fire, smelling of gasoline. But when she considered the troubling situation with his sick sister, it seemed a better idea to look into that a bit more before mentioning the teen's name.

She went behind the counter and pulled open a drawer where she had stashed the items she found at the bakery the day after the fire. Chief McArthur leaned over the counter to examine her finds.

First, the lighter with the NY logo on it. "This may have been what the arsonist—possibly Ryan Crosby—used to start the fire," Mary said.

"Or it may have just fallen out of his pocket when he was fixing the oven," Chief McArthur said pragmatically. It was a known fact around Ivy Bay that Ryan was *always* fixing the bakery's dilapidated oven.

She had obviously touched a nerve with that possibility. The chief liked Ryan. Who didn't? Ryan was a nice guy, with a great sense of humor and a warm personality. And, at times, a bit of a temper. But all in all, he had a lot of friends in the community, herself among them, and none would want to see him investigated as an arson suspect in his own wife's bakery.

She nodded. "Could be. However, there are other little pieces that don't seem like much by themselves, but when you add them up…"

Reluctantly, she filled him in on Ryan's kicking the oven and his offhand "eye for an eye" threat, in which he threatened to do to the oven what it had done to the burned brownies. His unexplained absence the night of the fire, and that she'd overheard Susan asking where her husband had been. Not to mention the fact that he'd been so agitated and belligerent when he showed up late at the fire. And now, the most recent clue. She reached into her pocket and pulled out the card she'd brought over from Susan's shop.

"And then there's this Ted Williams baseball card," she said.

"Cool," he said, turning it over in his hands to examine the sports treasure. But judging by the curious expression on his face, he wasn't exactly following the connection between the card and the arson.

"Ryan is a die-hard baseball fan, and his two favorite teams are the New York Yankees and the Boston Red Sox."

"Seriously?" Chief McArthur scratched his head in an apparent attempt to comprehend why someone would be a fan of both teams. Usually people loved one and hated the other.

"The connection is that the lighter has a New York logo on it, and the baseball card features a Red Sox player."

He met her gaze with a gentle smile and a slight tilt of the head. "I presume that would be your weak evidence?"

He had her there. "As I said, the bits and pieces alone don't seem like much, but when you add them together—"

"When you add them together, they look like a pile of circumstantial evidence."

Mary couldn't argue that. She didn't want Ryan to be the guilty party. In fact, she felt terrible about implicating her friend's husband in the fire but felt it was her civic duty to mention what seemed to her like a strong possibility. Even so, she prayed she had done the right thing in bringing his name to the attention of the authorities.

The chief picked up the lighter and stared at it for a long moment. "Then again, we should probably check it out." He held it aloft. "Do you mind?"

"By all means."

He stuck the lighter back in the envelope she had removed it from, tucked it in his pocket, and pointed to the remaining two items on the counter. "And what are these?"

Grateful that he had taken her suspicions seriously, even though they involved something of a stretch, she hesitated. These clues—or perhaps random artifacts—were even weaker than the others.

"This paper, from a roll of antacids, was found in the storeroom after the fire. I believe it was left there by a woman named Carol Bates." Susan had already mentioned the missing keys and her concern that Carol might have taken them. Mary went on to describe her only meeting with Carol, who had criticized Susan's frosting and then went on to accuse the baker of giving her food poisoning. On telling it, Mary had to admit that suggesting Carol might be a suspect came off as very weak. "I'm not saying she did it," she added. "Just that it seems odd for her to have gone into the storeroom when she had no business back there."

"If, indeed, she had gone in there."

"Touché."

Despite his skepticism, Chief McArthur jotted a note on his pad. "I'll check into it," he said, "and see if she can account for her whereabouts at the time the fire started."

He tapped the clear plastic bag on the counter.

"And this?"

If the other pieces of "evidence" were weak, then this one might be considered laughable. But the police couldn't check it out if she didn't bring it to their attention. She decided it was better to raise a false lead than withhold it and miss an opportunity to catch the culprit.

Once again, she described for him how a black vehicle with a blonde passenger had made its way slowly down Main Street with its lights off right after the fire started.

"Even if, as you suggested, they forgot to turn on their headlights," she said, coming out from behind the counter where she could pace off her nervous energy, "don't you think they would have stopped when they saw the fire? When they saw me trying to wave them down?"

Chief McArthur tilted his head as if she had a good point there.

"Anyway, when I was checking to see if Susan had left the butter on the prep table, I heard a noise." She explained that she hadn't mentioned the noise the night of the fire because at that time, the fire was considered to have been accidental. At least that's what Wyatt Heath had led her to believe. Mary laid a finger on her cheek while she recalled the moment. "The sound may have come from the arsonist hiding in the office area." She interrupted herself for a moment to describe the ring of flammable-smelling liquid that had been left on the floor. "Or the noise may have been caused by someone lurking outside." Or the orange cat. She didn't mention Tyson. Not yet. Maybe after she found out more about what he'd been doing that night near the shed. "Perhaps there was an accomplice."

"What makes you say that?"

She held up the plastic bag containing several strands of light-colored hair. "The passenger in the black vehicle had long blonde hair. The following day, I found this clinging to the gate behind the bakery." She paused theatrically. "Coincidence?"

"Maybe."

"Or maybe not."

After a moment, he conceded and plucked the bag from her fingers, depositing it in the pocket that held the lighter.

He retrieved his hat from the countertop and placed it on his head. With a show of gentlemanly chivalry, he tipped it to Mary. "Thanks for your help," he said.

She walked him to the door. "Will you let me know what you find out?"

He pressed his lips into a thin line before answering. "I'm sorry, Mary, and thank you for your help, but you know I'm not at liberty to discuss our findings in an ongoing investigation."

Mary took no offense to being left out of the loop. He was a by-the-book kind of police chief, and she appreciated how seriously he took his sworn duty.

The bell above the door jangled to announce his departure, and Rebecca returned to the checkout counter carrying an armload of books to feature as possible impulse buys. Mary helped unload Rebecca's arms and arrange them on the display table. Rebecca nodded toward the door Chief McArthur just exited. "Well, that was a one-way street."

Mary nodded in agreement. "True. But he's just doing his job."

God willing, his job would soon lead him to the arsonist and justice for Susan.

With a heavy heart, Mary returned to the bakery to inform Susan of her conversation with Chief McArthur. Honesty, in her book, was not only the best policy, but it was the only policy. She found her friend leaning over the desk with her forehead pressed against her hands.

"Are you okay?" Mary asked.

Susan dropped her gaze to a scrap of paper with a couple of dates scrawled on it. "For the moment," she said. "But the future is looking pretty bleak."

It hurt Mary to know that the news she came to share would only add to Susan's burden. As her friend, however, Mary needed to be totally up-front with her about what she and the police chief had discussed.

Mary perched on the edge of the desk and gave it to her straight. "I'm really sorry, Susan, but I had to be honest with him about what I'd found. Ryan may be totally innocent, and I pray he is."

She paused a moment to touch Susan's shoulder—a shoulder that must feel like it was carrying the weight of the world.

"And I pray that this won't affect our friendship," she added.

Susan looked up, her pale eyes showing surprise at the suggestion that she might hold Mary's honesty against her. She lifted her shoulder and turned her cheek to Mary's hand in a gesture of affection.

"Honey, I don't blame you. I've even had the same questions myself." Susan leaned back in the chair and stared at the framed photo on her desk that still showed a couple of smudges after having been wiped clean of soot. In it, Susan was laughing up at Ryan, who pulled her to him in a one-armed hug. "Besides, it was just a matter of time before someone noticed his mysterious absence the night of the fire."

Mary nodded, uncertain what to say. In the ensuing silence, she offered up an unspoken prayer of thanks that her friend didn't hold her actions against her, no matter how well intended they were. And she asked God to give Susan the strength to endure whatever might come as a result of it.

"Ryan has been surprisingly tight-lipped about his whereabouts that night," Susan said, "and I don't want to push the matter. But it should be all cleared away once he talks to Chief McArthur. Wherever he was that night, I'm sure he had a good reason for being there."

On the one hand, Susan's complete faith in her husband of almost twenty years could be a testament to a strong marriage built on hard-earned mutual respect. On the other, it could be a sign of gullible hope and blind trust. Mary fervently hoped it was the former.

At the moment, however, Susan seemed more concerned about the dates written on the scrap of paper.

"My landlord called this morning with an update on the time frame for making repairs to the bakery."

Mary wanted to hope for good news, but Susan's disappointed expression told her otherwise.

"It's going to take longer than expected. Much longer." She glanced at the paper in her hand, then her pale-blue gaze met Mary's sympathetic one. "The earliest he can get the contractor in here is late September. Maybe even mid-October."

More than a month away. Maybe two. Much too long to be without income. "Can't he find someone else to do the work? Maybe someone from out of town?"

Susan shook her head, the chain on her reading glasses swinging against her neck. "Apparently, construction is booming again, which has created a long waiting list. Besides, Roger prefers to work with Clayton Strong because he does good work, and he's local."

Her anxiety permeated the room, and Mary understood the dilemma that presented itself. The longer the delay, the less likely her friend would be able to get Sweet Susan's Bakery back up and running.

"What will I do if there is no bakery?" Susan's intense gaze beseeched her to come up with an answer to her unanswerable question. "Baking is what I know. I can't type fast enough to do an office job, and I can't afford to go back to school and learn something else." She paused, considering the possibilities. "A job as a cashier might buy Ryan and me a little time, but even that would eventually take us deeper in the hole. I have no idea how we're going to pay our bills."

Mary could feel the despair seizing her friend, tightening around her neck until the next words that came out of her mouth were barely more than a squeak.

"And then there are my employees. I paid them for this week, but next week…" She took a deep breath in an effort to clear the panic from her voice. "Alice is on a pension and works mainly to get out and socialize, to keep from being lonely. So she'll do fine without her earnings from the bakery. But Jasmine is saving for college. She needs a paycheck as much as I do."

That was so like Susan, to worry about others as much as herself. Mary wanted to cheer her up. To say the right thing. But she didn't want to just shower her with trite platitudes. All she could do was say what she believed to be the truth.

"I know this sounds like a cliché," she began, "but I really do believe this is an opportunity to practice faith. God *is* in charge, and He can turn even the most devastating situation into something good."

Susan smiled, but it didn't quite reach her eyes.

"Besides, you have all of us—your friends and neighbors— praying for you and willing to help out in whatever way we can."

At that, the smile made it the rest of the way up, and tiny crinkles formed at the corners of Susan's eyes. She rose and extended a hand to Mary. "Come on. Let me show you the progress we've made on the cleanup efforts."

As they walked through the shop, Mary was painfully aware of the nearly empty shelves in the storeroom, the lack of cheerful decor on the walls throughout, and the absence of baked goods, souvenir cookbooks and postcards, and jars of honey and jam for sale at the front. The kitchen had taken the greatest hit, with damage through the ceiling that left an open hole to the attic. Simpler to fix, but more visually disturbing, was the destruction to the wall that separated the kitchen from the cash-register area. Saddest of all were the empty glass display cases, one of which had been shattered, either from the heat or perhaps from contact during efforts to contain the fire.

After they'd made the rounds of the shop, they ventured outside where the cheery sun and colorful garden gave no hint of the damage and destruction that had been wrought inside. Once again, the restless feline acknowledged their arrival by disappearing between the fence slats into the neighboring yard—this time into Mary's yard.

"Do you have any idea who that cat belongs to?" she asked.

Susan shrugged. "Not a clue."

Stepping outside turned out to be a good way to end the tour. Nature had a way of doing that—of erasing pain and stress and reminding people that the world is bigger than whatever problems they might be going through at the moment.

Susan idly plucked a droopy leaf off a lacecap hydrangea bush. "Before the fire, Ryan and I had been talking about having an end-of-the-summer barbecue, to celebrate our twentieth anniversary with all our friends. Afterward, we couldn't imagine throwing a party with so much trouble on our minds." She paused a moment, giving it some thought. "But what better time to put on our party duds, surround ourselves with friends, and forget about this stuff," she said, gesturing toward the bakery. "Besides, it would be a nice opportunity to thank our friends for all the help and kindness they've shown us. And rejoice that no one had been hurt in the fire."

Mary smiled. Susan may have been knocked off-kilter for a while, but this disaster certainly wouldn't keep her down.

Susan stared off into the distance and started thinking out loud. "If we wait past next weekend, we'll be right in the middle of all the busyness of Labor Day weekend." She turned back to Mary and asked, "Would next Friday afternoon work for you? I know it's short notice, but I hope you'll say yes."

The eagerness in her voice pleased Mary. For these past few days, Susan had worn a stricken expression of bewilderment and distress. It felt good to see some of her bubbly effervescence returning.

"I wouldn't miss it for anything," she reassured her friend. "Would you like for me to bring some of my homemade sauerkraut for the hot dogs?"

"That would be wonderful. Better yet, bring your sister and Henry."

They both needed to get back to work, but neither of the women wanted to leave the sunny warmth of the yard, so they dawdled a few more minutes, going over the menu and planning games of horseshoes, volleyball, and badminton.

While they talked, a movement over Susan's shoulder caught Mary's attention. Beyond the Tea Shoppe, in the yard behind the hardware store, young Tyson once again lurked near the storage shed. His actions seemed sneaky, like he was trying to hide something. That, of course, riveted Mary's attention even more securely to whatever was unfolding over there.

"What—?" Having noticed Mary's gaze fixed elsewhere, Susan turned to see what had captured her attention. "Oh."

As if feeling the heat of their gazes on his back, Tyson turned and looked over his shoulder. When his eyes met theirs, the lanky teen quickly glanced away and hurried back into the hardware store.

Susan bristled at the sight of the boy. Mary could only assume she was remembering the sour attitude he had demonstrated when reminded of the ten dollars he had mistakenly shorted her. Telling Susan about his suspicious behavior the night of the fire would serve no purpose other than to heighten any lingering animosity between the two, so Mary kept her thoughts to herself.

After Susan returned to the bakery to continue her work, Mary hung back, saying she wanted to enjoy the sun for a few more minutes. But even the antics of a small brown house sparrow—intent on raiding the bird feeder of its favored millet seed—could not keep Mary's thoughts from returning to what Tyson had been doing by the shed.

Curiosity overcoming her, she let herself out the back gate and walked over to the small building where Tyson had bent his tall frame near the bushes. The fence kept her from going inside to satisfy her curiosity, but it didn't keep her from peeking into the well-groomed yard that everyone knew Amelia Shepard kept in tip-top shape.

Though nobody was in sight, Mary found herself casually glancing at her watch to cover for the fact that she was standing here, loitering behind the hardware store's property. As she turned to head back, she peeked over the white picket fence and craned just enough to see the corner of a can of liquid hidden behind a bush. Although she couldn't tell from this distance what kind of liquid it was, she could certainly make out the first four letters in red on the side of the rectangular can: FLAM.

Flammable.

Despite the gentle warmth of the sun caressing her bare arms, Mary felt a chill wash over her. She rubbed the goose bumps away, certain of one thing. Amid all the questions that the can had raised, there was one thing that was certain: She needed to be extremely careful how she handled this suspicious situation so it didn't blow up in her face.

SEVEN

—◆◆◆—

Later that morning, Mary had turned her attention to the upcoming learning session that would feature Tess and their ice-cream recipe. She needed to check in with Nicole for an update on the number of attendees to expect and to fill her in on the progress she and Tess had made so far.

She glanced at her watch. Almost noon. She could kill two birds with one stone by having lunch at the Black & White Diner and asking Nicole a couple of quick questions.

"I'm going over to the diner for lunch," she called to Rebecca, who was busily straightening shelves and turning their best sellers face out. "Want me to bring something back for you?"

Rebecca straightened and pressed the kinks out of her back with her hands. "No, but thank you. I'm going to run a couple of errands during my lunch break and pick up something to eat while I'm out. Have some Boston baked beans for me," she said with a grin.

Mary wasted no time getting over there. She needed to beat the lunch crowd so she could have a couple of minutes of Nicole's attention. As it turned out, everyone else in Ivy Bay must have had the same idea of eating before the noon hour struck. Fortunately, two empty tables remained, so Mary took the one in Nicole's station. She slid into the booth and studied the menu. No particular reason for doing so. Her taste buds had already made up their mind and clamored for the fried-fish sandwich advertised as "wicked good" on the daily-special flyer. Featuring fish rolled in homemade mayonnaise, then coated in cornmeal and fried until crispy, the sandwich always drew a crowd on the days it was featured.

Nicole popped over to the booth, her ponytail swinging with the energy in her stride. She took Mary's order, which included a side of baked beans, and suggested a drink she had invented: a lemon-lime soft drink flavored with a touch of cranberry juice.

Seeing that Nicole needed to hurry off to other customers, Mary quickly went over her questions about the ice-cream workshop.

"I'm glad you asked about the handout," Nicole said, enthusiasm bubbling over as it did every time they discussed the learning-annex series. "I charged the attendees a little extra to cover photocopying, so it would be great if you and Tess provide several different recipes for them to try at home. And if you can make three ice-cream flavors for tasting, and include the recipes in the handouts, people will just love it!"

"*Three* flavors?" It was already enough work perfecting and focusing on one unique flavor. Now their task had effectively been tripled.

"Yes, they say when you're teaching something new to a student, you should teach it three different ways so they can grasp the concept easier."

Right church, wrong pew. The teaching technique that Nicole mentioned actually referred to auditory, visual, and tactile presentations to cover each student's natural way of learning. She and Tess already had those covered with spoken instructions, written recipes, and a hands-on opportunity for each of them to take a turn at making the ice cream.

Mary realized this was going to be way more work than she had bargained for. However, she was a woman who went by the book—the Good Book, that is—when it came to keeping her word, so she would not back out on their arrangement. Instead, she mentally adjusted her plans for the workshop and expected she would be working a few more late nights until this learning session was done. Perhaps she and Tess could focus the majority of their efforts on the spotlight flavor, then take a shortcut on the other samples by showing the attendees how they could create other taste sensations merely by adding flavors to a vanilla base.

Nicole scurried off to get her sandwich, and Mary used the idle time to jot a few notes to herself. Perhaps she and Tess could consolidate the work by coming up with a base recipe and showing the attendees how to add ingredients to create their own favorite flavors.

A few minutes later, the door swung open and the woman Mary had met at Susan's bakery entered. Her eye shadow and lipstick were carefully applied, and her shoulder-length blonde curls bounced with more life than Carol was showing right now. She hovered near Mary's booth, her face pasty and colorless. A waitress asked Carol to wait another moment while she cleared a table.

Mary suddenly realized she had a large booth all to herself, so she invited Carol to join her.

After a moment's hesitation, in which it was clear that the woman was trying to place where they'd met before, recognition finally dawned, and Carol gratefully accepted. She settled herself heavily onto the bench seat and proceeded to dig through her purse until she turned up a ratty package of antacids. A small notepad escaped the overstuffed confines of her purse and tumbled unheeded to the bench seat where Carol sat.

Mary leaned forward, taking note of the blue lettering on white paper around the antacids. Same as the wrapper she'd found in the bakery storeroom.

Noticing Mary's interest, Carol hastily popped the tablet into her mouth. Just as quickly, she shoved the roll back into her purse and snapped it shut. She glanced around the room as if searching for something. Or someone.

Mary frowned at her odd behavior. Guilty conscience, perhaps? Did Carol expect Chief McArthur to show up and arrest her?

Nicole returned to the table to tell Mary her meal would be ready soon and seemed surprised to find that another diner had joined her. Ever the professional, Nicole whipped out her order pad and went through the daily specials again.

Carol waved her hand, clearly uninterested in the sumptuous fare. "I'll just have a cup of chicken noodle soup and half a turkey sandwich. Plain. No lettuce or tomato." Then she proceeded to grill Nicole about the food's freshness, or lack thereof.

The unpleasant implication rang clear—that she anticipated Nicole might serve her tainted food. Seeing Nicole's stiff glance and Mary's curious one, Carol hurried to explain.

"I got food poisoning the other day from a cupcake at the bakery across the street and would prefer not to repeat the experience."

Nicole bristled at the implied insult but kept her thoughts to herself. When she finally spoke, icicles dripped from her words. "All the food at Black & White is fresh. Every day."

After Nicole disappeared into the kitchen, Mary used the time to get to know Carol a little better and ask a few carefully chosen questions.

"Have you known Susan long?" Mary asked.

Carol snorted. "Long enough to know that her frosting could use some work." Apparently noticing Mary's look of disapproval, she backpedaled in an effort to smooth over her criticism. "Not saying it tastes *bad*, of course."

Mary pressed her lips together, stopping the flow of words perched on the tip of her tongue in defense of her friend's baking prowess. "You don't like her frosting because you got sick?"

"Because it tastes bland. Haven't you noticed?"

She hadn't, because she thought everything about Susan's cupcakes tasted fabulous. Not one to mince words, Mary decided on the direct approach.

"Do you have something against Susan?"

Carol seemed unfazed by the question. "Only against her frosting," she said. "And the fact that I got food poisoning from her cupcake. But I expect she's fixed that by now."

She had, but Mary refused to mention that Carol's comment had cost Susan an entire batch of cupcakes and frosting, as well as all the cream cheese stored in her refrigerator. All as a safeguard to prevent another illness that they both doubted had been caused by the cupcake. Carol seemed to harbor an air of competition when it came to cupcake baking, and Mary didn't want to give her a reason to gloat.

Nicole returned with their meals and gave Mary a warm smile as she set the plate in front of her. Carol received a frosty nod before Nicole turned on her heel and left them to their lunch.

Mary's fish sandwich was heavenly, almost enough to take her mind off the troubling conversation that had been brewing between her and Carol.

"I've been thinking about opening my own bakery," Carol declared. Not a surprise, given the thorough questioning she had put Susan through. She poked at her food as if checking for hidden bombs that might be lurking inside it. "The problem is that Susan has the prime retail spot, right in the middle of Main Street, where she can catch all the shoppers who want to pop in for an impulse purchase. The only halfway affordable property I've been able to find is on the outskirts of town where there's no foot traffic."

Ah. No wonder she'd made that comment about customers needing a choice of where to buy their cupcakes. A troubling thought occurred to her. Could Carol have set the fire to force Susan out of business, thus freeing up the prime real estate that she coveted for her own shop? The keys had gone missing shortly after she had been standing near the cash register where they'd been left. And then there was the matter of the antacid paper that had been left in the storeroom.

But if Carol had set the fire, would she have been so open about her interest in opening her own bakery? Mary pondered that a moment and decided that if Carol was guilty, she was either not very bright to be so forthcoming or, conversely, she was clever enough to use her supposed transparency as proof she had nothing to hide.

Carol took a bite of her plain turkey sandwich and carefully rolled it around in her mouth before she chewed and swallowed it. What did she expect to find in there? Razor blades?

Unable to hold back any longer, Mary got around to the subject she'd been wanting to address ever since Carol had walked into the diner. She set her fork on the table and met the other woman's gaze squarely. "I know you went into the storeroom at the bakery the day of the fire. It would help the investigation if you could explain what you were doing in there."

Carol seemed caught off guard. She frowned, and her eyes darted to the right as if she were recalling the memory. "How did you know that?"

Hmm. She hadn't denied it. Not one to tip her hand, Mary simply said, "We have evidence."

Carol's eyes widened as she blurted out her defense. "The cupcake," she declared. "It made me sick. Since my antacids had all been used up, I went to the storeroom to look for baking soda to settle my stomach. Susan owed me at least that much since it was her cupcake that caused my problem in the first place."

Mary narrowed her eyes as she took it all in, but Carol must have misread her expression as one of disbelief.

"Susan can check her security camera," she insisted. "That's all I did was go in there to look for some bicarb. Which I didn't even take, by the way, because the baking-soda boxes were still sealed. So I just left."

Susan didn't have a security camera at the shop, which was a shame, because it might have shed light on who had been sneaking around in there the other night. But Mary didn't bother to correct Carol on the matter.

"And I was sick for the rest of the night," Carol said, her voice becoming somewhat strident. "In fact, I got so dehydrated I had to go to the medical center where they hooked me up to a saline drip to replenish my fluids. If you don't believe me, you can check my medical records."

She lifted her chin as if daring Mary to do just that.

Actually, she couldn't because of HIPAA privacy laws, but it was a tempting thought. Interestingly, the whole time Carol had been declaring her innocence, she never once looked Mary in the eye.

Carol turned her attention back to the soup, eating a few spoonfuls, then pushing the bowl away as if the very sight of it offended her. Her lunch half finished, she abruptly excused herself, threw some cash on the table, and left in a hurry. Guilty conscience, perhaps?

Mary sat, unmoving on the padded bench, and watched as her lunch mate flung open the door and hustled outside.

She finished off her coleslaw and baked beans, reflecting on the odd conversation that had just unfolded. The diner had filled until patrons now stood by the door, waiting for tables, so Mary didn't bother to wait for Nicole to bring her check. She left some cash for her meal, then added a few extra dollars to cover the tip that had been shorted by Carol in her hasty departure.

Mary had just turned to leave when she noticed the errant notepad that Carol had dropped from her purse. Ordinarily, she'd give it to Nicole to hold until Carol's return, but the waitress was so busy running from table to table that she considered it might get lost in the shuffle. So she picked up the small pad and tucked it in her purse to give to Carol later.

Something told her they would be crossing paths again soon, whether Carol liked it or not.

After lunch, Mary headed over to the hardware store for a new extension cord—a longer one that wouldn't have to be run under the rug and create a fire hazard. Although the young firefighter Wyatt Heath had been mistaken about the cause of the fire in Susan's bakery, there was no doubt about the danger he had pointed out in her bookstore. Even though her shop had been updated in recent decades, it, like most historic buildings, could use additional electrical outlets. Someday, she might hire an electrician to add more, but for now, she could get by with an extension to take care of the few extra lamps needed to make her shoppers' browsing experience more enjoyable.

As she entered the hardware store, a flyer taped to the window caught her notice. Actually, it was the graphic of a baseball player in full swing that drew her attention. Bold

Helvetica type announced a sports-card trading show to be held at Liberty Elementary School over the Labor Day weekend. Smart marketing, she thought upon consideration of the show's venue...to hold it at the elementary school where it would draw not only young 'T-ball and softball players but their baseball-enthusiast parents as well. Not to mention the fact that Ivy Bay was known for its baseball fever. Ivy Bay even boasted its own team, the Blue Jays, which used a small stadium outside of town in Bayside Park.

In this case, the baseball-card show also drew a certain gray-haired woman with major curiosity about a baseball card that had been left behind after a fire. Where there were baseball cards, there would be collectors—knowledgeable enthusiasts who could tell her something about the card that was carefully tucked away in a drawer in her bookstore.

She pulled the heavy wooden door open and picked up a flyer from a small stack on a table by the door and made a mental note of the hours of the event. She glanced around the store and once again got the impression she'd stepped into a handyman's dream. The store held every imaginable tool, gadget, and gizmo any home-repair aficionado could ever want, all carefully labeled and organized in neat stacks and bins. And, as a pleasant surprise, there were unexpected items such as greeting cards, canning jars and lids, and cute sayings on metal plaques to hang by the front door. Her favorite was the verse from Joshua 24:15: "But as for me and my household, we will serve the Lord."

Mary knew from past experience that on the off chance something couldn't be found by the customer, Jimmy would know exactly where to locate it. She wouldn't need to bother him today since she knew the extension cords would be in the electrical aisle.

It took only a moment to find the right shelf, and another to compare between two cords before deciding on her purchase. On her way to the cash register, she passed plastic jugs of mold-removal spray for house exteriors. Though the color and everything else were different, the rectangular shape of the jug prompted a memory of the leaked liquid on the floor of Susan's office nook. On impulse, she decided that since she was already here, she may as well check out the cans of flammable liquids to see what Tyson might have been carrying out to the shed those times she'd found him lurking in the yard behind the hardware store.

She wandered a couple of different rows before she found some similar-looking metal cans in the furniture-refinishing area. Sure enough, there was the can just like the one Tyson had left beside the shed. Large red letters across the side cautioned, "FLAMMABLE!"

Setting aside the extension cord, Mary lifted the can of varnish remover and opened the cap. Almost instantly, the air filled with a strong, familiar odor that reminded her of gasoline. Most likely, this was what Amelia Shepard had detected the night Tyson had come home late, claiming the car had run out of gas.

Two disturbing thoughts occurred to Mary. The most obvious—and the one she'd been stewing over for the past several days—was that Tyson might have set the fire after his angry blowup when Susan reminded him that he owed her another ten dollars in change. Although Mary couldn't say for sure unless she compared the two fluids side by side, this one sure smelled a lot like the leaked liquid she'd found in Susan's office area. It was a stretch to think that a petty encounter could incur such an extreme form of retaliation. But if Tyson was as troubled as people indicated, it would be impossible to guess what he might be capable of doing.

The other, equally troubling possibility had been raised by Lynn Teagarden in their prayer meeting—that Tyson might be doing drugs. Only, in this case, he would have sniffed it rather than smoked it.

Mary's heart seized with a mixture of fear and compassion for the boy and whatever wrong choices he might be making lately. Although she took to heart the direction to *pray without ceasing* and frequently talked to God while working, socializing, or even driving, this time Mary felt compelled to close her eyes for just a few seconds and offer up an extra-earnest prayer. She silently asked God to watch over the teen and guide his choices.

A sinus headache brought on by the fumes of the open container brought a quick end to the prayer. When Mary opened her eyes, she found Jimmy standing at the end of the aisle, staring at her with open curiosity.

She supposed it did look odd, her praying over an open container of varnish remover. Anyone other than Jimmy might have assumed she was sniffing the stuff herself rather than praying for the boy she feared might be doing so. She quickly capped the container and put it back on the shelf. Even so, she didn't want her actions to trigger a discussion about the man's nephew and his questionable activities. Not yet. Not until she knew more about what Tyson was up to.

"Anything I can help you with?" Jimmy asked. "If you're thinking of refinishing some furniture, now's the time to do it while the weather is good."

She considered the possibility. The other day during Betty's gardening talk, when she'd seen the coffee table in the full light of day, it had been clear the antique piece could use some sprucing up. "The coffee table in the reading area of my bookshop is looking a bit dull and worn. I should probably strip it and revarnish it," she said, thinking out loud.

Jimmy came closer and picked up the can she'd been looking at earlier. "There are some people who swear by this stuff, but you really shouldn't use it. It's extremely flammable, not to mention toxic." He put it back and picked up the one next to it. "This one is nonflammable and safer to breathe, and it still does the job."

She accepted the can he passed to her.

"You should still use it in a well-ventilated area, though," he cautioned. "Preferably outside."

Mary thanked him for the advice and mentally added another task to her overflowing to-do list. Then she asked about his family.

Jimmy's face clouded over when he mentioned the medical ordeal his niece was going through, and she assured him that the prayer group had her at the top of the list.

"Tyson is on the list too," she added.

To her relief, Jimmy smiled and ended the conversation on a happier note. "At the beginning of the summer, the boy wasn't too happy about being 'forced' to work here. But he's been very quick to pick up everything I've taught him."

Jimmy's pride in his nephew was evident in his smile and in his nod of approval.

"That's wonderful," Mary said. Even if Tyson still had some issues to work through, it felt good to hear that he was making noticeable improvements since working at the hardware store with his uncle.

"His favorite is locksmithing, so I've been teaching him some of the tricks of the trade." Jimmy straightened his posture and hooked his thumbs through his belt loops. "Why, just last week, he helped Amelia out of a jam when she accidentally locked her keys in her car. Sure helped me out since I couldn't leave the store unattended, and I didn't want her to be stranded at the grocery store."

Mary adjusted her grip on the varnish remover and tucked the extension cord under her elbow. She followed Jimmy to the cash register where she paid for her purchases and considered the information he had just shared with her.

Could Tyson have used his newly learned locksmithing skills to let himself into the bakery?

Not only would she and the prayer group continue praying for the young man's sick sister, but she would make sure Tyson got plenty of prayer time as well.

EIGHT

The next evening, spurred by the flyer she saw at the hardware store, Mary sat at the kitchen table, opened up her purse, and pulled out the baseball card she had found at the bakery. Along with the card, she pulled out a small blue spiral notepad. For a split second, she wondered how it had got in her purse. But then she remembered that it was the notebook Carol had left behind at the diner.

Curiosity got the best of her, and she flipped through the pages. The notebook was empty except for the first page, where an address located way out on Colonial Road about a mile or two south of the Beacon Inn was written. Beneath it was the name Neil, yesterday's date, and a phone number.

Mary considered the note. She didn't want to be paranoid, but if Carol *was* responsible for setting the bakery ablaze, could this Neil person have played a role? Perhaps he had been her getaway driver in the black car? Mary stuck the pad back in her purse to return it to Carol the next time she saw her and turned her attention back to the baseball card. But although the page in the notebook was now out of sight, it was not out of mind.

Nearby, Betty puttered in the kitchen, preparing a dinner of roasted chicken with carrots and green beans. Normally, this meal would have included roasted potatoes as well, but Mary had read that nightshades such as potatoes, eggplants, and tomatoes can sometimes increase the pain of rheumatoid arthritis. So, as an experiment, Betty had decided to forgo those foods for a few days to see if it made a difference. With or without the nightshades, the vegetables her sister prepared were always delicious and perfectly seasoned, and judging by the yummy aromas wafting through the kitchen, tonight would be no exception.

"That beekeeper Leslie told us about came and gathered up the honeybees today," Betty said, her eye still on the pot she tended. "She was really excited to get them."

"That's wonderful." Wonderful for both beekeeper and bees. Deborah had a sterling reputation in the local apiary community, so Mary had no doubt the hardworking insects would be well cared for.

While Betty went back to stirring up delicious dinner smells, Mary set the baseball card on the table and removed the clear Lucite case from the black metal container. The card remained sealed inside the clear cover. She contemplated trying to figure out a way to pry it open, but ultimately decided that doing so might harm the value of the card.

She opened her laptop and did a quick Internet search of the Ted Williams card. Apparently, a fair quality card with creased or torn corners could sell for a few hundred dollars. A very good quality card could go for a thousand or two, and an excellently preserved specimen had been reported to sell for almost five thousand dollars. As with everything these days, their value could have fluctuated with the economy, but Mary knew one thing for sure: This card appeared to be in excellent condition. No creases, pen marks, or worn areas. Other than some expected yellowing that had darkened the paper over time, it appeared to be in perfect shape. There was no doubt this card would bring top dollar.

Setting aside the curious circumstances by which the card may have ended up behind the bakery counter, Mary knew that if it had been accidentally dropped by a customer, the owner must be frantically searching for it by now.

Tracking the limited information available to her, Mary typed Ribbie Collectibles into the search engine and followed the first link to an online dictionary of baseball terms that defined *ribbie* as "run batted in." The next link took her to an online baseball-card trader. It would be a while before dinner, leaving Mary plenty of time in which to prepare veggies for a salad, so she clicked through to the site's online store where she found a broad assortment of cards, acrylic storage cases, gift sets of lesser-valued cards assembled, and refractor cards that featured a colorful shine.

Unable to find where in the country the dealer was based, she gave up for the evening. "You think Emma would like a pack of Boston Red Sox baseball cards for her birthday?" she asked Betty.

Her sister lifted the lid on the pan of green beans, releasing a cloud of steam, and stirred. The smell of onions and seasonings wafted to Mary. "If you had asked me that thirty years ago, I probably would have said no," she answered honestly. "But Emma loves to play softball, and she and the family sometimes go to games in Boston, so I say, why not."

Betty had a good point about how times had changed. Mary's granddaughter not only loved the sport, but she was an excellent player as well. Mary could imagine the cards arranged artfully around the mirror in Emma's bedroom or tacky-puttied to the wall alongside her posters, dried flowers, and friends' photos.

Mary ordered an inexpensive assortment of cards featuring recent Boston Red Sox players for Emma and planned to complete the gift with a carefully chosen book from the shop. Although she hadn't been able to track the card dealer to a specific location, she considered the search a success.

Over the next week, Mary found her time gobbled up by work at the bookstore and preparations for the upcoming fire-safety and ice-cream workshops. Repair work on the bakery had not yet begun. Trouper that she was, Susan didn't let that get her down. She just pasted on a cheerful smile and used the downtime to prepare for her anniversary picnic.

Being surrounded by friends and family would be good for Susan. She needed their love and support right now. And, quite frankly, Mary would enjoy the break from her own responsibilities to spend a few hours laughing, eating, and socializing with like-minded friends and neighbors.

On Friday afternoon, Mary, Betty, and Henry mingled with guests on the Crosbys' patio while children in bathing suits ran squealing through the sprinkler at the far end of the property. Every so often, a breeze teased a happy tune out of the butterfly wind chime that dangled from the overhang that shaded the patio. To the left of the yard along the fence line, horseshoes clanked against metal posts or thudded in the dirt, depending upon the skill of the players. And on the other side, a group of teens and adults threw themselves into a heated game of volleyball as if an Olympic gold medal depended upon each hit.

At the edge of the patio, Ryan hovered over a barbecue grill that burped a cloud of smoke whenever he lifted the lid to flip the burgers. Decked out in his New York Yankees cap and Red Sox apron, he entertained some of the guests with stories from his experience as a coast guard reservist.

To look at him now, laughing and chatting, one would never guess his wife had just lost her business in a fire early last week. Perhaps the fact that no one had brought up the subject helped him to forget about it for a little while. On the other hand, if he had been the one to set the fire, his cheery demeanor could be the result of having accomplished the deed undetected.

Mary shivered despite the afternoon warmth and shrugged off the unwelcome thought.

Susan flitted among the guests, making sure everyone had plenty to drink and encouraging them to help themselves to the delicious goodies laid out on the picnic table. True to her down-to-earth personality, the small house and cozy yard lacked ostentation. What the place possessed in abundance, though, was a sense of welcome.

Betty ambled away to talk to Dorothy Johnson about some new books that had been donated to the church library. Henry excused himself and returned a moment later with two glasses of apple cider. He handed one to Mary.

"I see you're quite busy lately with the educational workshops you and Nicole are organizing," he said, and raised his glass in a toast to her efforts. Henry owed his six-foot height to his father's genes, and his lean muscles to working on his boat *Misty Horizon*. The silver of his hair seemed at odds with his youthful frame. Mary loved to hear his mild New England accent that was occasionally laced with the local "ayuh" in favor of "yes."

Mary lifted her glass to his and took a sip of the refreshing drink. "Thanks for reminding me. I have some flyers in my car advertising tomorrow's event. Perhaps some of the parents here would be interested in taking their children to learn about fire safety and toast marshmallows over the bonfire."

"Good idea. After you're done at the firefighter's talk tomorrow, come on over to the marina, and I'll show you the new depth finder I got for the boat."

When he wasn't fishing and supplying his fresh catch to local restaurants, Henry often took guests on tours of Ivy Bay or offered chartered fishing expeditions. And when he wasn't out on the *Misty Horizon*, he could often be found at the marina, doing maintenance work on the boat.

Mary smiled in response to his invitation. Although she wouldn't rank a depth finder at the top of her list of fun things to see, she enjoyed the enthusiasm Henry showed for anything that had to do with being out on the water that he loved so much. Besides, she was certain she would come away from the visit with a new tidbit of knowledge and some pleasant companionship. And Henry's diversion would be welcome after helping out at the bonfire.

"Thank you. That would be interesting."

He nodded. "Give me your car key, and I'll get the flyers for you." A sudden surge of activity attracted his attention to the barbecue grill where Ryan and a couple of the neighbors loaded burgers and hot dogs onto platters. "I'd better get a wiggle on if we want to find a dry seat before the kids in swimsuits start claiming them."

"That's okay. I'll get the flyers," Mary said and motioned him toward the line forming near the grill. "But I wouldn't mind if you nab a hot dog for me."

She opened the gate and skirted the side yard to head to her car when a black sedan pulled up behind her Impala. The vehicle looked very similar, if not identical, to the one she saw leaving the fire with its lights off. When it came to a halt, the back door swung open.

Tyson got out wearing a scowl and baggy below-the-knee shorts. He pulled the front passenger door open for his aunt Amelia, offered her an obligatory elbow, and seemed bored by the whole chivalry business. Mary suspected he'd been prompted to open doors for ladies. He might not like it now, but she had a notion he'd be grateful in the future for the manners training he was receiving this summer.

Jimmy usually drove a pickup truck for work-related errands, and they took Amelia's car for all other trips. Mary recalled Jimmy's proud declaration that the teen had unlocked Amelia's car so she could retrieve her keys. Had Tyson driven this car the night of the fire—the night he came home smelling of gasoline? And if he had been the one driving down Main Street with his lights off, who had been sitting in the passenger seat beside him? His sister, perhaps? Jill had mentioned at prayer group that the siblings were very close.

But close enough to be partners in crime? And, if so, what could be their reason for doing such a horrible thing?

Mary retrieved the flyers and walked with the Shepards to the backyard where food had unified the previous scattered activities of the group.

After everyone had eaten their fill, the younger children played tag, teenagers clustered in groups, the women sat around the picnic table sipping raspberry lemonade, and the men congregated over by the grill where Ryan—hatless for a change—shared cigars with a couple of friends. Henry declined with a polite wave of his hand.

Susan glanced in her husband's direction, then quickly turned her attention back to chatter about whose children would be assigned to which teachers for the upcoming school year. Mary knew from previous conversations with Susan that her business neighbor didn't care for Ryan's smoking, but since he only did it on special occasions, and never in the house, she wouldn't complain.

Boisterous laughter burst out among the men, and Ryan dug into his pocket, presumably for a lighter. Coming up empty, he wedged the cigar between his teeth, turned up the propane on the grill, and bent over the flames to light it. An uneasy feeling settled in Mary's stomach as she watched with trepidation.

Mere seconds later, Ryan straightened abruptly, yanked the cigar from his mouth, and swatted briefly at his face.

Mary rose from her chair and reached for the ice bucket. Susan must have also noticed her husband's gaffe, for she grabbed the container of ice from Mary's hand and took it to him.

Several of the women clustered around, expressing concern and asking if he was all right.

"I'm fine, I'm fine," he said, obviously embarrassed by all the attention. But despite his protests, he took a couple of ice cubes from the bucket and swept them over his forehead and cheeks to cool his warm skin.

When he turned back to the crowd gathered around him, a collective gasp rose from among the onlookers.

The sparse brown wisps of hair that rimmed his face had transformed from fine, straight strands to kinky coils that had lightened to an odd shade of caramel brown. And his eyebrows, normally as thick and bushy as his hair was thin, now pointed weird, spiral bristles in all directions.

He blinked a couple of times, water from the ice dripping off his face, and looked for all the world like a cartoon character who'd just opened a package from Acme Explosives.

With all eyes fixed on him, silence reigned while Ryan wiped the remaining water from his face. His hand touched the crispy brows, and an expression of concerned puzzlement crossed his features.

At that moment, Tyson walked past and paused from typing a text message on his phone. "Dude," he said as if that one word encompassed it all. "You stick your finger in a light socket?"

The mood lightened as abruptly as the sun returns after a summer storm. It was apparent that Ryan had suffered no harm from the silly accident, and his friends' relief erupted in a hearty chorus of good-natured laughter.

It was only when Ryan joined in the hilarity that Susan visibly relaxed and Mary felt her own tensed muscles unclench.

In an attempt to prolong the fun, and maybe draw attention away from Ryan's embarrassing error in judgment, Henry reached into the box of cigars and handed him one still wrapped in cellophane.

"I'll have mine medium rare," he said, and laughter exploded anew.

Mary placed a hand on her chest and turned to Susan. "Is your heart still pounding too?"

Susan nodded and forced a grin. "With Ryan around, you never know what's going to happen next."

At that moment, Chief McArthur arrived in uniform and knocked politely at the gate before letting himself into the yard.

Susan seemed glad for the distraction and bustled into hostess mode. "I'm so glad you could come," she said, gathering up a paper plate and plastic cutlery for her latest guest. "Would you rather have a hamburger or a hot dog? Betty brought some delicious tomatoes from her garden. Come over here and fill your plate."

The police chief's expression tightened, and he shook his head. "Thank you," he said, his tone serious, "but I'm not here to enjoy the party. I'd like to speak with Ryan a moment, though."

He met Ryan's gaze and jerked his head toward the side of the yard in a signal for him to step away from the group so they could talk privately.

The mirth of a moment ago squelched down to an awkward tension among the partygoers. The only ones who seemed oblivious to this latest development were the children who ran through the yard shouting, "Olly Olly oxen free!"

While the two men spoke in hushed tones, Susan stepped toward them, her feet moving like leaden blocks, and Mary instinctively followed her.

As they approached, Chief McArthur said, "I'm sorry, Ryan, but considering the nature of the charges, I have to do this."

He turned Ryan away from him and pulled a pair of handcuffs from his back pocket.

"You have the right to remain silent," he began. The rest of his words were drowned out by Susan's fervent protests.

NINE

The next day, Mary threw herself into work at the bookshop, grateful that Saturday's changing of the weekly rental tourists did not hamper the flow of shoppers. She needed to stay busy, to keep from fretting over the situation with Ryan. Despite the growing evidence against him, Mary wanted to believe he was innocent.

Susan hadn't handled her husband's arrest well. But, under the same circumstances, who would?

Needless to say, the party broke up soon afterward. Mary had stayed behind until Susan's parents arrived to stay with her. Fortunately, her mother's presence had been a calming influence. By the time Mary had left, she was convinced her friend would get through the night, though probably without much sleep, while Ryan spent the night in jail.

About an hour before the scheduled fire-safety talk, Mary drove over to Little Neck Beach where Wyatt Heath and a couple of firefighters were stacking driftwood, a couple of broken lobster traps, and dry scrub in a fire pit.

The firefighters had dressed in navy-blue slacks and blue T-shirts with the Ivy Bay Fire Department insignia on the back and left chest. Wyatt wore red suspenders, an affectation the others did not share. A red pumper truck idled by the road, in part to be on hand to suppress the fire if needed and partly to draw the attention of passersby who may not have heard about today's safety talk. Nicole hadn't arrived yet.

Mary pulled a couple of webbed lawn chairs and a bag of marshmallows from her car and carried them to the area where attendees would congregate. The children and their parents should be fine sitting on blankets, but it wouldn't hurt to have a few chairs available for weary grandparents.

Nicole must have had the same idea. Apparently having been able to slip away from work a little early, she showed up a few minutes later carrying a toddler on one hip and dragging a couple of chairs with her free hand. Her husband, a slim man with a shy demeanor, lugged several more chairs and kept a close eye on a little girl who scampered along in front of him.

"You and Chip must be on the same wavelength," Nicole exclaimed. "We were just leaving the house when he said, 'Will there be enough chairs for people to sit on?'"

It didn't surprise her that Nicole hadn't thought to bring the extra chairs herself. It was fast becoming apparent that, although Nicole was a whiz at coming up with ideas for the learning sessions, the planning aspects of putting together these workshops seemed to slip past her. Mary shook off the impatience that had briefly overcome her and reminded herself that Nicole was an absolute dynamo at the diner who remembered multiple orders and performed several tasks at once to serve her diners quickly and efficiently. As with any skill, it must have taken her a while to learn to be a top-notch waitress, so it would take some practice to get the learning-annex details ironed out.

The important thing was that the featured speaker had arrived, chairs were available for guests, and she, Nicole, and Wyatt were offering a valuable service to the residents and tourists who were already starting to arrive and claim their spots with blankets on the sand.

Mary made her way through the small but growing group of people and handed out the printed fire-safety tips Wyatt had provided. Nicole shook out a blanket, and she and Chip settled the children on it.

At the appropriate time, Wyatt got off to a nervous start in which he self-consciously twisted his mustache, stammered, and said a lot of "you knows." After a bit, he pulled out a scrapbook of fires he'd attended, and that's when he finally warmed up. Although he'd only recently been certified as a professional firefighter, the pictures he showed the crowd dated back more than a year. At that time, he explained, he had been a volunteer in training and hadn't been qualified to ride the fire trucks, but he drove his own vehicle to the fires, helped unpack and repack hoses, and took photos.

He opened the scrapbook and held it out for folks to see the image of a half-burned couch that had been set ablaze by a smoker who had nodded off in front of the television. Another showed flames shooting out of a chimney because the home owner had neglected to remove the creosote that had built up inside it. Then a kitchen fire with blackened cabinets and a charred pan of grease on the stove.

That last image brought to mind the scorched walls of Susan's bakery. Too bad the young firefighter didn't have any advice on how to prevent fires started by arson.

Wyatt moved on to some outdoor photos. A brush fire started by a home owner burning leaves during a burn ban. Then a shed set ablaze after a pile of used cleaning rags had self-ignited. And a tree house accidentally set afire after children had played with matches.

Pausing dramatically, Wyatt straightened and snapped his red suspenders. Then he proceeded to caution the children never to play with fire.

Mary sat back on her blanket, her arms behind her to brace herself, and let her gaze rest on the stretch of sand, beach, and small dunes topped by sprigs of sea grass. She wished Henry could have joined them, but at least she'd see him after the learning annex. This late in the afternoon, the sun's warmth had started to wane, and a cooling breeze mingled the scents of salt, fish, and coconut sunscreen.

A pair of shorebirds quarreled over possession of a scrap of food, prompting several slim-legged plovers to go skedaddling across the sand. The sounds of the birds, along with beachgoers calling to each other and the constant *whoosh* of waves upon the shore, forced Wyatt to raise his voice to be heard by those at the back of the small group.

Mary made a mental note to borrow a portable speaker the next time they scheduled one of these talks to be held outdoors.

"…playing with my uncle's lighter and accidentally set my parents' garage on fire."

She sat up straight, her mind no longer drifting, having caught the tail end of what Wyatt was saying. Had he been talking about himself?

"I was a kid," he said, "like you," and pointed to a boy about six or seven years old. "I thought I knew what I was doing and that I could make the fire stop whenever I wanted."

A little girl raised her hand. "But you couldn't?"

Wyatt shook his head. "No. I could have been killed. Or my family. We were fortunate that all we lost were my mother's antique sewing machine and my brother's and my bicycles."

A couple of children who had been distracted during his talk suddenly took notice of the loss of bicycles. And a middle-aged woman near Mary said to her companion, "My grandmother had a treadle sewing machine. It got passed along to my cousin because I don't even know how to thread a needle."

Wyatt went on to encourage the children never to start smoking, saying that cigarettes accounted for a large number of accidental fires every year. A preteen asked if Wyatt smoked, and the firefighter replied that since he knew it was bad for his health and dangerous to life and property, he had never even tried it. The boy's mother seemed to appreciate his confirming what she'd apparently been trying to drill into her son.

Nicole leaned over to Mary. "People seem to be getting a lot out of this presentation."

Mary nodded in assent. What *she* was getting out of it was a peek into Wyatt's history with fire. He had gone on to tell the audience that his close call in the garage that day had triggered his desire to become a firefighter. But had it instead triggered a desire to become a fire *setter*?

He tucked a few scraps of paper into the bonfire pit in preparation for the marshmallow roasting to come, and Mary's thoughts turned to the introduction Tess had offered in which she had bragged about his 100 percent attendance at all of Ivy Bay's fire calls since his fire-school graduation.

And then there were the courtesy fire inspections he had offered to business owners, she recalled. The work of an overeager beginner, or of a pyromaniac casing out potential sites for fires?

Mary gave herself a little pinch and mentally derailed that train of thought. Just because he went a little overboard with his red suspenders and mustache twirling, that didn't mean he was guilty of such a heinous crime as arson.

The kindling ready to ignite, Wyatt knelt and pulled a silver lighter from his pocket. He ran his thumb over the flint wheel twice, but nothing happened.

Her curiosity piqued, Mary rose from her blanket and joined him at the pile of brush, where she knelt and cupped her hands behind one of the bits of paper he had added.

"This should block the breeze," she said, fully aware that his problem was with the lighter rather than the tinder.

He flicked the wheel again, and this time, the spark caught. When he extended the flame to the paper, Mary's breath caught in her throat at what she saw in his hand.

Wyatt looked up from his task and met her gaze. "You okay?"

Not really, but she nodded anyway, too surprised to speak.

He held the lighter to the kindling until it caught, then snapped the lid closed and stuck it in his pocket. But not before Mary got a good look at it.

The broad Zippo case sported the letters FDNY—very similar to the lighter found at the bakery.

Mary supposed it was reasonable enough that he should have such a lighter. He worked as a firefighter, and the heroes of the New York City Fire Department represented the risks and sacrifices of firefighters all across the country. But why would a nonsmoker carry a lighter? And why would a young man carry the larger size common to smokers of his father's and grandfather's generations rather than a disposable lighter or matches as his peers did?

She thought of one of her bookshop customers who considered herself a connoisseur of books. Quite elitist about her choices, not only in the subject matter but also the medium, Rosa adamantly insisted on reading only mysteries, and only in hardback. No paperbacks or electronic readers for her.

Could it be that Wyatt considered himself an elitist when it came to anything fire-related, including lighters?

He stood and held out a hand to help her up, a slight frown marring his handsome features. "Is something wrong?"

With that simple question, Mary realized she'd been staring, studying him as if to determine whether this polite young man could possibly harbor the heart of an arsonist.

As the warm fire glowed, Wyatt wrapped up his talk and invited people to come ask questions or toast marshmallows.

Thrilled with the success of this workshop, Nicole chatted happily about her ambitious plans for future events.

"Perhaps we should take things a step at a time," Mary suggested. "Let's not bite off more than we can chew."

But that didn't slow Nicole down. Her next big idea involved asking Amy Stebble to offer a back-to-school segment on teaching your child good study habits.

"The concept is excellent," Mary said. Trying not to step on her dreams, but rather to offer some perspective, she asked, "Do you think Amy will have time at the beginning of the school year for an additional commitment?"

At the edge of the group, Chief McArthur spoke with one of the families. He tipped his head in their direction, which sent Nicole off on a new tangent.

"Then let's ask the chief of police to talk about how to practice safe Christmas shopping! Last year in Hyannis, my mother had her car broken into. Maybe he could offer some prevention tips."

"That's a good idea. But perhaps we should wai—"

Before Mary could even finish her suggestion to wait until they could rate the success of the first three learning annexes, Nicole had asked her husband to watch the children and darted through the crowd to speak to Chief McArthur.

A few minutes later, they returned to where Mary was helping Chip supervise the children who were toasting their sugary treats over the fire. Apparently, Nicole had forgotten to buy marshmallows, so the kids twirled sticks speared with orange circus peanuts instead—the closest thing they'd had in the pantry to marshmallows. Mary smiled at Nicole's creativity. Despite the fact that the candies bloated into bizarre, strangely colored shapes, they worked almost as well as regular marshmallows. And the kids seemed happy with the unusual treat.

"Mary, you'll never guess! Chief McArthur offered us something even better: He'll host the workshop at the police station and give everyone a tour afterward. Isn't that fantastic?"

Indeed, it was. They arranged a tentative date for mid-September, and Nicole excused herself to chase down her son who had wandered too far away from his dad.

The chief lingered. He seemed to want to say something but apparently couldn't find the words. He lifted his dark sunglasses, revealing dark circles under his eyes.

Mary knew without his saying so that he hadn't slept well last night. She decided to just go ahead and address the subject directly.

"How's Ryan?"

Chief McArthur nodded as if to indicate she had touched the source of pain that filled his eyes. "He was released on bond this morning."

Yesterday, after Susan's parents had arrived, the first thing they had done was offer to lend her the money to get her husband out of jail. Mary was grateful they'd been in a financial position to take care of the matter so quickly.

Chief McArthur drew in a deep breath. "I've seen some difficult things during my career. Dealt with some rough cases. But arresting Ryan was one of the hardest things I've ever done." He paused, and when he spoke again, his voice was softer. "Ryan Crosby is a good man. I hope this doesn't ruin him."

Mary touched his arm. "No one blames you."

She hoped Susan wouldn't blame *her* either. Her friend had been understanding when Mary had first told her about handing the evidence over to the police. But now that her husband had spent the night in jail, would she feel the same?

"What happens now?" Mary asked.

He straightened the baton at his belt. "He's not in the clear yet, because the investigation is still ongoing."

She asked the question that had been nibbling away at her thoughts ever since she had found the lighter. The question loomed even larger now that she'd seen Wyatt's lighter and considered the possibility that the firefighter might even have a small collection of lighters.

"Do you think Ryan did it?"

A muscle in the chief's jaw twitched while he measured his response. "He gave us an alibi, but we're still checking it out."

Mary tipped her head back to meet his gaze. Her heart lifted to think that maybe their suspicion of Ryan was all a big mistake.

"An alibi? That's good news." She remembered that yesterday's cookout had been in part to celebrate the Crosbys' twentieth anniversary. Perhaps Ryan's curious absence the night of the fire had been prompted by a desire to buy Susan an extra-special anniversary gift. "Was he working overtime?"

"I can't share the specifics," the chief said, an answer Mary had expected. "It's a private matter between Ryan and Susan."

Taking note of that last bit, she prayed that her supposition about the anniversary gift was correct.

She also prayed for Chief McArthur, who was still clearly hurting over having to arrest a friend.

Mary walked over to the marina to meet up with Henry who said he'd be working on his boat today. She wore deck shoes, appropriate for being around boats, but not so good for walking in sand. When she reached the paved walk, after making her way up Little Neck Beach, she paused to empty the sand out of her shoes.

The several-blocks walk provided picturesque glimpses of past and present in old and new buildings. The theme carried out onto the water with old wood-hulled fishing boats and newer fiberglass pleasure boats. One enterprising businessman had built a replica of the historic *Mayflower*, which he had outfitted with air-conditioning and modern plumbing for harbor dinner cruises and wedding parties.

She walked past one of the old shanties where a construction crew was finishing up for the day. The truck parked out front read Clayton Strong Contracting. As she passed, Clayton walked out, carrying an old plank of lumber on his shoulder.

Some of the squat little buildings along this strip had been turned into restaurants or souvenir shops. This one was a dilapidated bait-and-tackle shop getting some much-needed weatherproofing.

"This just goes to show prayers work," she called out to him. "It's good to see business is looking up for you."

He threw the nail-studded board into the bed of his truck, removed the ever-present green cap with his company's name above the bill, and walked over to her with his hand stuck out. "I appreciate the prayers you and your prayer group have been offering up on my behalf."

Mary reached to shake his proffered hand, but he seemed to think twice about it, wiped his hand on his wash-faded jeans, then took her hand in a quick but firm grip.

"It means a lot to us to remember our fellow church members in prayer, and we love to see such positive results," she said with a sweep of her arm toward the little shanty. "I hear you're booked solid with work for at least the next month or two."

He frowned and ran a hand through his hair. "I don't know who told you that, but unfortunately, they're wrong."

Mary could have swallowed her tongue. She certainly hadn't *imagined* Susan telling her work couldn't begin on the bakery for at least several weeks. "But aren't you contracted to do the repairs on Sweet Susan's Bakery?"

He nodded and returned the cap to his head. "Yes, and I'd like to get started, but I'm waiting on Roger to give me the go-ahead to begin work. Maybe it's the overall economy, but business is slow everywhere. The only reason I'm working on a Saturday," he said, indicating the shanty where a couple of his workers were packing up for the day, "is so I can leave weekdays open to go calling on some of my past customers. See if they need any work done."

How unfortunate for Clayton. And how odd. Perhaps Susan's landlord was waiting on his insurance claim before starting.

Whatever the case, Mary planned to ask her prayer group to keep Clayton and Susan on the list. And she would add one more name; it sounded like Roger Cline could use a little divine intervention to get his insurance payout in a timely manner.

Now that Henry's maintenance chores were completed, Mary happily accompanied him on the *Misty Horizon* for a sunset ride through the harbor and into Ivy Bay. A few seabirds circled the boat, looking for handouts or perhaps to snap up some chum spread as bait. Unable to resist their pleading squeals, she tossed bits of bread crust from their picnic supper into the air and watched their aerial gymnastics to be the first to grab them. Most of the birds, however, seemed to know that bedtime was coming and had retreated to shore to roost for the evening.

True to his word, Henry gave Mary a thorough indoctrination on the benefits of depth finders for watermen. Since certain fish favored different depths, Henry could more specifically target their preferred feeding levels with his newly upgraded device. In deeper waters, it could alert him to the presence of an occasional underwater sandbar or rock ledge where smaller fish fed on plants and larger fish fed on the plant eaters.

Despite its technical nature, Mary found the gadget's features fascinating and was pleased when Henry let her try her hand at it.

"Either you're pretty good at this or I'm a really good teacher," Henry said with a wink. "Either way, I'm rather proud."

"As you should be." She rubbed her knuckles against her shoulder. "I wouldn't have my vast knowledge of Ivy Bay and everything water-related if not for you taking me out in your little rowboat when we were kids."

Though she had only spent summers here during her growing-up years, she and Henry had forged a lifelong friendship based on those early days of exploring the forested areas and smaller waterways of Ivy Bay. Back then, it seemed as though Henry knew everything there was to know about all the creatures and plants that lived in the water or anywhere near it. She had sometimes teased him about being a walking encyclopedia when it came to any factoid about the sea life in this little town.

"I may have taught you about the scientific side of nature, but you taught me to enjoy God's beauty in it." He gestured to the west, in the direction of Plymouth, where the sun had started to settle over the marshland.

They watched while the orange-and-yellow glow inched itself below the horizon. When it was over, the air hung heavy with the significance that they were merely two tiny beings in a world that owed them nothing. How awesome, she marveled, that God—the Creator of all this glory—should incline His ear to them when they spoke His name.

The silence continued for a heavy moment. Mary finally broke it by referring back to his comment that she had taught him to enjoy the beauty of nature.

"And don't forget all the wonderful mystery novels I introduced you to," she said, steering them toward the less-intimidating, man-made world of classic fiction and interesting folks.

"Ah, yes, our beloved Agatha Christie. And let's not forget Raymond Chandler."

They chatted for a moment about some of their favorite current authors' latest titles and agreed that they would never have enough time to read all the books on their bucket lists. Just as she would never have enough time to finish the sorry-looking knitting project she'd been working on for the past couple of years.

She filled Henry in on Ryan's release and shared that Chief McArthur was having a difficult time with his role in the arrest. She didn't mention what he'd said about Ryan's alibi being a matter between husband and wife.

Henry nodded and didn't say anything, but Mary knew he'd soon be paying a visit to both of them to check on them and see how they were doing.

Daylight fading now, Henry took the *Misty Horizon* back to the dock, where Mary helped him tie down the boat.

When they stepped onto the pier, she noticed that they had pulled in next to a party boat decked out in green, white, and red streamers. The bow of the *Buona Sera* sported an image of a beautiful sunset over the harbor, a lone ship silhouetted against the sky. Something about the name seemed familiar, but she couldn't remember where she'd heard it before.

A sun-leathered man of about forty stepped off the boat, his short-cropped dark hair glistening with sweat and sea spray. When he saw Henry, he smiled and waved.

"*Amico mio!*" he said in Italian, which Mary guessed meant "my friend." His words thick with a Mediterranean accent, he asked, "How you doing? You enjoy the sunset with the pretty lady?"

"Indeed, I did." Henry clapped the man on the back while they shared a guy moment. "Allow me to introduce you to my friend, Mary Fisher. She spent her summers here as a child and recently decided to move here for good."

Mary smiled at his words. It wouldn't matter how long she lived here.... Because she hadn't spent her whole lifetime in Ivy Bay, she would always be viewed as a "recent" import to the community. Her roots here might not be deep, but they were becoming more firmly planted with each passing day.

"Mary, this is Gino Azzara. He knows everything there is to know about fishing, which he teaches to all the guests who go out on his boat."

The name rang a bell, and Mary strained to place it.

"I am new here too," Gino said proudly. "Only twelve years in America." With a grin, he added, "The fish, they don't care I don't speak so good English."

She imagined his guests didn't care either. His outgoing personality must surely cross all language and cultural barriers.

Henry stood back and surveyed the boat. "You got her cleaned up very nicely. Was she out of the water long?"

"A week!" Gino said with a grand sweep of his arms. "Seven days I say to nice people, 'No, I can't take you fishing. Don't give me your money.' Seven days I don't have a *buona sera*—a good evening." He leaned in to Henry as if to confide something, fisherman to fisherman. "The barnacles, they could wait, yes. But the loose board? No, she has to come out now. Then I gotta paint the hull and fix the motor. How they say? It's a bummer."

Now Mary remembered. This was the father of the little girl who had taken a barnacle to school for show-and-tell. The family Amy Stebble had asked the prayer group to pray for. "You must be Bibi's father."

At mention of the child's name, all the concern and worry left the man's face.

"*Si*. Bibiana." He lightly kissed his fingertips and joyfully flung them to the air. "She's gonna change the world someday. That's a smart one, my girl."

"She sounds delightful." If the girl was anything like her father, she must be quite the charmer.

He narrowed his eyes at her. "How you know my Bibiana? You a teacher?"

"No, her school principal told us about the problem with your boat and asked our prayer group to pray for you."

Gino smiled and took her hand in both of his, then tossed a glance at Henry as if to see if he minded. "You are good people," he declared. "Your prayers make good things happen. See?" He gestured to his boat. "She's all ready to go back to work and make the tourists happy."

"That's wonderful," Mary said. "I'm so happy for you."

After all the bad things that had happened these last couple of weeks, they could use a little good news.

TEN

·—◆◆—·

After church on Sunday, Pastor Miles stood in the vesti-
bule and shook hands with Mary and Betty. Mary noticed he took care not to squeeze her sister's hand.

"Your idea for the Honor Your Calling program has
captured the enthusiasm of everyone who has worked to
bring it together," he said to Betty. "Are you sure you won't
consider joining our panel of speakers? You are such an
inspiration, and I'm sure everyone would love to hear how
you serve God through your enjoyment of decorating with
antiques."

When Jill Sanderson's ten-year-old son Benjamin had
asked about the significance of Labor Day, Betty had tried to
explain the importance of working hard to honor the job that
God has called each of us to do. Before long, that conversation
had developed into a program of testimonials, with church
and community members scheduled to share stories of how
they honor God by following His calling in their particular
lines of work. In addition to recognizing and encouraging
people to follow God's direction in their daily lives, Betty had
wanted the program to show that people don't have to be
celebrities to have important jobs. And, of course, she saw the

event as a way to recognize and thank individuals for the jobs they do on behalf of many others.

"Thank you for asking," Betty said softly, "but we already have so many excellent speakers lined up. Why don't I serve as an encourager this time...from the pew?"

What a gracious way to acknowledge that even the audience plays an important role during the church's special functions. Mary smiled at her sister, but a speck of concern tugged at the corners of her lips. Betty had been exceptionally busy lately—delivering the gardening workshop for the learning annex, picking up some of the slack around the house so Mary could devote more time to the upcoming ice-cream workshop, preparing for Grace Church's special Labor Day program, and keeping up with the usual activities that routinely filled her calendar. Mary suspected Betty had declined Pastor Miles's request so she could allow her aching body some much-needed rest.

The pastor nodded in agreement and thanked her again for her contributions to the program.

Mary led the way to the car. "Sam's Seafood?"

Betty settled herself on the passenger seat. "I thought you'd never ask."

The restaurant by the marina could be described by some as a "dive" where fishermen congregated, but that didn't seem to matter to the after-church crowd that swarmed the place for sourdough bread and crispy fried seafood.

Mary's description of yesterday's boating trip with Henry and their chance meeting with Gino Azzara was interrupted several times as friends and acquaintances called out greetings. After they'd eaten and counted out bills to leave by their empty plates, Betty dragged her purse off the table and accidentally knocked the tip onto her chair.

"I've got it." Mary bent to retrieve the money. The action triggered a memory of the last time she'd scooped up something a lunch companion had left behind. Carol Bates's notepad, with the address written in it. "Feel like going for a little drive before we head home?"

Betty tilted her head in the affirmative, but her expression was one of both curiosity and skepticism.

They drove down Shore Drive and eventually, Mary headed south on Colonial Road. Once they passed Beacon Inn, the businesses thinned out considerably.

Betty crossed her arms over her chest. "This isn't just a 'little drive,'" she said. "It's a quest. You're at it again, aren't you?"

Betty's pretended annoyance at being taken on an outing with a hidden agenda didn't fool Mary. Her sister loved to watch her puzzle out some of the mysterious happenings that occurred in and around Ivy Bay, and Betty frequently piped in with helpful suggestions of her own.

"Whatever do you mean?" Mary said and cut a mischievous grin at her sister.

She slowed the car to check the address at one of the few business properties along this stretch of road. A red-and-white For Rent sign graced the tiny yard.

They got out and walked to the front porch, where a large white molar beamed at them with its glittery, painted-on smile and beckoned them in with a toothbrush held aloft by a skinny wire arm. A sign on the front door announced the nature of the business:

Neil Bouchard, DDS

Hours: Monday through Friday, 8:00 AM–5:00 PM

The phone number's last four digits were spelled YANK, and Mary chuckled at the dentist's lack of sugar coating about the nature of his business. With good cause, she wondered if his forthrightness was the reason behind this now-empty building.

"Even if he were open on Sundays, which he isn't," Betty said, "you wouldn't be able to see Dr. Bouchard today because he retired a couple of months ago."

Mary paused in front of the door and stared at the sign. *Neil.* She pulled her cell phone and Carol's notepad out of her pocket. Sure enough, the name on the pad matched the first name of the dentist, even down to the spelling. She checked the phone number on the paper against her keypad and confirmed that the last four digits spelled out YANK. But, if Dr. Bouchard was somehow involved in the fire, what would be his motive? A man in love following the whims of his attractive-yet-slightly-neurotic girlfriend?

"What? Are you going to call him anyway?" Betty seemed surprised at her apparent relentlessness.

Calling him hadn't been Mary's intent, but now that she thought of it, that wasn't such a bad idea. Going by the date on the page, Carol had apparently used the number as recently as a week or two ago. If it was still connected, the voice-mail message might give a clue as to the reason Carol carried the contact information of a retired dentist in her purse. Or the number might be forwarded to ring to another number and connect her to a live person. She had no idea what she'd say if someone answered.

"Couldn't hurt," she said while punching in the numbers.

Inside the building, the ringing of the phone echoed in the empty reception area. A man moved past the window to answer it, noticed the two of them standing on the porch, and pulled open the front door a second later.

"Hello?" he said into the phone, then smiled and motioned that he'd be with them in a minute. The solitary word reverberated in Mary's ear.

"Um, hello." She pointed to her cell phone and snapped it closed. "That was me."

All her years of reading caught up to her and urged her to change her grammatically incorrect statement to "That was I," but it would have sounded so stiff and formal that she just let it slide this time.

The man appeared to be about ten years younger than Mary, perhaps in his early fifties. His curly, sandy-colored hair revealed few traces of gray, and when he smiled, his teeth gleamed so white they rivaled the smile on the giant molar mascot.

Taking his cue from Mary, he disconnected the phone and stepped out onto the porch to join them. He stuck out his hand. "Neil Bouchard. How may I help you?"

He was a big man, and his biceps were huge. Possibly from yanking all those teeth over the years? Mary instantly liked him, even though everything about him—right down to his movie-star good looks—was over the top.

"I'm sorry for bothering you," she said. "We were out for a Sunday drive and happened to notice your For Rent sign."

Betty's eye roll was subtle, but Mary noticed it. She only hoped Dr. Bouchard hadn't caught it as well.

The dentist's eyebrows drew together as he assessed them. Mary could only imagine what he must be thinking. Two ladies of retirement age, dressed in their Sunday go-to-meeting clothes, inquiring about renting a dental office.

"Are you a dentist?" he asked, addressing his comment to Mary. He must have seen Betty's hands and known they lacked the strength and flexibility to perform such a demanding job.

"Actually, no, I'm a bookseller." She introduced herself and Betty and assured him she was not interested in moving her bookstore out here. However, she thought, if the damage to the bakery couldn't be fixed in a timely manner, Susan might need someplace else to set up shop, even if it was on the outskirts of town. Better this than nothing. "It is possible, though, that a friend of mine might be looking to move her business."

Bouchard ran a hand through his impossibly tidy curls and seemed to be putting two and two together. "Your bookstore is right next to the bakery that burned, isn't it? Is she looking for a new place?"

"Not yet. I thought I'd mention to her that this place is available." She paused. "Just in case."

"That's interesting. Another baker was out here just a couple of weeks ago. Said she was planning to open her own cupcake shop and seemed really interested in renting the building." A frown marred his perfect eyebrows. "Haven't heard back from her, though, so tell your friend it's still available if she's interested."

Mary recalled the first time she'd seen Carol, who had been questioning Susan about the ins and outs of running a bakery, all while planning to become her direct competition.

Carol had admitted to wanting to open her own bakery, but that the only affordable property she could find was on the outskirts of town, far from the coveted foot traffic along Main Street.

He gave them a quick tour of the place, pointing out how the electrical connections and plumbing could be easily converted to accommodate the needs of a bakery.

Mary took his card, thanked him for his time, and returned to the car.

Betty shot her an approving smile. "It appears you're hot on the trail, Miss Marple."

———

That evening, Mary popped over to the bookshop to pick up some paperwork and put a few things in order so she could hit the ground running first thing in the morning. She'd brought Gus along to keep her company and to avoid that creeped-out feeling of being alone in the shop after dusk. She never felt unsafe here, but it did get terribly quiet with Rebecca and Ashley gone. Gus watched, bored, from his position on the armchair near the shop's fireplace. He yawned, and for a brief moment, his fangs made him look like a creature from a horror movie.

After Nicole had wrangled Chief McArthur into promising a class featuring shopping-safety tips and a tour of the police station—which Mary considered a fabulous idea—Nicole started listing a dozen more future workshop possibilities.

And then when Mary had mentioned in passing her conversation with Gino Azzara, Nicole had squealed with delight. "Gelato! Maybe he could join you and Tess and show people how to make ice cream, Italian style. Everybody will love it because gelato is lower in fat than regular ice cream."

Never mind the fact that they didn't even know if Gino could make gelato. Mary had tried to point out the pitfalls of adding too many cooks to the soup pot of speakers for this workshop, but Nicole had developed a sudden case of deafness when it came to hearing her concerns. Gino was now unofficially a featured speaker on the learning-annex program, which, if he accepted their invitation, would require changing the flyer that had already been printed and displayed all around Ivy Bay.

So here she was, working late to try to keep up with bookshop responsibilities that had been pushed aside to attend the fire-safety workshop and plan for the ice-cream session.

Not only that, but tomorrow, Ashley was scheduled for the Children's Reading Adventure at the library. When Mary had told Rebecca of librarian Victoria Pickerton's prayer request for a healthy turnout, Ashley had overheard and immediately volunteered to read for "the little kids." Victoria had been thrilled by her willingness to help. And, quite frankly, Mary wouldn't miss her little friend's performance for the world.

After about an hour, she stretched and decided to call it an evening. Her focus was shot, and she wanted to go home, slip into her pajamas, and get started on the new knitting mystery that had just arrived the other day. She might not be much of a knitter herself, but she sure loved reading about knitting aficionados who also had a talent for sleuthing.

Mary had just reached for Gus's carrying case when the cat perked his ears toward the back of the shop. "No, you can't go out," she said. "It's time to go home."

With a flip of his fluffy gray tail, Gus stalked to the back door, his front legs moving stiffly. A low growl emanated from deep in his chest, then ended as a higher-pitched yowl.

By now, his tail had bushed out until it looked like he'd been electrified. As if by osmosis, Mary picked up his mood, and tiny electric shivers zoomed over her skin.

"What is it, Gus? What do you hear?"

Naturally, he didn't answer, so Mary did the next best thing. She followed him to the door, pressed her ear to the wood, and tried to quiet the heavy beating of her heart. Her nerves on edge since the fire next door, she could take no chances if a prowler was lurking out there. Her breath hissed slowly in and out as she listened to hear what might have sent the cat on alert.

"*Yeeeeooooowwwww!*"

Mary's feet quite literally left the floor. Rattled, she staggered back and placed a hand to her heart. "Did you really have to do that?"

Gus nonchalantly twined himself around her ankles, and an answering call echoed from the yard.

Of course. The stray cat that had been hanging around for the past couple of weeks. The nervous tension that had been building in Mary all week suddenly dissolved, and her legs felt strangely like spaghetti noodles.

She leaned against the door, and another yowl sounded from outside. "Well, Mr. Romeo, it sounds like your girlfriend is lonely."

Actually, Mary had done the responsible thing and taken Gus to the vet shortly after she adopted him, so there would be no little Guses running around. But that didn't stop him from being curious about other cats whenever he encountered them.

She glanced down at the floor where a few bits of kibble remained in his food dish. Maybe his visitor was hungry.

Now that the thought had entered her mind, she wouldn't be able to go home until she had done something about the stray. She grabbed a few kibbles and stuck them in her slacks pocket, then put Gus in the carrying case so he wouldn't slip outside with her. She eased the door open.

In the hazy light that filtered from nearby streetlamps, she could see the fuzzy orange creature slinking toward the back gate. In one easy jump, it scaled the fence post, then hopped down on the other side.

Curious to see whether the cat would return home, thereby letting her know it wasn't a stray after all, she decided to follow it a short distance to see where it might go.

She opened the gate and turned left, her shoes making little noise on the grass and gravel, and followed it past the bakery yard to the Tea Shoppe. There, it leaped up and walked along the white rail fence, its tail waving like a banner to lead Mary along.

Just as the cat crossed the fence into the yard behind the hardware store, the shed door flung open, spilling light from a single incandescent bulb. Startled, the cat jetted itself out across the yard, dove under a clump of hostas, and scuttled along until Mary could no longer track its escape.

At the moment, the cat was the least of her concerns. Emerging from the shed, Tyson Shepard paused and glanced first one way, then the other.

What was he doing at the hardware store so late on a Sunday evening? Mary stood immobilized, watching and waiting to see what the teen would do next. Since his eyes were accustomed to the light inside the shed, and an overgrown butterfly bush stood between them, she doubted he could see her in the dusky shadows. She held her breath anyway.

Tyson peeled off a pair of rubber gloves and dropped them to the floor of the shed, then headed back to the hardware store. She watched while the shop door opened, and he disappeared inside.

Rubber gloves! To prevent leaving fingerprints behind, maybe? If Tyson was, indeed, the person who had set fire to the bakery, he could be planning his next arson. Sickened by the thought and worried for the next potential victim, she knew she had to do something.

But what?

The hostas rustled, their leaves swaying as the cat meandered through a row of them along the fence to the open shed. When the little orange furball stepped out into the yard, Mary pulled some kibble out of her pocket and eased toward the feline.

"Here, kitty-kitty."

Slowly, she opened the gate and let herself into the yard, her hand outstretched to beckon the skittish creature a little closer. The cat's ears swiveled forward, and it eased toward her. It stopped at the open shed door, blinked, then squinted its eyes as if it had encountered something distasteful.

Mary eased forward and scooped the cat up into her arms. To her relief, it didn't try to wriggle away. It was a young cat, barely more than a kitten, and it wore no collar. She stroked its soft fur and offered it a bite of the kibble, which it devoured and begged for more until the stash in her pocket was gone. The poor little thing's ribs felt like a washboard under Mary's gentle fingers, leading her to the conclusion it hadn't eaten much lately.

Probably a throwaway. It wouldn't be the first time that someone with an unwanted litter dropped off a puppy or kitten in this area, probably hoping a tourist would take it home with them.

"Don't worry, sweetie," she said, and kissed the top of its head. "We'll find you a good home."

Standing at the entrance to the shed, she could understand why the cat had wrinkled its nose. A strong chemical smell burned her eyes, and she wiped away the stinging tears.

Concerned about the cause of the strong fumes, she shaded her eyes and leaned closer to the open door, hoping to get a glimpse of what Tyson had been doing in there.

Other than the rubber gloves he had dropped at the entrance and the can of solvent she'd seen him with on earlier occasions, nothing else seemed amiss. At the front of the shed were the usual gardening supplies and storage items. Farther back in the narrow structure, something stood about chest high in the middle of the floor, but the single low-watt lightbulb shone too dim for her to discern what it might be. Apparently growing impatient with the lack of action, the cat squirmed in Mary's arms.

Unable to see anything in the shadowy interior, she decided against entering the building. It wasn't her place to pry, but the rubber gloves, flammable liquid, and Tyson's suspicious behavior were enough to warrant a frank discussion with the boy's uncle. She felt certain that, no matter what was going on out here, Jimmy would do the right thing.

For right now, though, she would focus on finding out whether she could find this little orange cutie in her arms a place to call home. As she turned to leave, a firm hand grasped her arm.

Mary screamed, and the cat scrambled away, leaving angry scratch marks on her skin.

"Be quiet! You're going to have the whole neighborhood after us."

Mary drew in a breath for another scream and prepared to fight off her attacker. But when she turned to face him, she was both surprised and relieved to discover it was only Tyson. Her breath came out in a long *whoosh*.

"What are you doing here?" he demanded. "Why are you snooping around Uncle Jimmy's shed?"

Mary straightened to her full height of five feet one. As regally as she could muster, she said, "I wasn't snooping. I was"—the teen eyed her warily—"looking." Now would be a good time to redirect the focus of their conversation. "Perhaps I should be asking what *you* are doing out here."

Tyson scowled and backed away. At first, Mary thought he might run, but he shoved his hands into his pockets and focused his scowl on the ground. He seemed so troubled. And then she realized his scowl had merely been an attempt to hold back an emotion that he obviously didn't want her to see.

Her voice softer now, she approached him slowly, as carefully as when she had coaxed the cat to come to her. "If you have anything to confess, you can tell me. I'll see to it that you get help for whatever problem you're going through."

Silence, but he seemed to be thinking about what she said.

"If you're in trouble, you can tell me. I only want to help."

Tyson lifted his head, his brows drawn together in confusion. "What? I'm not in trouble."

"Then what's all this?" she said softly and gestured toward the shed.

After a brief hesitation in which he studied her as if to determine whether she was telling the truth about wanting to help, he shrugged. "Can you keep a secret?"

She paused. "You're putting me in a difficult spot."

"Can you?" he persisted.

Mary spoke carefully, weighing her words so she neither made any false promises nor scared him into clamming up. "It depends on what it is. If your secret involves the law or someone's safety—"

He shook his head. "No, it's not that." Tyson stepped around her and disappeared into the dark recesses of the shed.

Mary heard the sound of wood scraping against the concrete floor as he dragged the large object she'd noticed earlier to the front where she could see it. Under the dim light, a beautiful wooden rocking chair sat atop a shipping pallet. She stepped into the shed to get a better look.

"Don't touch it," he warned. "It's still wet."

Low to the ground, the chair featured a tall back and curved armrests that seemed as though they would embrace the person fortunate enough to relax there. The stain had been removed from the headrest, arms, seat, and rockers, and still reeked of the fluid Tyson had soaked them with. But the part he hadn't done yet—the ornately carved rungs—showed a dull, dark finish that had been worn in uneven patches over the years.

Mary didn't claim to be an antiques expert, but she had no doubt the chair was old. Very old. "Where did you get this? It's beautiful."

Tyson grunted. "It's not beautiful yet. But it will be when I'm finished with it. Anyway, I *hope* it will." He carefully avoided Mary's gaze and stared at the chair instead. "It belonged to my grandmother. She used to rock my sister and me in it when we went to visit her. Then she passed away about four years ago and left it to my sister. But it just sat in the attic, collecting dust."

Dust notwithstanding, the piece reminded her of her own grandmother's rocker that held a special place of honor in the bookshop. Often, when she sat in the rocker, she experienced a quiet moment of sweet nostalgia. Judging by Tyson's unsuccessful attempts to act matter-of-factly about his family's treasured heirloom, he must also feel the stir of long-ago memories.

Mary wasn't one for leaping to conclusions, but Tyson's surreptitious behavior almost had her wondering if he had perhaps stolen the chair. That didn't make sense. A teen might take a car for a joyride without permission, but she couldn't imagine what might motivate a young person to abscond with furniture.

"I'm fixing it up for my sister," he said in answer to her unspoken question. "She planned to use it to rock babies after she and her husband start their family. But she's been really sick recently, so I figured she could use it now."

Of course. When his aunt Amelia had asked the prayer group to add Tyson to their list, she had mentioned that Tyson's sister had been going through chemotherapy.

"I'm sorry about your sister," she said and touched his wrist before considering that he might not care for that. But he didn't seem to notice. "A lot of people are praying for her." Although she didn't say it out loud, she added, *and you.*

"Thanks."

Obviously unused to discussing issues of such magnitude, he seemed uncomfortable talking about the difficulty his family was going through. So Mary did him a favor. She switched the subject to something he could discuss without fear of letting her see his fear and sadness.

"It's a very kind and thoughtful thing you're doing for your sister," she said, "but I don't understand why you're being so secretive about it."

"It's supposed to be a surprise." Tyson twisted his mouth as he considered his next words. "If Uncle Jimmy knows, he'll tell Aunt Amelia. And Aunt Amelia calls or visits my sister every day. I don't want to take the chance of her spilling the beans. Especially if the chair turns out looking terrible."

He looked at his feet.

"I don't want her to get her hopes up, then be all disappointed if I don't do it right."

"I'm sure she'll adore it, because she'll see the love you put in it."

For the first time, Tyson actually smiled. "Yeah, she'd probably be all excited even if it looked like a kindergartener refinished it."

"It sounds like you two have a very close relationship."

"We do, but I haven't seen her as much since she got married last year. Her husband's a nice guy, so I'm happy for her. It's just hard getting used to not having her to hang around with all the time like we used to."

A slight breeze stirred, freshening the air in the shed and reminding Mary that the fumes in here were toxic. Touched by Tyson's thoughtfulness, but concerned that he might get sick from breathing the strong chemical, she made an impulsive offer. One which she was certain Betty would agree to.

"Look, you can't continue sneaking out here to work on the chair in this airless shed." She led him outside where they could breathe a little better.

"It's okay," Tyson said. "Uncle Jimmy just thinks I'm coming out here to sneak a smoke. After I'm finished with the rocker and he sees that it was all for a good purpose, he won't mind."

"No, that's not what I'm talking about. I'm worried you're going to get sick from these awful fumes." She waved a hand in front of her face, but the acrid smell persisted.

He started to act a little cocky at the suggestion that he wasn't macho enough to endure a bit of varnish remover, but when Mary suggested it would be unfortunate if both his sister *and* he were to be sick, he changed his attitude.

"Come finish the job in my backyard," she urged. "Your secret will stay safe, and the work area will be well ventilated." She thought of the nontoxic refinishing liquid she had bought to use on her coffee table. "And get rid of that nasty stuff you're using on the chair. I have something you can use that won't fry your brain cells."

Tyson rubbed his forehead. "I *have* been getting headaches lately," he said, as if finally putting two and two together.

He wisely accepted her offer. After she gave him directions to the house, he pointed to the red streaks marking her arms.

"You're bleeding," he said. "We've got some ointment in the shop for that, if you want it."

Indeed, she was bleeding. And it stung like the dickens. "Thanks, but I'll wash it at the bookstore, then take care of it at home. Wouldn't want to give your secret away," she said, indicating the questions that might arise if Jimmy was there when she followed Tyson into the hardware store for the salve.

Mary cast a quick glance around the area, but the orange cat was nowhere to be found.

Too bad. She'd really like to thank the sweet little kitten for leading her to the truth about Tyson.

ELEVEN

◆

The next day, Susan came to the bookshop to buy a novel, to distract her at night from the stress of all that had happened lately.

"Do you have anything that's not a mystery?" she asked. "My mind is already so active at night that I don't want to give it more to think about. Perhaps something relaxing. A story that will both cheer me up and help me sleep."

"Of course," Mary said. "Someone just traded in a pile of paperbacks, so I may have just the thing for you."

She led her to a pile of romance novels.

"You'll never go wrong with the classics," she said, pulling out a Jane Austen title. "Or here are some faith-based love stories. Everybody loves Janette Oke. You can't help but fall in love with the hero, right along with the heroine."

Mary turned to pass the small stack of books to Susan for her to peruse, only to find her friend brushing away a tear.

"Thank you," Susan said with a sniff, "but I don't think I can handle any romantic stories right now."

Caught off guard, Mary did the only thing she could think of at the moment. She set the books down and wrapped Susan in a sympathetic hug.

"Oh, Susan, I'm so sorry." She stroked the back of her friend's short dark hair. "Whatever I said, I didn't mean to upset you."

Susan returned the hug with a tight squeeze, then stepped away and pulled a crumpled tissue out of her purse. "You didn't say anything wrong. I'm just being a silly goose."

"You're not a silly goose. If something's upsetting you, you have the right to cry."

Susan dabbed her eyes and stuffed the tissue back in her purse. "Do I ever," she agreed. "Mary, you are such a dear person. I'm so fortunate to call you a friend."

She stepped away from the reading area where a couple of customers relaxed, books on their laps, and gestured for Mary to follow her. Then she glanced around in a way that made Mary think of Tyson's secretive mission last night.

"I have to talk about this to somebody, and I know you'll keep it to yourself." Susan looked Mary in the eye. "You will, won't you?"

Mary doubted this was a matter of the law or personal safety. "Of course. You can trust me."

Susan paused and looked for a moment as though she might change her mind. But she finally blurted out, "I think my husband is seeing another woman."

Mary blinked, taking in the unexpected revelation. Like most people, Ryan was no angel. He showed a bit of temper at times, as evidenced by his kicking the oven two weeks ago, and Susan had mentioned his tendency to forget birthdays and anniversaries. But all in all, he was a good, churchgoing man. A well-respected pillar of the community. To her knowledge, Ryan loved his wife dearly. So much, in fact, that Mary had actually believed he could have set the fire to get an insurance payoff so Susan could upgrade her bakery equipment.

Mary didn't know what to say. What came out was, "Ryan? There must be a mistake."

Susan shook her head. "He had told me he was scheduled to work overtime the night of the fire. But when I called his company before going to bed to tell him good night, the person who answered the phone told me Ryan's name was not listed on the work roster." She waited a moment to let it sink in. "Ryan had taken the entire afternoon off."

"Things aren't always as they seem," Mary reminded her, all the while hoping Ryan wasn't foolish enough to sample the grass on the other side of the fence when he already had a wonderful wife who adored him. And hoping this wasn't further evidence against him as an arson suspect.

Susan reached into her purse, this time pulling out a carbon copy of a form that had been filled in by hand. "I found this while I was doing laundry. It's a receipt for a rental car."

Mary looked at the paper and noticed the car had been rented and returned on the same day, August 22. "Well, this is very curious, but it doesn't necessarily mean he had another woman with him."

"This was in the other pocket." Susan handed her a scrap of paper with a woman's name—Tootsie—and a phone number scribbled on it. "That's Ryan's handwriting."

"Oh."

"He didn't even give me a card for our anniversary. The cookout was supposed to be part of our anniversary celebration. How could he forget?"

This did not look good. Mary's conversation with Chief McArthur flashed through her mind, confirming that Susan's suspicion might not be so far-fetched after all. The chief had mentioned that Ryan's whereabouts on the night of the fire were a private matter between husband and wife. At the time, Mary had assumed Ryan had been working overtime to buy an anniversary gift for his wife. But could he have been with another woman instead? Even David and Samson in the Bible had been known to succumb to the allures of forbidden women.

And then she remembered. August 22 had been the day of the fire. She took another look at the receipt. He had rented a Ford early that afternoon and returned the vehicle shortly before the fire started.

A *black* vehicle.

When Ryan had been released on bond, Mary had desperately hoped the charges against him would soon be dropped and Chief McArthur would announce they'd found the *real* arsonist. Unfortunately, the bits and pieces of evidence, albeit circumstantial, sure seemed to be piling up against Ryan.

She wondered if the woman whose name was written on the slip of paper Susan found was a blonde. Could that woman be the same one Mary had seen in the black car that night? Mary had told Chief McArthur about the mysterious black car and its long-haired passenger that night, but so far, no leads had turned up.

"Excuse me a minute." Mary went to the front of the shop to retrieve her cell phone and returned a moment later. She punched the number into the phone and waited until it went to voice mail.

A husky-voiced woman happily announced that she was off having fun somewhere and to please leave a message. The voice reminded her of a cross between Kathleen Turner and Marlene Dietrich.

"No answer." Mary didn't bother to leave a message. She just snapped the phone closed.

Despite all of this, she wanted to caution both Susan and herself not to jump to conclusions. "Don't borrow trouble. We don't know who Tootsie is or what this phone number is about." She handed the paper back to Susan. "As for your anniversary, you've mentioned before that Ryan has a tendency to be forgetful at times. Even if he had remembered to get you a card or gift, it could have been overlooked during all the commotion at the cookout."

She didn't bother to state the obvious—that being arrested had a way of making a person forget a lot.

"He *is* forgetful," Susan said. "But that doesn't excuse him for being out at night until after I went to bed and not even bothering to tell me where he was going."

"Have you tried asking him?" Mary tried to return the receipt to Susan, but she pushed it back, her palms open.

"He just gives me a vague nonanswer, which I can't decipher." She nodded her head toward the paper she had just refused. "That receipt may hold the answers I need, but I'm afraid of what I might learn."

She grasped Mary's arm, beseeching her with her eyes.

"You have a way of finding out information. Will you go to the car-rental company and ask if"—she hesitated—"he had someone with him?"

Mary's husband, John, had never given her cause for concern about his fidelity. For that, she was incredibly grateful. John had been a good husband, and he had left her with many happy memories. She could only imagine the agony that Susan was living, wondering whether the man who had once promised to love, honor, and cherish her had gone back on his vow. Mary wanted to help Susan find the peace of mind she needed. The kind of peace of mind Mary had enjoyed in her own marriage.

"I'm sure the rental agent would think it odd if I go in there asking questions," she said. "However, as their customer's wife, you could go and clarify a few questions about the bill. Maybe find out a few extra pieces of information while you're there."

"No, I'd probably just break down and start crying." Just the mere mention of losing control prompted her voice to crack. "Would you go with me?"

Susan had been through so much this past week. Mary's fear was that the information they turned up might only add to her emotional burden. Then again, if she were in Susan's shoes, she'd find that not knowing would be a bigger burden than seeing the truth, not matter how cold and hard it might be.

"Of course. I'll be there for you."

Perhaps, she thought, this car rental could provide information needed to solve the arson. More than that, Mary prayed it would absolve Ryan of wrongdoing. But a sickening feeling in the pit of her stomach told her it might do just the opposite; it might prove him to be the guilty party. Both in the bakery fire and in his marriage.

The approach of Ashley's library reading that afternoon inspired excitement for the little girl and a welcome relief for Mary. Relief to be focusing on something positive and happy for a change.

The sound of gargling drifted from the back room where Ashley prepared her throat for the rigors of reading aloud. Gus had followed her back there and watched, his tail flicking with interest. At first, Mary had wondered whether he wanted to get to his food bowl, but the curious tilt of his head indicated he was just trying to figure out what this strange, new language meant.

"I'm ready," Ashley announced and popped over to the children's section where she collected the books she planned to read. All eight of them.

Rebecca picked up her purse. "I'm sure there are plenty of books at the library you can choose from."

"But the library may not have *these* books."

Mary tried not to let Ashley see her smile. Sometimes the child seemed so much older than her years. Seven, going on thirty-eight. Her young friend would most assuredly be insulted to think that Mary found her cute ways amusing.

Wisely, Rebecca didn't even bother to mention that there probably wouldn't be time to read all the books tucked under her daughter's arm. She held open the front door and turned back to Mary. "You coming?"

"In a minute. I'll lock up and put the sign on the door." Mary picked up her keys and spooled off a couple of strips of tape to use for the sign. "You two go ahead. I need to stop by the yarn shop on my way over."

After they left, Mary smiled as she taped up the paper Ashley had printed: "We'll be back soon. While you wait, please join us at Ivy Bay Public Library for a special reading by Miss Ashley Mason."

After Mary locked up, she headed over to the aptly named Yarn Store. Rebecca and Ashley had gone to the library early to have the girl's reading selection approved by Victoria Pickerton prior to the Children's Reading Adventure. Mary idly wondered what color reading glasses the librarian would be wearing today.

Happily anticipating the feel of soft wool in her hands, she crossed Water Street and happened to see Carol Bates carrying a takeout bag from Pizzeria Rustica. Thinking of the notepad Carol had left behind at the diner, Mary called to her and tried to wave her down. Apparently preoccupied, the other woman didn't even bother to acknowledge Mary's friendly hello.

Mary shrugged it off and pushed open the door next to Paul Becker's law office. No problem. She'd give the notebook to Carol later…along with a few strategic questions to determine whether she had tried to kill the competition from Sweet Susan's Bakery.

Inside the yarn shop, Mary entered a kaleidoscope of colors, textures, shapes, and—oddly enough—hopes and dreams, love and friendship. Total strangers turned to one another to ask opinions of angora versus cashmere and advice about needle size and yarn tension. Each project the customers worked on provided opportunities to connect with other needle crafters who shared their joy of knitting, as well as with the fortunate recipients of their gifts of time and love.

Yarn almost always proved to be a wonderful way to detangle one's mind, a benefit Mary welcomed at the moment. She loved the varied colors and textures and never ceased to be amazed that a clump of animal-hair fibers could be transformed into beautiful sweaters, shawls, hats, and vests. Well, on *other* knitters' needles they transformed into those beautiful creations. On Mary's needles, they looked like an interesting clump of animal fibers.

But no matter how novice her attempts, the process relaxed her. The click of the needles and the counting of the stitches never failed to clear her mind so she could process whatever the day's developments had brought. Today, she would pick up some yarn and look at patterns for her next knitting project, assuming she ever finished the current one in this lifetime.

Mary finally settled on cheerful skeins that blended pale yellow, mint green, blue, pink, and white, along with a pattern for a baby blanket. She knew of no one in the family way, nor did she have any idea of gender, but she fully expected at least a couple of announcements and births to take place before she ever finished the project.

Her package carefully tucked under one arm, she left the shop and saw Carol again, this time leaving the pharmacy and carrying a bottle of pink liquid. Carol twisted off the cap, lifted the concoction to her lips and took a sip directly from the bottle. Then she wiped her mouth with the back of her hand, recapped the bottle, and went on her way.

Sympathy gripped Mary's heart. Carol had been a bit peculiar both times Mary had crossed paths with her, especially when it came to her impression that Susan stood in the way of her dream of opening her own bakery. But now Mary wondered if her crabby attitude came as much from physical discomfort as it did from her grudge against Susan.

She watched the woman disappear down the street. There was no doubt Carol had a health issue, but Mary could not allow sympathy to cloud her thinking. Until information arose to clear her of setting the bakery on fire, Carol's name would remain on Mary's list of possible suspects.

When Mary entered the library, Victoria was assigning the order in which each of the volunteers would read. Children milled about, most seeking books to check out and a couple of boys horsing around while waiting for the program to start. It looked like it would be a few more minutes before it began, so Mary went searching until she found exactly what she wanted.

A medical journal.

TWELVE

———◆◆———

Scheduled to read third, Ashley had surmised to Mary that the librarian was saving the best book—her selection—for last. Mary agreed that her little friend's conclusion was a very strong possibility, mainly because it was a story most of them had never heard before.

Three seats remained open near Susan. They slid into the chairs next to her, and Mary commented that she was glad to see Susan getting out.

"Well, it's not like I have a job to keep me busy," Susan said morosely. "The least I can do is be here to support Ashley, who always tidies up my displays whenever she comes into the bakery." She twisted her mouth. "When she *used to* come into the bakery."

Mary assured her that the bakery would soon be tempting customers with fresh cinna-lobsters and iced raisin bread.

"Don't forget my world-famous blueberry muffins," Susan joked.

Conversations quieted when the first reader, a mother in her thirties, who had dressed up like Beatrix Potter, launched into *The Tale of Peter Rabbit*. After a moment, Mary found her mind wandering back to the scraps of paper Susan had shown her this morning. Mary had tried the woman's number a second time, with the same unhelpful result, and attempted to do a reverse lookup on the Internet. But the best she could find out was that it was a cell phone number.

Mary didn't want to believe Ryan could be seeing another woman on the sly, but all the evidence—flimsy as it might be—pointed to exactly that. Could he have rented a car so his old clunker wouldn't be noticed while he consorted with his girlfriend? Or maybe even to impress the girlfriend into thinking he owned the late-model car? And then there was the question of whether the woman on the voice-mail greeting, who had declared she was out "having fun," could be the same woman Mary had glimpsed in the black car leaving the scene of the fire. It was bad enough to consider that Ryan might have been with a woman who was not his wife, but worse to ponder the possibility that the pair may have teamed up to torch the bakery and use the insurance money to start a new life together.

When it came Ashley's turn to read, Mary was pleased that she and Victoria had settled on an obscure title, *Greedy Greeny*, a humorous story that taught the importance of moderation when eating watermelon.

Proud as any honorary aunt or stand-in grandparent, Mary noted that Ashley's voice never quavered, and she showed no sign of stage fright. The little girl with the big personality was much braver than Mary had been at that age.

After the reading concluded, Susan agreed with Mary's high praise, and Ashley got swallowed up in a hug by her mother and the two of them.

They were preparing to leave when Mary asked Susan if there were any updates on when repairs would begin on the bakery. Perhaps Clayton had been able to let her landlord know he was now available to take on new work.

Until the work was completed, Susan needed a source of income to buy groceries for her family and pay household bills. She considered hiring her temporarily to help out at the bookstore, but there was neither enough work nor enough cushion in the budget to warrant a temporary hire. For now, she'd have to make do with keeping her ear tuned to any whispers of job openings in Ivy Bay.

Susan shook her head in response to Mary's question. "Still the same, as far as I know. Problem is, I can't keep waiting around for progress to happen." She pushed a hand through her short dark curls and left a tendril near her temple sticking up like an antenna. "I need to file an insurance claim, but I can't find the policy anywhere. You didn't happen to see it during the cleanup, did you?"

"No, I put all the paperwork I found in the top desk drawer. Your agent should have a copy in his office. Why don't you go on over there now and ask him to look it up for you?" Mary glanced at her watch. "The insurance office doesn't close for at least half an hour."

Many businesses in town got their insurance through Ivy Bay Mutual because it offered reasonable rates and personal service.

Susan slowly shook her head, as if the very thought of processing the paperwork seemed too great a task to tackle. "I don't know. Maybe tomorrow."

Mary recognized the feeling of being overwhelmed that Susan must surely be going through. After John had died, Mary had initially succumbed to the devastation of grief. The multitude of decisions that needed to be made, uncertainty about the future, and the need to reassure others that she was doing "just fine" had seemed like too much to handle. And the relentless details involved in filing so much paperwork had her wishing she could just hibernate for six months and come back once everything was settled. About a year later, after she had shared those feelings with Betty, her sister had confided that she, too, had experienced the same sense of being overwhelmed after the death of her husband, Edward.

So Mary did what she wished someone could have done for her back then. She made a decision for Susan.

"Come on," she said, stretching out her hand. "I'll go with you."

———

The visit to Brad Overly's office at Ivy Bay Mutual netted a copy of the insurance policy and bad news.

"I wish I had something better to tell you," he said about the dollar amount on the form. "This figure is based on the depreciated value of the equipment you lost in the fire, and I'm sorry to say it doesn't cover your lost sales while you're temporarily out of business."

Temporarily. From his lips to God's ears. And the shorter her friend's time away from work, the better. The longer it took to get the bakery back up and running, the less likely Susan would be able to bounce back. In fact, the longer the wait to start repairs on the building, the more tourist dollars she would lose.

Susan nodded at the information Brad supplied. It was clear to Mary that this was not news to her. Susan had not expected the policy to replace everything that had been burned. All she had said she wanted was enough to see her through to get the bakery up and running again.

"Then there's the matter of the arson." The barely thirty-year-old agent twisted his green silk tie. He seemed sincerely sorry for Susan and the trouble she was going through, but they all knew he was bound by the restrictions of the policy. "Until the police matter is settled with your husband, our hands are tied."

Susan shot a look of sheer surprise at Mary, then turned back to the dapperly dressed man. "You think Ryan did it."

Clearly, she'd had such faith in her husband that the possibility of his guilt had never crossed her mind. To Susan, it had simply been a matter of *when* Ryan was cleared, not *if*. And she had obviously assumed everyone else shared her confidence in her husband.

It was interesting, Mary thought, that Susan could entertain the possibility that her husband might have been with another woman, but not that he would set fire to the business. However, now that she'd learned of the small insurance payout, Mary understood the lack of motivation for Ryan to have done it.

Unfortunately, as the fire investigator had informed them, it's a simple matter to prove arson but not so simple to prove who did it. If Ryan was not cleared soon, a trial could turn out to be a lengthy process. Time that he and Susan could not afford.

"It's not about what I think," Brad said. "It's purely business. I'm sure you understand."

Susan leaned forward in her chair and rested her cheeks in her hands. "Yes, and I'm sure you understand that this puts us in a huge squeeze."

"I do," he said softly. "And this is exactly why I've been after you, your landlord, and several other business owners for quite some time now to increase your coverage."

Brad drew invisible circles on the paper with the capped end of his pen. Zeros. Exactly what Susan would get from him until or unless the arsonist was found and Ryan cleared of wrongdoing.

Mary thought about the woman's name on the slip of paper found in Ryan's pocket.

Or, if not wrongdoing, at least until Ryan was cleared of burning the bakery.

"It's too bad I can't turn back time," he told Susan, "but even then, I couldn't have forced you to sign for more coverage. Fortunately, your landlord listened to me in time to protect his assets. I really wish you had done the same."

Susan stood and shook his hand. "Not as much as I do."

Mary walked with her to their shops by way of Water Street to Main. When they passed the dentist's office, Susan half joked that having a tooth pulled would have been more fun than what she'd just gone through.

"But I'm glad you were there with me," she told Mary. "Maybe I'll have a better outcome the next time I go into Brad Overly's office."

"I sure hope so."

"It's ironic. I wanted to buy full coverage for the bakery, but Ryan didn't want to pay the higher premium. He said Brad's suggestion to buy more insurance was just an attempt to get a bigger agent's commission." They passed the pizzeria, and the smell of oregano and pepperoni wafted out to them. "I think it annoyed Ryan that Brad was wearing an expensive suit, and there he was in his worn-out work pants. Not to mention me being covered in flour."

She wasn't covered in flour today. If the arsonist wasn't found soon, it could be quite a while before she baked another batch of her "world-famous" blueberry muffins.

It had been a poor business decision to opt for minimal insurance coverage for the bakery. But Mary actually saw the good news in Ryan's insistence that they ignore Brad's wise advice. His choice convinced Mary that the insurance money could not have motivated him to set fire to the bakery.

Ryan might not be innocent when it came to his personal relationships, but she felt almost certain he was not guilty of torching Sweet Susan's Bakery.

———

After dinner that evening, Mary and Tess met in Betty and Mary's kitchen to sample the practice batch of ice cream and take notes to improve their creation. Since joining forces to come up with an interesting workshop and concoct their "ultimate" ice-cream flavor, Mary was pleased to find their friendship growing closer.

She'd always respected Tess's business acumen, but more than that, she liked how Tess saw each customer as an individual—a friend she hadn't met yet. Her warmth and openness were infectious, and it was difficult not to get caught up in her positive attitude. So what if they did more laughing than ice-cream making during tonight's prep session? The important thing was that they were having fun. So much fun that Betty came in from the garden, washed the dirt off her hands, and joined in the noisy camaraderie.

A short while later, Tyson showed up with the half-stripped rocker in the back of his aunt's car. The women *oohed* and *aahed* over the graceful lines of the antique chair and assured the teen this would be a fabulous gift for his sister. Still filled with the silliness of their laughter-filled "girls' night," the three of them raised their right hands and swore an oath of secrecy over Tyson's refinishing project. In exchange, they let Tyson sample the ice cream and made him promise not to divulge their secret recipe.

The women watched for a few minutes while he went to work on the rocker. The furniture seemed to transform before their eyes, as the layers of dull, time-blackened varnish melted away from the wood. Underneath all the scratches and irregular wear, a reddish-brown hue emerged, leading them to conclude that the chair had been crafted out of cherry wood.

Tyson wiped the sweat from his forehead with the back of his arm, his devotion to the job—and to his sister—obvious in his determined strokes of the rag over the brightening wood. Mary silently gave thanks that she'd discovered what he was up to before he did permanent damage to his health from working in the unventilated shed. She was also thankful his surreptitious activity had not been related to the fire but had been motivated by love for his sister.

They left him to finish his work and convened in the living room to finish their own. Mary and Tess sorted through the many pages of notes taken over the course of several ice-cream batches and taste testings to determine just the right balance of chocolate and their secret ingredient, cayenne. Betty joined them and tossed out ideas of names for their unusual ice cream.

"Choc-cayenne?" Betty waved her hands before they had an opportunity to nix it. "No, that's too 'on the nose,' as you would say about some of the mystery clues in the books you read. How about Choco-Zinger?"

Tess considered it a moment. "That's a possibility." A polite way of saying, "We'll think about it until something better comes up."

Betty picked up a copy of *Cape Cod Living*. "I'm not crazy about it either. I'm sure that the minute I turn my attention to something else, the perfect moniker will come to me."

Mary smiled. Prayer did that for her. Anytime she was stuck on finding an idea or a solution to a problem, a momentary pause for prayer almost always gave her the answer. Not always the answer she wanted, but an answer nevertheless.

"I'm so glad we kept everything in writing," Tess said. "Otherwise, we'd be up the creek with half a paddle."

Mary and Betty both swiveled their heads toward Tess at her distorted cliché. Neither bothered to correct her, but the misspeak made Mary want to dig out that book of Casey Stengel-isms she had at home and read through it for more fun with words.

"After all the changes we made," Tess continued, "I'm sure we'd never be able to remember the right measurements." She sorted their notes in chronological order and stacked them on the coffee table.

Gus brushed past their legs, letting them know he wanted to be the center of attention, but they had a bit more work to do, so Mary idly rubbed his back and turned her focus to the order of their presentation.

"So I'll start with the basic vanilla recipe," Mary confirmed, "and you'll cover how to add other flavorings."

"Right. Did I tell you? After you mentioned that Nicole wanted Gino Azzara to touch on how to make gelato, I bumped into his mother-in-law, Lucia, at the farmers' market selling beautiful hand-embroidered tablecloths. She said Gino may know where to find the fish in Ivy Bay, but he can't find his way around the kitchen."

So much for that idea. Nicole wouldn't be pleased that her idea for Italian ice cream didn't pan out, but Mary considered it was for the best.

Tess made a little victory salute. "However, Lucia often makes gelato for her family, so she said she'd be happy to join us as a guest speaker."

Mary didn't want to rain on Tess's parade, but she had to voice her concern about loading the workshop with too many speakers and confusing attendees by bombarding them with multiple recipes.

"I'm sure Lucia is very knowledgeable about making gelato, but I'm wondering if adding another speaker will make our program run too long."

Tess touched a finger to her chin. "I thought about that too, but Lucia seems to think her accent might be too thick for people to understand, so she'd rather hand out the recipe, give tastings, and be available to answer questions. I don't think her part will add more than ten additional minutes to our program, but it should provide an interesting bonus to the workshop."

"Sounds good." Although Mary hadn't met Lucia, she felt certain her portion of the workshop would add value to the overall learning for the participants. Besides, Mary wanted their workshop to be everything that Nicole had envisioned.

"I invited Lucia to join us tonight, but she couldn't come. She said she has it all"—Tess tapped her temple—"up here."

Obviously impatient with their talking, Gus hopped up on the table and walked across their work as if to say, "Look at me! I'm more important than these silly papers you keep pushing around."

Naturally, all three of them gave him the doting attention he wanted. After a moment of that, he'd had enough and jumped down off the table, scattering the previously organized papers in his wake.

"It's okay. I've got it." Tess pulled them back together and sorted them into two piles. One to keep, and one to throw away. She placed the keep pile—recipes, speaking notes, and handouts—in an envelope and handed them to Mary.

With their work on the ice-cream workshop finished, Tess turned to the subject that never drifted far from Mary's mind lately.

"Any news on the bakery fire?"

Betty stopped flipping pages in her magazine to listen to Mary's reply.

"Unfortunately, no arrests other than Ryan's have been made." Mary quickly went over the items she'd found at the bakery during cleanup after the fire. She didn't mention her initial suspicion of Tyson, nor did she point out Carol Bates's peculiar behavior. And since Wyatt Heath, the new firefighter, was a friend of Tess's and her family's, Mary didn't bother to bring up the curious connections she'd found between him and the lighter she'd found. As for the most obvious suspect, almost everyone in town must have heard about Ryan's arrest, so Mary didn't spend much time going over that part. But she did reveal that she'd seen a black car with its headlights off leaving the scene of the fire and that Susan had found a car-rental receipt in Ryan's pocket. To bring up the slip of paper with the woman's name and phone number would have served no purpose other than to sully the man's reputation even further, so Mary left that part out as well.

Betty had already heard about the suspicious black car, but this was the first opportunity Mary had to share about Ryan's car rental. Her sister laid down the magazine and leaned in.

Tess seemed saddened to hear what appeared to be further evidence against Ryan. "Like everyone else, I hope these are just terrible coincidences. Everyone who knows Ryan likes him a lot. And I'm one of them."

As were she and Betty.

"Even so," Tess continued, "I'm quite impressed by your sleuthing skills. You have quite a knack for putting puzzle pieces together."

Betty chuckled. "She should. She's read enough mystery novels to qualify for a PhD in amateur sleuthing."

Tess had started gathering up her belongings, but she seemed in no hurry to leave. "Your talk of the rental car reminds me of the time Blake and I flew down to South Carolina for a family reunion. It was during the dog days of summer, and we rented a car to get around town. A *black* car." She turned her hands upward in a questioning gesture. "No one bothered to tell us Northerners how hot a black car can get in the South."

"I've heard that," Betty concurred. "Black must draw the heat."

"Exactly. And we didn't think to leave the windows cracked, which made the car even hotter. After the reunion picnic, we went back to my great-aunt's house and stayed a couple of extra days."

"Is that the aunt who loves to cook and taught you to make ice cream?" Mary asked.

Tess tilted her head at Mary. "Yes. I'm amazed you remember that."

Betty wasn't. "No detail is too small for Mary to remember," she said on a teasing note. "Unless it's the occasional dozen eggs I ask her to pick up from the farmers' market."

Mary laughed. "That was just one time, and I only forgot because I kept thinking about the steamed clams you had promised to make for dinner that night." Turning the subject back to the story Tess had been telling, she said, "You must have been relieved to return to the moderate temperatures of a Massachusetts summer after all that heat and humidity."

"You can say that again." Tess sat on the edge of the sofa as she prepared to finish her story. "The problem was that, just before we were to leave, Aunt Ada noticed that her favorite casserole dish was missing. The one we'd taken to the picnic. We turned the house upside down looking for it and eventually had to give up and hope she'd find it later."

"I hate when I misplace my favorite kitchen items," Betty said. "Especially those special pieces you can't replace."

"Indeed. She'd had this casserole dish for decades and always used it for family gatherings." Tess stared out the window as she recalled the memory. "Blake and I had to leave, believing that the casserole dish may have gone home with the wrong family, but we expected it would turn up eventually." Tess shook her head and quirked a smile at the memory. "Well, it did."

"In the laundry room?" Betty asked. "I still have no idea how my hand mixer ended up in there."

"No. The next afternoon we were scheduled to fly home, so we returned the rental car. When Blake opened the trunk of that hot, sweltering car to make sure we'd left nothing behind, there was the casserole dish—half full of egg salad."

Mary wrinkled her nose and fanned the air in front of her face. "The smell must have been horrendous."

"There isn't a word to describe it. I nearly retched, right there in the parking lot. If it weren't Aunt Ada's favorite casserole dish, I would have dumped the whole thing right into the trash can."

"What did you do?" Mary and Betty asked in unison.

"The only thing I could do. I took it into the bathroom, flushed the contents, and tried to wash the dish the best I could. But after two days in the hot South Carolina sun, the nastiness had baked onto the dish like a rock."

Tess laughed and held her stomach at the thought of the nauseating memory.

"The whole time, Blake stood outside the bathroom door, shouting that we were going to miss our flight if I didn't hurry up. So I grabbed up that dripping wet dish with hardened green egg salad still clinging to the sides, and plopped it in his hands for him to carry. Let me tell you, people gave us wide berth at the airport."

By now, Mary and Betty had joined in the laughter. Like all wives, Mary remembered those days when she had scurried to get the children ready for church and, like Blake, John had "helpfully" tried to hasten them along. Judging by the misty tears of laughter in Betty's eyes, she had gone through similar experiences with Edward. But Tess's version of manly impatience took the cake. Or egg salad, as the case may be.

"Can you imagine what would happen if that had occurred today?" Tess said. "I'm sure we would have been detained by TSA authorities for trying to board the plane with a toxic chemical."

That comment set off another round of hysterical laughter, and the women tried to outdo each other with their made-up scenarios of the casserole dish glowing like hazardous waste. And of Blake and Tess wielding the dish like a weapon while shouting, "Stay back! We have egg salad, and we're not afraid to use it."

Their laughter was still ringing when the back storm door squeaked open.

"Miz Fisher?" Tyson poked his head into the living room. "I'm sorry for just coming right in, but I knocked three times and nobody answered."

"No problem," Mary said, rising from her chair.

"I'm ready to leave now. Do you and Miz Emerson mind if I leave the chair on the back deck to finish drying? I can put it at the far end, out of your way."

"That's fine. Are you finished already?"

He shook his head. "No, ma'am. I just got it down to the bare wood, then stained it. It'll need a couple of coats of polyurethane after this."

The women trekked out to the back deck to inspect the progress he'd made, then insisted he have another dish of ice cream before he left.

Tess, convinced they'd finally got the right combination of flavors for their ice cream, left shortly after him, leaving Mary and Betty to resume their usual evening routines.

While she and Betty put the ice cream away, but not before Betty dipped a spoon into the container for one more taste, Mary's thoughts returned to the car-rental receipt Susan had found in Ryan's pocket. What if, like Tess and Blake, he or his presumed passenger had left something behind in the car? A clue, perhaps.

Pondering the possibilities, she scrubbed at some food stuck to a dinner plate and was grateful it was only a bit of gravy that washed off fairly easily and not stuck-on egg salad.

With a renewed sense of determination, she decided a trip to the car-rental company would be in order for tomorrow.

Not so much to inquire about a supposed female passenger as Susan had wanted to do, but to see what other clues the car might offer up.

"I've got it." Betty smacked her lips and dropped the spoon into the dishwasher. "The perfect name for your chocolate and cayenne ice cream."

Mary lifted her head from her task.

"Fire and Ice Cream."

THIRTEEN

The receipt lay on the counter between Susan and the car-rental agent, a pretty woman with her sleek brown hair pulled back in a ponytail so tight it doubled as a temporary face-lift.

The place looked like it had been in operation since production of the first Model T Ford. Though clean and tidy, the mom-and-pop establishment showed few signs of modern technology. Rows of olive-green filing cabinets lined the wall behind the counter, and an IBM Selectric typewriter sat on a desk in a small office nook. And the telephone, with a coiled cord that tethered the receiver to its clunky black base, harkened back to at least the 1970s. Everything in here looked older than the woman working the equipment. Even her uniform and name tag—Carmel—looked like they had time traveled here from another era.

Mary hoped Susan's nervousness wouldn't trigger suspicion. She had coached her to ask to see the car first and put off any questions about the mystery woman until later.

"My husband rented this car two weeks ago. I was wondering if I could take a look inside...." Since neither of them had thought of a valid reason for asking, Susan simply let her voice trail off.

The woman across the counter studied the receipt, her eyebrows raised. Mary couldn't tell whether her raised brows were due to surprise or to the pull of her ponytail. After what seemed like an excruciatingly long time, Carmel reached into a file cabinet and pulled out a folder marked August 22. She flipped through the day's rental papers until she found Ryan's paperwork with several other sheets stapled to it.

"Of course. People leave stuff in cars all the time. The worst was when someone left half a bushel of steamed crabs in the trunk." She squinted at the memory of it, reminding Mary of Tess and her egg salad. "This vehicle went into the shop for maintenance after your husband took it out, and no one has rented it since then, but I'm sure it's been cleaned already. If anything had turned up, we would have called, but you're welcome to take a look anyway."

"Thank you," Susan said. "I'd really appreciate it."

The agent disappeared out a side door to retrieve the car, leaving them standing there to wait for her return. The folder lay open on the age-battered wooden counter.

Mary turned the folder to take a closer look at the papers Ryan had signed. The contract, waivers, disclaimers, and a photocopy of his driver's license. Nothing seemed out of order here. Susan peered over her shoulder, apparently searching for some sign of the woman who had given Ryan her phone number.

Mary, however, found her gaze drawn to the rest of the papers that lay fanned out on the open folder. Miller. Smith.

Herrick. She nudged Ryan's documents aside to reveal the one beneath it. A familiar name.

A black vehicle pulled up to the door where Carmel had exited earlier, and Susan hurriedly pushed the folder to the other side of the counter where Carmel had left it.

Mary considered snatching the folder back to see if any of the other rentals that day had been for a black sedan. Perhaps a bit of a stretch, but her curiosity had been aroused. But before she could do anything about it, the side door opened and the agent motioned for Susan to follow her.

"You're in luck," Carmel said. "The new guy parked this in the wrong place, and it didn't get cleaned. So it's possible what you're looking for may still be there."

She led them to the black vehicle. A small, late-model Ford pickup.

"This is a truck," Mary said. "Didn't Ryan rent a sedan?"

Carmel shook her head, and her ponytail flipped over her shoulder. "Nope. This is the one." She glanced inside the building where a couple with two small children stood waiting at the counter. "Go ahead and take a look while I help these other customers. Let me know when you're finished."

She disappeared inside, leaving them to their search.

A truck. Definitely not the black sedan Mary had seen cruising slowly past the bakery with its lights off. A sense of relief swept over her. Who knew what Ryan had been up to that night? Whatever it happened to be, Mary was certain this was not the vehicle she had seen the night of the fire.

Susan stepped back from the truck, seemingly undecided about where to start looking.

Mary went straight to the passenger's side and pulled open the door. She didn't know what she expected to find. Maybe a hair? A dropped earring?

Nothing. Not quite enough to put Susan's fears of marital infidelity to rest, but encouraging, nevertheless. Mary swept her hand under the seat, and Susan followed suit on the driver's side. The glove box brought up the usual rental-car information, and the bed of the truck offered only a few fallen leaves.

Mary went to the driver's side and slid in behind the steering wheel. She sat there, imagining herself to be Ryan and wondering if he might have left something in here and where he would have put it. The dashboard was bare.

Carmel had left the key in the ignition, so Mary turned it to the first notch. The dash lit up, and a global-positioning device opened to the welcome screen. In contrast to the company's antiquated office and reception area, this truck came with all the latest bells and whistles, including satellite radio. They obviously invested their money where it mattered most to customers.

Mary touched the Okay button, agreeing not to operate the GPS device while driving on the road, and the screen switched to a map showing their current location. Then she touched the Menu button that offered the option of entering a new address or pulling up a previous destination. She chose the previous destination, and a lone address showed up on the display.

Chelmsford, Massachusetts. On the other side of Boston, at least an hour and a half's drive from here. The late-afternoon rental would have given Ryan enough time to drive to Chelmsford, quickly do whatever he'd planned to do or meet whomever he'd arranged to see, and return home just in time to learn of the fire at the bakery.

"May I see that receipt again?"

Susan handed her the paper, and Mary did some quick math from the starting and ending odometer readings to determine that Ryan had driven 97 miles. The distance to the Chelmsford address was 93 miles. If he'd made a side trip, neither the time nor the mileage would have allowed anything other than a rest stop or quick bite at a fast-food restaurant.

Mary pulled a ballpoint pen from her pocket and wrote the address on the palm of her left hand.

A moment later, Carmel returned. "Did you find what you were looking for?"

Susan shrugged. "Not really. Were you the one who rented this truck to my husband?"

Mary winced, hoping the car-rental agent wouldn't notice Susan's abrupt change of subject. Personally, she'd found that a less obvious approach to questioning proved most effective for finding the answers she sought.

Fortunately, Carmel was focused on getting the truck back to the lot for cleanup. "No, I wasn't working that day." She slid into the truck and started the engine. "Is there anything else I can help you with?"

Clearly disappointed that Carmel wouldn't be able to tell her whether Tootsie had accompanied her husband on his surreptitious outing, Susan shook her head and thanked her for her help.

When they turned to leave, Susan said to Mary, "Well, that was a giant waste of time."

Not completely. Mary had discovered the good news that Ryan could not have been in both Chelmsford and Ivy Bay at the same time. Chief McArthur had probably already investigated Ryan's alibi, but she was relieved nevertheless that this bit of evidence might clear Susan's husband of setting the fire. She was sorry for Susan's sake that it still left unanswered questions about the woman whose phone number had been found in Ryan's pocket.

Mary curled her fingers in on the address written on her palm. "Have faith," she urged. "It may take some time, but the truth will eventually come to light."

To facilitate the process, Mary would pass along to Chief McArthur the evidence that Ryan had been in Chelmsford the night of the fire, returning to Ivy Bay just after the fire was being set.

Susan quickened her step as they returned to Mary's car. "Not soon enough, if you ask me."

With Tyson and Ryan cleared as suspects in the arson—at least in Mary's mind—that left only two others that Mary knew of with motives to set the fire: Wyatt Heath, the firefighter whose zeal for fire could be interpreted as somewhat obsessive; and Carol Bates, the dyspeptic would-be competitor for Susan's cupcake business.

They got into the car, and Mary pulled onto Route 6. Thinking of Carol reminded her of something she needed to do.

"Would you mind giving me Carol Bates's phone number?" she said to Susan. "I need to give her a call."

That evening, Mary and Betty watched Tyson Shepard apply the first layer of polyurethane to the rocker. The stained surface took on a vivid reddish-brown hue that gleamed in the rays of the setting sun.

"That looks fabulous," Mary said. "Your sister will be so happy to receive such a beautiful gift."

Tyson stood back and admired the chair, obviously pleased with his efforts. "It'll look even better after I add the second coat."

Gus put his paws on the storm door and meowed to be let out.

Betty moved to open the door, but Mary stopped her. "Better not. You know the first place he'll go is to the rocking chair. And, *poof*! Tyson's sister will get a cat-hair chair."

Tyson grinned. "Might keep her warm on cold days."

During the time he'd been working in their backyard, Mary and Betty had come to know him better and enjoy his company. Mary had been delighted to discover his amusing sense of humor. He'd warmed up a lot since his surly reaction to Susan a couple of weeks ago over the ten dollars he'd accidentally shorted her.

Gus meowed again, more insistent this time. Betty rubbed her hands and wrists. "You two carry on," she said. "I have things to do inside."

She closed the door behind her to stop Gus from crying to go out.

Mary knew the "things" Betty had to do were to take a hot soak in the bathtub to relieve her aching joints, followed by an early bedtime. After Mary saw Tyson off, she would go in and make some herbal tea for her sister.

"Uh, Miz Fisher?" The teen awkwardly looked at the ground rather than meet her gaze. "Aunt Amelia said you and your prayer group have been praying for us—for my sister and me."

She turned and leaned against the deck rail, staring at the walkway to the garden that transfixed the boy. "Yes, we've been praying for all of you."

He blew out a long sigh. "I think it's working. The doctor told my sister he's already seeing some improvement. She might not need to have the full round of treatments, after all."

"That's wonderful. I'm so glad to hear it." Unable to contain herself, Mary threw her arms around Tyson's neck and gave him a heartfelt hug.

The gesture seemed to both surprise and please him, and he leaned down from his six-foot height to return the hug along with a bashful smile. "She's real happy about that, and she wants to go to the church near her house and thank God for the healing that's already started. The only thing is, she doesn't belong to a church, and she doesn't know anyone over at Grace Church."

"Betty and I go there. We'd be happy to introduce her to the members. I'm sure she'll enjoy Pastor Miles." She leaned an elbow on the deck rail and carefully phrased her next statement. "And we'd love for you to come too. Grace Church has a very active youth group."

He dipped his head noncommittally, leaving her to wonder whether he'd take her up on the invitation.

"Thank you. I'm sure she'd like that. Do you suppose"— he wiped at a spot of furniture stain on the palm of his hand—"I mean…would you come to her house and pray with her? Miz Emerson, too, if she feels up to it. That way, my sister could get to know you, and the prayers might help her to keep getting better." He paused a moment and cleared his throat. "It would mean a lot to her. To both of us."

The love Tyson had for his sibling was as evident as the stain he kept trying to rub off his hand. He'd clearly been worried about her health, and it must have been hard for him to ask for this favor.

"We'd be very honored to come and pray with her. And with you too, if you'd like to join in."

Tyson smiled, and for the first time, Mary noticed just how handsome the teenager was. Amazing how a smile could transform a person's appearance like that.

"Awesome," he said. "The rocker should be ready in a few days. Maybe you could come with me when I give it to her?"

He waited for her answer and seemed hopeful. In a way, he reminded her of her son Jack at that age, who would have been mortified to be caught doing anything the least bit sentimental. Mary deduced that their presence might also be intended to keep the gift giving from becoming a too-mushy event.

"We'd be thrilled," she assured him. "In the meantime, please tell her about Grace Church's special event tomorrow evening called 'Honor Your Calling.' It's to recognize the contributions of God's people in the workplace."

They went inside, and Mary wrote down the time and date so Tyson wouldn't forget.

After he left, she remembered the call she needed to make. She pulled the scrap of paper from her purse on which Susan had written a phone number for her. Mary picked up the receiver and punched in the numbers.

Her research the other day had opened Mary's eyes to some interesting possibilities, but she didn't know whether this would provide the answer that was needed. She wouldn't know for sure until this person was put through a test.

The phone rang twice, and a woman picked up.

"Hello, Carol? This is Mary Fisher." She hesitated only a moment in which she wondered if she might be overstepping her bounds. But she had prayed over this and knew she was doing the right thing. She plunged ahead before doubt could overtake her. "We need to talk."

FOURTEEN

◆◆◆

The following day, Mary stood at the counter in the bookshop and sorted through the many notes she and Tess had jotted down for their ice-cream concoction. Although Tess had discarded the earliest versions the other night, one of the test copies had been overlooked.

Concerned that the wrong recipe might make its way into their presentation, she balled up the old one and tossed it toward the recycling bin. Her aim left a lot to be desired. The wad of paper bounced off the rim and landed on the floor. If her granddaughter Emma, the softball player, were here, she would most certainly have something to say about Mary's nonexistent pitching ability.

She would pick it up in a minute. But first, she punched holes in the remaining pages and inserted them into a three-ring binder.

Mary started to reach for the trash on the floor but was interrupted when Susan burst into the bookshop, doing a happy jig. Her friend clutched something in her hand and waved it in the air.

"I finally found my keys!"

"That's terrific. Where were they?"

Ever since the fire, Susan had been using her husband's shop key whenever she needed to go into her bakery and do some work. She had confided to Mary that she hadn't made a copy to replace the missing one yet, because she didn't know when—or even whether—the shop would reopen.

Susan set the keys on the counter and lifted her palms. "In my jacket at home. Can you believe it? But I'm a little befuddled as to how they got there. I never put my keys in my jacket pocket, and they were definitely on the counter next to the cash register the day of the fire."

Mary's thoughts fled back to that fateful day. The last person she'd seen near the register had been Carol Bates, who had complained of being food poisoned by Susan's cupcake. The likelihood of her returning to put the keys in Susan's jacket seemed very slim.

While she and Susan tossed around probable scenarios, little Ashley puttered around them, busying herself with organizing the checkout counter. First, she tidied the stack of learning-annex flyers, then rearranged sticky notes around the cash register, and finally returned Rebecca's pack of sugar-free gum to her purse.

Next week, when Ashley started back to school, Mary would miss her little friend's company in the bookstore. She'd see her occasionally after school or on holidays and weekends, but it wouldn't be the same. She would certainly miss the almost daily dose of Ashley's giggles, smiles, and helping spirit.

The little girl moved closer and lifted Mary's arm to dust the counter under her elbow.

That's when Mary remembered. Sweet, helpful Ashley had accompanied her to the bakery the morning of the fire. She must have noticed the keys that Susan had absentmindedly laid on the counter when she suddenly got deluged with customers.

While Ashley had performed her self-appointed tasks, Mary had seen her "straightening" a jacket on a hook. Apparently, the thoughtful child must have put them in Susan's pocket and forgotten to mention what she had done. Mary broached her question carefully, making sure the little girl knew she wasn't being accused of anything.

"Ashley, when you were straightening up at the bakery a few weeks ago, did you happen to put Miss Susan's keys in her jacket?"

The little girl stopped her cleaning and vigorously bobbed her head. "They were gonna get lost, so I put them in Miss Susan's pocket to be safe."

Well, that answered one question but raised another. If Susan had the keys all along, how did the arsonist enter the bakery without it looking like a break-in?

Ashley had apologized for her role in the confusion, but Susan insisted that everything had worked out for the best after all. Then she promised to bake the little girl whatever kind of cupcake she wanted in payment for being so helpful.

After Susan left, Mary returned her attention to the workshop notes. With the ice-cream learning annex set to take place in a few days, she wanted everything in order. But when she paged through the information, she discovered the most recent version of the ice-cream recipe missing from the meticulous collection of notes. All that remained was one early attempt in which she and Tess had added too much sugar to compensate for their heavy-handed use of cayenne.

A moment of panic threatened to overwhelm her. All but the final version had been either too spicy, too bland, or even merely mediocre. It hadn't been until they tried that final time that she and Tess got the blend of chocolate and cayenne just right and the flavors popped. What good would it do for them to give a workshop that featured boring ice cream? Mary's conscience wouldn't allow her to take their attendees' registration fees for an unsatisfactory recipe.

"Oh no." Mary forced herself to relax, then remembered what she usually did in situations like this. She prayed.

She sat on the chair behind the counter, lowered her head, and began with a silent heartfelt thank-you for the recipe she and Tess had created. Then she followed with a request to lead her to the errant paper.

When she looked up, she calmly tried to recall exactly where she had been and what she had been doing, and when she had last touched the paper. Then she let her gaze roam around the small area where she had been working.

Yes, she was positive she had put it in the binder. She quickly flipped through the pages again.

Rebecca looked up from the window display she was working on. "Something wrong?"

"I can't find my recipe, and it was here just a few minutes ago."

"Well, it couldn't have gone far. I'll help you look."

Ashley playfully backed away. "It wasn't me this time."

Mary laughed. "Don't worry, sweetie. The thought hadn't even crossed my mind."

They looked everywhere. All around the counter. In the binder. Ashley even checked in Rebecca's purse in case she had absentmindedly put it in there along with the gum.

Mary stood back and sighed with frustration. "Tess was counting on promoting this flavor as her special of the month."

There was nothing special about the test-run recipe that had found its way into the binder.

Her hymn tune this week, "Come unto Me," played from a shelf beneath the counter. How appropriate.

Ashley tilted her head. "Your purse is ringing."

Mary retrieved the cell phone and glanced at the caller ID. Nicole. She pressed the connect key, and Rebecca and Ashley went back to their work.

"Mary, I just had this great idea!" No hello. Just bubbling over with enthusiasm.

Mary felt her muscles tighten at the news. "Really?"

She listened while Nicole detailed her latest brainstorm. This time it involved the added feature of sprinkles for the ice cream. That was certainly doable, given that the workshop would take place at Bailey's Ice Cream Shop, and they could incorporate any ingredients Tess had on hand. But sprinkles might not taste so good with the cayenne flavor. Maybe she and Tess could let the workshop attendees taste a small sample of the plain ice cream with sprinkles before they added the "fire" to the chocolate.

"Sure," she said into the phone. "I suppose we can make it work."

"What about crumbled pralines? Don't you think that would taste astounding on ice cream?" A crunching sound came through the phone. "My husband brought some home last night, and it's delicious!"

"I don't think Tess has any praline crumbles at the shop." Mary also doubted the taste would combine well with many flavors other than vanilla.

"That's okay. I'll ask Chip where he found them. All you have to do is buy the pralines and beat them with a mallet until they're the right size."

All she had to do…

Mary drew in a deep breath. "No, actually Tess and I already have our time planned out to the minute until this learning annex takes place. We'll just do without praline sprinkles this time."

There! No waffling, and no reason for Nicole to misread the fact that Mary absolutely would not be taking on this extra task. Mary had once read in a self-help book that saying no at the beginning of a sentence was the best way to make your intention clear. And in this case, she thought it worked very well. At least she hoped so.

A pause stretched out between them. "Oh," Nicole finally said, clearly surprised that Mary hadn't run with the idea. But then she took a breath and Mary could tell Nicole had come to her senses when she said, "It's no big deal. Your ice cream is so delicious, no matter what the toppings."

Mary smiled into the phone and said, "Thanks, Nicole."

"Thank you, Mary. And I should probably go. My break is over. See you soon!"

Nicole hung up before Mary could tell her the recipe had gone AWOL, but at least Mary felt confident there were no hard feelings. She prayed the recipe would turn up in time for the upcoming learning annex and that God would provide both Nicole and Mary with wisdom.

———

When Mary returned home that evening, Betty wiped her hands on a dish towel and handed her a brown padded envelope. A sloppy, handwritten scrawl spelled out Mary's name and address. The post office box return address had been similarly scribbled in the upper left corner, and a blurred postmark adorned the right corner.

It didn't feel like a magazine. Rather, a rectangular lump shifted around inside. Mary gently pressed the envelope, trying to guess at the contents.

Betty good-humoredly flicked the dish towel at her, but despite the playful gesture, Mary could tell she wasn't feeling up to snuff. "Just open it already," Betty urged. "I'm dying of curiosity."

Happy to oblige, because her own curiosity had switched to high gear, Mary slid a finger under the flap and pulled out the receipt first. The company name Ribbie Collectibles curved inside a graphic of the tip end of a baseball bat.

"Oh, I remember now. It's the baseball cards I ordered for Emma's birthday."

Betty took a seat beside her on the sofa and watched her go through the contents of the envelope. She picked up the package of cards and turned it over in her hands. "Nice. I think Emma will like these."

"I hope so. I'll give her something else to go along with it, just in case." She stared at the receipt. Something about that tip of the bat looked vaguely familiar. Mary had seen this before, but had trouble putting a finger on it.

After a moment, a sneaking suspicion occurred to her and goose bumps rose up on her arms.

———

Grace Church's special Wednesday night event had drawn a good-size crowd. Not bad, considering how many local families were enjoying last-minute vacations, preparing for the start of a new school year, or working long hours to squeeze a few more dollars out of tourists before they headed back to their hometowns.

Mary loved the beauty of this church. The white vaulted ceiling compelled people to look up, a perfect metaphor for a life of looking up to God for His guidance, love, and protection. And the rows of stained-glass windows on either side of the building filtered the day's fading sunlight before it fell in colorful patches across the pews. The beams of light reminded her that the Bible's message should subtly and pleasantly color every aspect of her life.

A computer-printed banner with the words *Honor Your Calling* hung from the podium where Pastor Miles welcomed the congregation and went over the agenda for this evening's proceedings. It was too bad Betty hadn't felt well enough to come tonight, especially since the idea for this program had been hers to begin with. Mary opened the bulletin and scanned the names and bios of those who had agreed to speak. Elderly Strom Engle was slated to talk about the fishermen of Ivy Bay and the role of Seafarers' Hall in helping watermen who were temporarily down on their luck. Jill Sanderson would speak about how being a mother is an important calling from God. And Chief McArthur had agreed to share a story of God's presence the time he had organized a search crew to find a lost autistic child. Even Wyatt Heath was here, invited by Tess, to talk about his calling to become a firefighter.

A movement to Mary's left distracted her, and a young woman with a pretty pink bandanna around her head slipped into the seat beside her. Mary scooted over. Recognizing her as Melody, the friendly gal who had attended Betty's gardening workshop a couple of weeks ago, Mary beamed a welcoming smile.

After Chief McArthur's compelling story about the amazing coincidences—God's leading, perhaps?—that led him and searchers to the lost child, he fielded a few questions from the audience.

The young woman leaned in and whispered to Mary, "He's such a kind man. Chief McArthur has helped my little brother through a couple of periods of teenage rebellion."

Mary nodded. "His heart is in the right place. He wants to help people. Make a difference in their lives."

"My brother started drifting into trouble last year." Melody toyed with the loop of scarf that hung over her shoulder. "I hope his summer job will keep him out of trouble. Give him a sense of accomplishment." Her pretty green eyes met Mary's directly. "My biggest wish is that he'll come back to church. The way we were raised."

Remembering what Tyson had said about missing his sister's presence since her marriage last year, Mary smiled and ventured a guess. "Are you Tyson Shepard's sister?"

Melody's eyes opened wide. "How did you know?"

Pastor Miles walked up to the podium, and Chief McArthur stepped down. "Let's give a hand for the blessings God has bestowed through the work of devoted public servants like our own Chief McArthur."

Amid the applause and "amens," Mary winked at Melody as if to imply that was a secret she would keep. Of course, she would tell her later. But for now, she marveled that, of all the people in this church, young Melody had ended up sitting beside her. Mary thought back to the interesting circumstances Chief McArthur had relayed in his talk, and wondered once again … *Coincidence? Or God's leading?*

Wyatt Heath took the podium next. He opened with the Firefighter's Prayer. "When I'm called to duty, God, wherever flames may rage…"

A collage of images tumbled across the projection screen behind him while he finished reading the prayer. Ivy Bay firefighters spraying water on a brush fire beside the road. There was the picture he had shown at the beach bonfire of flames shooting out the top of a chimney. And an image of firefighters back at the station, repacking hose on a pumper truck.

Most of the photos featured dramatic action scenes of firefighters working to suppress fires, leading Mary to wonder what fueled Heath's passion to go "wherever flames may rage."

After the prayer, Wyatt started by correcting a common misconception. "Just so you know, I'm not a fireman. A fireman was someone who stoked the boiler of a steamship or railroad steam engine." He waited for the soft chuckles to finish rippling through the audience. "You might also use the term for a baseball player who replaces the starting pitcher. Or a fireman could refer to a pyromaniac."

He pressed the clicker to pause on an image of himself in a bright-yellow coat and shiny new helmet, clutching a certificate of graduation.

"I, on the other hand, am a fire*fighter*. My buddies in the fire department and I fight fires."

He pressed the clicker again, this time landing on an image, which had been scanned from a newspaper clipping, of a soot-faced man in his mid-thirties. The angular face bore a striking resemblance to Wyatt's. The man wore black turnout gear striped with yellow reflective tape, dulled by ash and smoke. A fire-resistant hood hung down beneath a helmet with the station number and white letters: FDNY. He looked tired. And perhaps a bit proud of his accomplishment.

"This is my uncle Cal," Wyatt said. "He was a New York City firefighter. From the time I was a little kid, I looked up to him. Copied everything he did. And I figured that if he worked with fire, then fire must be a cool thing."

He went on to tell the story of how, at age six, he had sneaked his uncle's lighter out to the garage where he tried to flick a flame from it the way he'd seen Cal do. But Wyatt's small fingers hadn't been strong enough to turn the thumbwheel, so he had rolled it on some discarded newspapers until it sparked. The resulting fire consumed a sewing machine and two bicycles before he finally worked up the nerve to alert his parents and uncle to what he'd done.

"Understandably, my father wanted to burn my hide," he said with a grin. "But Uncle Cal was the one who set me straight." Wyatt turned and bestowed a fond gaze on the image of his uncle. "The next weekend, he took me to New York and gave me a tour of the fire station where he worked. He made me understand the serious damage fire can cause. From that time on, I wanted to be just like my uncle and experience the thrill of riding a fire truck as it barreled down the street with its sirens blaring."

The audience's attention remained riveted on Wyatt. The young man's sincerity resonated in his words as he described camping trips with his beloved uncle, who had shown him the proper use of a lighter for starting campfires.

He paused for a moment and lowered his head. When he looked up again, his eyes were red. And when he spoke, his voice cracked with emotion.

"On September 11, 2001, Uncle Cal showed the world what a true hero is. That day—and my uncle's supreme sacrifice—forever changed my perspective of what it means to be a firefighter." Wyatt rubbed his nose with the back of his hand. "That's when I learned that being a firefighter is not about fighting fires and riding fire trucks, or even getting your picture in the newspaper," he said with a sweep of his arm to the projection screen. "It's about serving others."

Wyatt reached into his pocket and pulled out the FDNY lighter he had used to light the bonfire on the beach last weekend and held it aloft for all to see.

"This lighter is the only thing I wanted of my uncle's belongings. It reminds me of the mistake I made that God directed Cal to turn into something positive. What I do for the fire department and its citizens, I do to honor God…and the man who truly knew what it meant to serve others."

Something rustled at the other end of the pew, and Dorothy pulled a tissue from her purse to dab at her eyes. Beyond her, Nicole sat with her family. She sniffled and put a hand on her little boy's bouncing leg.

A hush fell over the congregation, and Mary felt the full impact of what Wyatt had just shared. As she looked into his sincere, tear-filled eyes, the questions and concerns she had harbored about his motives fell away. This was not a man who sought the adrenalin rush of fighting fires or the adulation of others. This was a man who, as he had said in the Firefighter's Prayer, wanted "to fill my calling and to give the best in me." For the first time, she truly understood that his interest in the fire department was not about chasing thrills and glory, but about honoring his uncle's memory.

With a heart full of relief and joy, Mary knew this could not be the man who had started the fire in Susan's bakery.

FIFTEEN

———◆◆◆———

Mary flagged down Chief McArthur in the church parking lot. She had tried to call him soon after the trip to the car rental agency, but he'd been in a meeting at the time and suggested they talk after church. After she thanked him for his inspiring message tonight, she filled him in on the information she had learned at the car-rental agency.

He rubbed a hand over his jaw while she described the pickup truck that did not match the black sedan she'd seen the night of the fire. Since he'd already heard Ryan's alibi—a matter between husband and wife—she supposed he'd already made up his mind that Susan's husband was innocent of setting the fire. But, just to make sure, she gave him the address she'd found on the truck's GPS device. She also told him about the mileage readings and the pickup and drop-off times, as well as what else she'd seen in the folder for that day's rentals.

Chief McArthur wrote the address on a small pad of paper, and Mary prayed it would be enough evidence to clear Ryan of arson. The sooner he was cleared, the sooner Susan would be able to collect her insurance check.

At home, Gus lay curled up on the sofa beside Betty. The television blared instructions for a do-it-yourself patio project, but Betty appeared not to be listening. She drew her gaze away from the window when Mary walked into the room.

"Hey, Bets. Are you feeling better?"

Betty managed a weak smile. Rather than answer, she switched off the television and asked how the Honor Your Calling event went.

Her sister's lack of response worried Mary. Betty must be in a lot of pain and didn't want to trouble her by talking about it.

So Mary obliged and gave a quick overview. "You'll love this," she added. "Someone got the brilliant idea to tape tonight's event. Pastor Miles said the DVD will be ready for you to borrow by Sunday."

That got a smile out of Betty. Despite her discomfort, every honey-blonde hair lay in place, and a boatneck top and clamdigger shorts gave the impression of a fashionable lady prepared to board a yacht for a day of sailing. In addition to keeping a tidy house, Betty was always particular about her appearance. It saddened Mary that the rheumatoid arthritis had not been particular about who it struck. No one deserved to go through such trouble. Least of all, Betty.

A short while later, Betty excused herself to get ready for bed, and Mary pulled out the laptop computer. While she waited for it to boot up, she made some herbal tea for herself and for Betty to take to bed with her and retrieved the Chelmsford address she had shared with Chief McArthur.

She sat down and took a sip of the ginger tea, then typed the address into the search program. Several offerings popped up with reviews for a home-style restaurant near Route 495, but no Web site for the restaurant existed.

A click on the first site showed several positive reviews, many of them exclaiming over the restaurant's signature homemade rolls. All the reviews dated back to last year or earlier. On the next site, a satisfied diner commented on the friendly attention given by Gordy and Thelma Brodbeck, the owner and his wife.

Mary was about to close out when she noticed an online article from the *Chelmsford Bugle*. The headline declared, Gingham and Lace, Country-Style Restaurant, Closes after Fifty Years in Business. One of the elderly owners had passed away two years ago, and his widow was preparing to retire from the business. The final day of operation was eight months ago. Mary searched for a more recent listing at the address, but none existed, so she could only assume the building still sat vacant.

She shut down the computer. Why would Ryan Crosby drive more than an hour and a half out of town to an empty building? A rendezvous point, perhaps?

The thought both puzzled and distressed her. Why would he meet a girlfriend at a vacant building, unless… She got up and found the scrap of paper with the woman's name and phone number on it. Unless Tootsie also didn't want anyone to know about their meeting.

"Please don't let it be what I'm thinking," Mary whispered.

Once again, she punched the number into her phone. This time, someone answered.

Talk in the shop the next day kept going back to one subject: Ashley's teacher assignment for the upcoming school year. The little girl had received her notice yesterday, and Mrs. Pace was all she could talk about.

"Some kids say she's mean," Ashley confided in a low tone, "but she just makes people work hard and act like adults."

Some people would chuckle at the thought of a seven-year-old acting like an adult, but such behavior would be natural for Ashley. And Mary had a notion her little friend relished the idea of learning from a teacher who expected students to work hard.

Near the end of the day, Mary suggested Rebecca leave early and take Ashley to finish shopping for school supplies. Mary took care of the remaining customers and finished some of the preparations for the ice-cream workshop. She clenched her jaw, sorry that the recipe hadn't turned up as she'd hoped. Fortunately, Tess had taken the news like a trouper and suggested an alternate recipe. The "Peachy Keen" substitute wouldn't have the same dramatic effect as their "Fire and Ice Cream" concoction, but it was delicious, and Mary expected attendees would be happy to try out the recipe.

She headed to the back of the shop to retrieve the cat carrier when she found Gus over by one of the reading chairs, his bottom end pointing skyward and his head hidden under the chair. His tail twitched the way it did whenever he found something fun to play with, leading Mary to wonder if another cricket had found its way into the shop.

He lay down on his side to reach farther under the chair and batted furiously at something. If not for a small life potentially at stake, Mary would have just stood back and enjoyed watching the cat play. Instead, she grasped Gus around the middle and lifted him away from whatever "toy" he had managed to find. She rubbed his ears in apology for disrupting his fun, set him beside his carrier, and gave him a treat.

Careful to stay clear of whatever might leap out at her, Mary got down on her hands and knees and peered under the chair. No crickets, thank goodness, but there appeared to be a wad of paper just out of reach. Ashley must have been trying to teach him to fetch again, an impossible endeavor, but the game usually entertained both pet and child.

Mary rose to her feet and lifted one side of the chair, while Gus watched intently from nearby. A small kick sent the paper ball scooting across the floor, and he shot after it, batting the toy as if he were Pelé on a soccer ball.

Curious to see if this might be a picture that Ashley had drawn, Mary opened it up and smoothed out the wrinkles. The crinkling sound set her cat's tail twitching again.

"Two cups heavy cream. One cup milk. Six egg yolks…"

Mary gasped. Here was the final, handwritten version of the "Fire and Ice Cream" recipe! The one she'd been searching everywhere for.

Still holding the crumpled paper, she considered how it might have gotten under the chair. Then she remembered taking the old version out of the folder full of papers and filing the newest one in the binder. She must have balled up the wrong one by mistake. Either it got kicked away from the recycling bin by someone passing through that area, or Gus had mistaken it for a plaything and carried it off for a game of cat soccer.

Regardless of how the recipe found its way under the chair, Mary was grateful to have found it in time. Looking up, she murmured a thank-you, then rewarded Gus with another of his favorite kitty treats for having led her to it.

Elated to be able to proceed with the learning-annex program as originally planned, Mary tucked Gus into his carrier and headed home to pick up Betty and the casserole and cookies they had prepared for a visit to Tyson's sister.

When they arrived at Melody's house, she parked behind Tyson's car and he led them to the den where Melody sat in an uncomfortable-looking wingback chair that appeared to have been handed down. Many times.

The rest of the place was small and cheery, like its owner. Nothing fancy, but very welcoming. A cluster of framed photos perched on the fireplace mantel, and the den furniture was arranged to promote easy conversation.

The girl looked as worn-out as the chair she sat in. With effort, she rose and greeted them warmly. A checkerboard sat on a small table between her seat and a straight-backed chair that had been brought in from the dining room. Her side of the game board appeared to be winning.

Tyson had already coached Mary and Betty on what to do. The stated purpose of the visit was to pray with Melody. The gift giving would come later. Their job, when the time was right, was to distract his sister while he brought in the rocker.

Even so, he hovered nearby, shifting from foot to foot. Mary concluded he must be anxious to present the rocker, so she took the cookies and casserole to the kitchen and suggested they get right down to praying.

He directed them to the more comfortable seats on the sofa and took the dining chair for himself. Seeing the siblings together, Mary was struck by their uncanny resemblance to each other and marveled at the miracle of genetics that God had created in them.

Melody surprised her by asking to go first, then proceeded to thank God for the doctors and medical staff who administered her treatment and for her husband, friends, and family who gave her love and emotional support. She reached over and squeezed Tyson's hand.

Mary followed, asking for a speedy recovery for the sweet-natured girl who had so quickly captured her heart and offered a few Bible verses to reinforce her request. As for Betty, the Honor Your Calling session from the other night was still on her mind, and she asked God to show Melody how to honor Him, both during her healing and after she was fully restored.

The room went silent, and Mary wondered how Tyson felt about praying aloud. Should she close the prayer, or wait for him to chime in?

He cleared his throat. "God," he said with only a slight hesitation in his voice, "You gave me the best sister in the world. Please make her well again so that someday she'll be the best mother and grandmother in the world. Amen."

The prayer wasn't the most glamorous or eloquent that Mary had ever heard, but it ranked right up there with the most heartfelt.

"Amen," the rest of them said together.

Tyson stood and looked at Mary and Betty before announcing, "I gotta get something out of my car."

Betty slanted a sly smile in Mary's direction, and Mary returned with a gentle elbow to her sister's arm to warn her not to give away their secret.

While Tyson was outside retrieving his gift, Melody suddenly sat forward. "Oh no. I meant to ask if we could pray for Carol Bates. She's a lady I met at the medical center a couple of weeks ago."

At the mention of Carol's name, Mary's ears perked up. Her quizzical expression prompted Melody to continue.

"When I showed up on that Tuesday morning to get some blood work done, she was already there, slumped in a chair in the waiting room. As gray as the cat in your store. The poor woman said she had been terribly ill with stomach trouble all night."

Mary already had an inkling what that was about, but thought it wouldn't hurt to have Melody confirm it. "Did she say what her trouble was?"

"Apparently, she had a case of food poisoning and was very dehydrated. I sat with her and kept her company until the nurse took her back to give her some IV fluids."

"That was very kind of you," Betty said, echoing Mary's thoughts.

Melody shook her head. "After I came home from church last night, I realized my job—for now—is to heal. And while I'm doing that job, God is calling me to honor Him." She smiled as she considered what she had just said. "It's all about serving others. That's how we honor God."

Her gaze drifted off to the window, and Mary hoped Melody couldn't see what her brother was doing outside.

"I didn't realize it at the time," she continued, "but I was able to honor Him by comforting someone who felt worse than I did at that moment." A smile crossed her lips. "And my payment was that I found a new friend that day."

It did Mary's heart good to hear this. Not only had Melody looked beyond her own suffering to reach out to someone else, but last night's Honor Your Calling testimonials had given her a sense of purpose as she continued to battle her health problem.

Although more than double the younger woman's age, Carol would most certainly be blessed to have such a positive-minded friend. And Melody's story matched what Carol had said earlier, which told Mary that Carol had been too sick the night of the fire to wreak havoc on the bakery.

"We've talked on the phone a few times since then," Melody said, "but I don't think Carol is getting much better."

"No?"

"Last I heard, the doctors were considering some possibilities, but most of them sounded very serious."

"Let's pray for her now," Mary said. "God willing, it may turn out to be something that's easily treated." Until then, she promised to keep Carol on the prayer list at church.

Toward the end of their brief prayer, in which Melody thanked God for using her health problem to lead her to a new friend, the front door eased open. Tyson bowed his head and waited until they were finished.

"You mind holding the door while I bring it in?" he asked Mary.

She got up, and Melody started to join her, but Betty motioned the girl to stay seated.

Tyson entered the house carrying the beautifully refinished rocking chair. Although Mary had already seen it drying on the deck, the piece now took on a new luster, as if it had been specially designed for this house.

Melody took a quick breath and put a hand to her chest. "Is that...?"

He set the chair in the middle of the room so she could see it from all sides. Gently grasping her elbow, he guided her to the chair and urged her to sit. "Nana Shepard's rocker," he said, answering her unfinished question. "She wanted you to have it, and I wanted you to have it in good condition."

She eased herself into the chair. Her fingers curled around the graceful bend of the arms, and she hesitantly pushed her feet to set it rocking.

"Oh, Tyson," she said, her voice tight with emotion.

From the first time Mary had met Melody, the girl had worn a cheerful smile. People who knew her always mentioned her strength and positive attitude in getting through her medical ordeal. And even at this young age, small smile lines bracketed her mouth, a sign that she must have had an even more bubbly personality before her illness had tamped down her effervescence.

And now, for the first time, cheerful, strong, hold-it-all-together Melody succumbed to the emotions swirling around her.

She broke down and cried.

SIXTEEN

⸺◆◆⸺

Friday morning, Mary woke up thinking about what she had planned to do that afternoon. The birthday gift for Emma sat on her dresser, waiting to be wrapped, a tangible reminder that today heralded the beginning of the weekend-long trading-card show. The flyer had advertised three days of baseball cards, memorabilia, and seminars for enthusiasts of the game, and she was itching to go and learn what she could about the Ted Williams card that had been found after the fire.

"Want to go with me to the baseball-card show this afternoon?" she asked Betty at breakfast.

"Oh, I wish I could. Madeline's hosting the book club at her house later today, and I promised I'd be there to help her set up." She slanted a coy smile at Mary. "Besides, Madeline just redecorated her master bedroom, and I can't wait to see what she did with it."

A highly acclaimed local artist, Madeline Dinsdale fascinated everyone with the creative twists and turns she took on everything she touched. Mary had no doubt Madeline had transformed her bedroom into a work of art.

"Take a picture for me," Mary suggested. "I'd love to see what she's done with it."

Before heading off to work, Mary located the trade-show flyer and the Ted Williams rookie card and tucked them in her purse. Most of the scheduled activities were set to begin at three o'clock today. Ever curious, she wished it were already in progress, so she wouldn't have to wait. If business was slow at the shop today, as she expected for the Labor Day weekend, she might slip over to the elementary school as soon as the show opened to see what else she could ferret out about the Ted Williams card and the person who had dropped it.

As the morning lumbered on, Mary distracted herself by speaking in rhymes with Ashley.

"Ashley, my dear, would you bring the calculator here?"

"I can't find it. We may have lost it, I fear."

"Is that it?" Mary said, pointing to a bookshelf. "Near the book called *Jokes and Zingers?*"

In a playfully petulant pose, Ashley poked out her bottom lip. "So sorry. We'll have to count on our fingers."

Throughout the morning, Mary found herself laughing until her eyelashes grew moist with happy tears. Better that than the sad tears that threatened to sneak out every time she remembered her little sidekick would be in school next week, working hard for her "mean" teacher rather than making up silly word games with Mary.

The game made the time go faster, and a few customers even got in on the act.

"May I interest you in a literary tome?" Mary asked a man who had told her he was an English professor.

"Why, thank you. I'll need something to read after I return home."

Mary rubbed her chin with her thumb and forefinger, playing the part of a scholarly person, then handed him a volume she thought he might like. "Your rhyme is fine, but how about some iambic pentameter?"

"Thanks for the book," the gentleman said, taking the novel she offered. "I must hurry. No time to banter."

At mention of iambic pentameter, Ashley's eyebrows had drawn together. And when his final word didn't quite rhyme with the unfamiliar term, she cocked her head to one side. "Huh?"

The professor patted her on the head. "Poetic license. It's a legal way to cheat."

A lightbulb went off over Ashley's head. Still rhyming, she said, "Really? That's pretty neat."

Mary raised an eyebrow. "But not for your schoolwork."

"Right," Ashley agreed. "'Cause learning's a perk."

About an hour later, Mary gathered up her purse to go to lunch, then decided she'd better check to see if Gus's food dish had plenty of kibble. But her approach to the rear of the shop revealed that the door to the back room had been closed, cutting off access to his fishy fare.

Gus sat facing the door, his ears pricked forward in rapt attention as he stared intently at the sliver of light along the floor. He slid one furry paw under the door, then hopped back in such a comical manner that Mary couldn't withhold her laughter. Amused, she watched a little longer, wondering if he'd found yet another cricket.

A moment later, an orange blur darted beneath the door, then withdrew just as quickly.

That was no cricket. Nor could it have been a mouse or any other wild outdoor creature that might have found its way inside.

The movement repeated, and this time, Mary saw that it was a paw. An orange paw. Gus smacked at it and twitched his tail.

"Ashley?"

The girl appeared beside her as if out of thin air. How did she do that? It must be a gift of children and animals.

"Yes, ma'am?"

"Did you bring an animal into the shop?"

Ashley studied Mary closely. Apparently discerning that this was merely an inquiry and not the beginning of a scolding, she nodded in the affirmative. "That's Pumpkin. She was thirsty, so I let her come inside and have some of Gus's water and food."

Hearing his name, Gus broke his door-watching focus and looked up at the little girl.

"He doesn't mind sharing," she added.

Mary slowly opened the door and found the small orange cat that had been hanging around out back lately. The water bowl was low, and the food bowl had been licked clean.

Startled by her entrance, the little interloper dashed between Mary's legs and rocketed through the store, Gus in hot pursuit. When he caught up to her, they reversed roles, this time with Gus in the lead as they played chase around the book stacks.

"That's why I closed the door," Ashley said somberly. "Pumpkin doesn't know her inside manners yet."

Mary recalled the night she had followed the cat to the yard behind Jimmy's Hardware and found Tyson lurking around the shed. At the time, the animal had worn no collar and its ribs had jutted out sharply, camouflaged only by its thick coat of fur. Since Ashley was now referring to it by name, it was possible that someone had adopted it since that night and slipped a collar and name tag onto its neck. Her gaze followed the little orange blur and decided the name fit the cat...for the color, if not for the shape.

"We need to take her back outside," Mary suggested, "so she can go home to her family."

Ashley shook her head. "She doesn't have a family. I named her so she wouldn't feel like a complete orphan."

The girl's insight tore at Mary's heart. No pet should go through life without even a name to call its own.

A moment later, the cats tired of their play, and Ashley scooped up Pumpkin in her calm grasp. The young cat's body draped like a towel over a waiter's arm, showing Mary just how gentle and trusting the animal could be.

"I wanted to keep her, but Mom says we have all the animals we need." Ashley looked thoughtful. "She's prob'ly right."

With a maturity beyond her years, Ashley neither tried to plead her case to keep the stray, nor did she declare the unfairness of not being able to take it home with her. Instead, she carried the cat to the chair nearest the fireplace and sat down with it on her lap. A true nurturer at heart, she wrapped her arms around the juvenile kitten and began to rock.

"Pussycat, pussycat, where have you been?" she asked in a singsong chant. "Have you been to London to visit the Queen?"

Almost like a human baby, the cat laid its head against Ashley's chest and relaxed into the rhythmic rocking movements.

The scene tickled a memory in Mary's heart.

"Ashley, you won't have to worry about Pumpkin being an orphan much longer. I think I know just the right family for her."

———

After a quick phone call to make sure the potential adopter was home, Mary arrived at the small, well-tended house with Gus's carrying case in one hand and a takeout lunch from the Black & White Diner in the other. A separate bag contained some kibble and kitty treats.

The front door opened upon her approach, sparing her the dilemma of finding an extra hand with which to ring the doorbell.

"Mary! It's so good to see you. Please come in." Melody took the lunch bag from her and pushed the door open wider.

Inside the cozy living room, the hand-me-down wingback chair had been removed. In its place, the rocker swayed gently, evidence that it had been in use until a few seconds ago. A hand-knitted afghan had been draped across the arm of the chair, and a paperback mystery novel lay open, its pages facedown on the side table.

Melody looked tired and thin, but not quite as pale as before.

"You really didn't need to bring lunch. I would have been happy to make something for us." Melody opened the bag and inhaled deeply. Her eyes closed in bliss. "But I have to admit, my cooking wouldn't taste as good as this smells." She took the bag to the dining room and returned a moment later.

Mary set the carrier next to the rocker, and her young friend's gaze traveled to the mischievous orange paw that swatted at the fringe of the afghan.

"Please don't feel obligated to take her," Mary said. "If Pumpkin is not a good match for you and your husband, I'll keep her until I find the right fit."

Since many strays ended up in shelters or, worse, victims of wild predators or unfortunate encounters with car tires, she had promised Ashley she'd find Pumpkin a home. If Melody said no to taking this sweet pet, Mary had a couple of other possibilities in mind. But she really hoped this would be the cat's forever home. Something told her the two needed each other.

"This is the same kitten I saw at the bookshop the day of your sister's gardening talk." Melody sat in the rocker and leaned forward to speak to the cat in a soft tone that bordered between sympathy and baby talk. "Aw, you sweet little thing. You are such a cutie pie."

Slowly and gently, as if determined not to frighten the cat, she unlatched the door on the carrier and pushed it open.

Pumpkin accepted the invitation and stepped two front feet out of the carrier, her nose stretched forward to sniff Melody's jeans. Unlike her hyperactive explosion at the bookshop, the orange cat now gave a long stretch, then delicately launched herself onto Melody's lap.

In a gesture that seemed more automatic than calculated, Melody pulled the afghan around Pumpkin and leaned back. The rocking began, and the cat squirmed under the blanket to snuggle against her chest just as she'd done with Ashley. A rumbling purr filled the silence and touched a tender spot in Mary's heart.

Melody's eyes closed, and for a moment, it seemed as though she'd forgotten about everything else but cuddling her new feline friend. Her hands stroked the animal's furry ribs, and when she opened her eyes, concern filled them.

"She's skin and bones."

Mary nodded. "She could use some TLC."

Pumpkin chose that moment to lick Melody's wrist, as if to indicate her new owner could also use some tender loving care. Yes, this certainly seemed like the perfect match.

Melody kissed the top of Pumpkin's head. "And she needs some food to get her back up to the proper weight."

Mary told her where she had put the cat food she'd brought and suggested Melody feed small meals at first, until Pumpkin's shrunken tummy got used to having regular meals. With God's blessing, they should both gain the weight they needed for strength and good health.

Still purring loudly, the cat rose up and rubbed her face against Melody's chin, a gesture intended to show that she was claiming the young woman as her own.

Melody laughed, the sound both joyful and a bit rusty from lack of use lately. "I'll take good care of her," she promised.

Something told Mary the cat would also be taking care of Melody.

Pumpkin had found her calling.

———

It was almost four o'clock before their unexpectedly brisk business slowed enough for Mary to head over to the elementary school for the baseball trading-card show. She took a moment to give thanks for today's almost constant ringing of the cash register, then called good-bye to Ashley and Rebecca before walking the two blocks to Liberty Elementary.

The sun was making its last hurrah before summer faded, and Mary flapped the front of her sleeveless knit top to fan away the heat she'd worked up during her brisk walk. The gesture reminded her of what Betty had told her upon entering what Mary had referred to as her sister's fancy phase. "Horses sweat, men perspire, and ladies *glow*." She smiled and decided she must be glowing like a neon sign.

The sprawling brick school building brought back memories of Mary's early days in Ivy Bay. As a child, she had loved what she called the "princess tower" roof over the turreted entrance. Although her family had moved away from Cape Cod before Betty started kindergarten, Mary had plenty of opportunities to roam the school's stately grounds, play on the playground equipment, and attend "Summer Fun" classes with Betty and Henry during their vacations. She had enjoyed learning basic art techniques, pottery making, and how to make simple, child-safe recipes. Sometimes, when

Henry had taken the lead through the old school's winding halls, Mary had been slightly envious of his easy familiarity with the building. And when his teacher Hazel Pritchard had taught one of their summer classes, Mary had found herself wishing she lived here so Mrs. Pritchard could be her teacher all year long.

Mary got in the short line for the trade show and paid her three-dollar entry fee at the door. A sign at the registration desk stated one dollar from each ticket would go toward buying new base bags for the school's softball field.

The printed program indicated that vendor tables would be set up throughout the school's broad halls, and that classes would take place in the auditorium. She had missed the Card Collecting for Beginners session that would be repeated several times throughout the weekend and another on the advantages of selling cards through brick-and-mortar stores. The next, What's It Worth?, was scheduled to begin at four thirty. She pushed a hand into her pocket, and her fingers closed around the case with the Ted Williams card inside. Yes, that class would be perfect!

With twenty minutes to spare before the program began, Mary decided to roam the halls first and check out the offerings before claiming a prime seat in the auditorium. To her surprise, she actually enjoyed browsing through the cards—old and new—as well as examining books about the sport. In addition to cards, books, and card-storage supplies for collectors, most vendors also offered key chains and other inexpensive doodads decorated with team logos.

While she perused the various styles of card protectors, including one similar to the case in Mary's pocket that the seller claimed to be fireproof, a movement at the next booth caught her attention.

She turned, and a large dog looked up at her from its bed on the floor. Its elegantly tapered head featured lovely eyes rimmed in brown and a long, aristocratic nose. Its well-brushed creamy-yellow hair parted at the center of its head and flowed like silk over its long ears and down the rest of its long, lanky body.

Curious who owned the beautiful Afghan hound, Mary let her gaze wander to the vendor declaring the authenticity of a baseball card to his customer.

The vendor Roger Cline wore a baseball cap over his thin, limp hair and a long-sleeved henley shirt over his scrawny frame. A green shirt, this time. Although the building's air-conditioning blew cool air through the vents, the constant opening of the front doors resulted in a temperature that Mary found warmer than comfortable, leading her to wonder why the man persisted in wearing shirts intended for fall and winter weather. Even more curious was his unexpected appearance at this baseball lover's event. His physique was hardly what one would describe as outdoorsy or athletic, so she assumed that, as a sports enthusiast, he must fall into the category of an armchair fan as opposed to an actual participant in the game.

On the table, a hand-printed sign sat propped against a bag of doggy treats, asking that people get permission before petting Bruce. The dog's name triggered a note of familiarity in the back of Mary's mind. After a moment, she recalled the day at Susan's bakery, when the prayer group, Roger, and others from the community had gathered to help clean up after the fire. Dorothy had mentioned the landlord had a dog named Bruce.

"What a beautiful dog you have." Mary approached the table, a growing awareness taking root as she focused on the man's awkward facial features. "And what a nice surprise to find you here, Roger."

The other customer had already stepped away, but Roger ignored her comment and didn't bother to make eye contact with her. He simply turned his attention to a passerby who barely heeded Roger's offerings. When that didn't work, he tried to interest a mother and child in a starter pack of collector cards.

His uneasiness and pointed attempts to avoid talking to her raised Mary's curiosity. She already had an inkling of what was going on, but his odd behavior compelled her to stick around this booth until she flushed out some more details.

Lined up like rectangular soldiers in front of Roger, packs of cards similar to the set she'd bought for Emma were displayed in precise rows. As she leaned in to get a closer look at the cards, she finally noticed what had seemed so odd about the landlord.

In the shadows beneath the bill of his baseball cap, all that remained of the sunburn he'd received during his fishing trip the day of the fire was a small, crusty area on the bridge of his nose where the skin had peeled away. And, oddly enough, no tan. But what captured her attention was one pale-brown eyebrow that lacked the outer arch.

From her nursing days back in Boston, Mary knew that thinning eyebrows, and especially those missing the outer third of the arch, could be a sign of thyroid dysfunction. But in this man's case, only one brow showed this irregularity. Both, however, were either unnaturally short or curling in all directions.

The image of Ryan Crosby trying to light his cigar from the grill flashed through her mind. Roger's eyebrows had faded to an odd caramel color like Ryan's, and bits and pieces of the puzzle Mary had been gathering over the past couple of weeks clicked into place. The landlord, noticing her scrutiny, flashed her a nervous glance.

Had those frizzled eyebrows resulted from being too close to the fuel-soaked tinder when setting fire to the bakery? And if so, what might he have gained from torching his own building? She looked down at the program in her hand and considered the upcoming workshop that touted the benefits of selling from a brick-and-mortar store. It would take a hardened person with no regard for his victim to follow through on such an evil deed, but the payoff would have been an easy way to break the lease and set up his own shop in what Carol Bates had called a prime retail area.

The program crackled in protest under Mary's fisted grip as she recalled what Brad Overly at Ivy Bay Mutual had told Susan: "Fortunately, your landlord listened to me in time to protect his assets. I really wish you had done the same."

Interesting timing on Roger's part. How very convenient.

Mary recalled the landlord's appearance at the bakery the day after the fire. Those ineffectual strokes of the broom had not been a generous attempt to help Susan but rather an effort to find the valuable card he had dropped the previous night.

The dog, apparently deciding it was time for a snack, rose up on his hind legs in search of the treat bag on the table. Bruce's buttery-yellow hair cascaded down over his slim body and almost touched the floor. Still standing upright, he braced one paw against his owner's shoulder in a gesture that seemed almost like a human resting a hand on his buddy's shoulder, and the animal peered over the table in search of his treat. As he moved, Bruce's long golden ears swayed against his neck, reminding Mary of a woman's flowing tresses.

Before she could stop herself, a small gasp of recognition escaped her lips. "The blonde," she said, pointing at the dog.

The black car with its lights off. That was the landlord. Bruce—Roger's almost-constant companion, according to Dorothy—must have been the passenger in the black car the night of the fire. In the dim light of the streetlamps, the dog's long, carefully groomed hair had understandably led Mary to believe the getaway driver's companion had been a woman.

For the first time since she'd approached his table, Roger looked directly at her. The awareness in his squinting eyes indicated he knew she had put the rest of the puzzle pieces together.

He reached to retrieve some note cards from the table, and Bruce returned to all fours, his slender nose sniffing the table for the expected treat. When Roger stepped out of the booth area, Mary laid a hand on his arm.

"Wait. I want to ask you—"

He yanked his arm from her grasp, and the hurried motion raised his sleeve to his elbow, disclosing a healing burn on his forearm.

Time hit the Pause button while they both stood there, frozen, their eyes glued to the telltale mark. Along the length of his arm, brown hairs coiled in bizarre corkscrews in areas where they hadn't been seared off.

Her hand still clutching his sleeve, Mary looked up into defiant blue eyes filled with anger and fear. Like a wild animal wary of capture, Roger lunged past her, shoving her aside with ruthless abandon, and entered the auditorium.

Mary staggered back against the table, and the cards in their protective cases clattered from their carefully arranged stacks. Bruce, apparently disappointed that no one had followed through on his hint for a treat, shook himself until his hair rippled like waves and trotted after Roger into the auditorium.

Stunned, and a little embarrassed by what must have looked to others like a personal dispute, Mary laid a hand on her back where it had impacted the table's edge. She doubted the skin had been broken but expected a bruise would show up later.

A glance in the direction Roger had disappeared showed a sign propped on an easel by the auditorium door. A photo of Roger's face smiled from the sign, and bold lettering announced that R. G. Cline, owner of Ribbie Collectibles, was next on the agenda to speak to the crowd of avid collectors who wanted to learn tips on how to price rare cards.

Still shaken by her altercation with the landlord, Mary reached into her purse and pulled out her cell phone. Chief McArthur picked up on the second ring, and she quickly explained what had happened.

"Please come quickly," she said. "I'm not sure how long he'll stick around."

Rather than wait passively for Chief McArthur's arrival, Mary entered the auditorium where Roger held court at the podium. Bruce sat nearby, his posture erect and elegant, looking like a cross between Lady Godiva and a British castle guard.

Mary took an aisle seat on the front row where she could see and hear everything.

Roger hesitated in his description of card flaws and watched while she finished getting situated, but he quickly recovered and continued on with his lecture. When he got to the part where he cautioned that even a slight splitting of the paper at the corners could devalue a card, Mary raised her hand to ask a question.

As she expected, he ignored her and pointed to an elderly man in a wheelchair. "Did you have a question, sir?"

The man looked at the people around him, then pointed a finger at himself. "Who, me?"

Undeterred, Mary rose from her seat and raised her hand again. Again, Roger pointedly ignored her. Not to be outdone, she moved forward a few steps until she stood on the raised edge of the dais. She reached into her pocket, withdrew the card, and held it aloft for all to see.

"I have a 1939 Ted Williams rookie card," she declared loudly enough for the people on the back row to hear. "And it's protected in this high-quality Ribbie Collectibles case."

Instantly, the slight murmur of individual conversations ceased, and all eyes riveted to the card in her hand. Especially Roger's.

"I'm not a professional like yourself," she said, "but I have done a bit of research on the Internet." Still holding the card above her head like Norma Rae with a Union sign, she dragged out the moment and watched Roger's face go pale.

"Can you tell me if I'm correct in valuing this card at more than three thousand dollars?"

Roger swallowed, and his Adam's apple plunged and bobbed like a floater on Henry's fishing line.

"And is it your opinion that I should hold on to this card to let the value increase even more?" Now she played to the audience. "Or should I take advantage of this lovely trade show and perhaps sell it to another Red Sox fan?"

He stood numbly, apparently stricken mute, while the rest of the audience murmured and nodded agreement that she'd have no trouble fetching a lot of money for the rare card. Maybe more. Mary could tell Roger wanted to say something—do anything—but that she had caught him totally off guard.

Two rows back, a heavyset man in a red plaid vest stood and jabbed a beefy finger in her direction as he made a bid.

Soon a small bidding war ensued among three eager collectors who had left their seats to join the small crowd that clustered around Mary for a peek at the valuable card. When a fourth bidder joined the melee, Roger finally managed to snap out of his stupor.

He ripped the microphone off his collar and flung it aside before jumping down off the low dais. By now his color had changed from a sickly white to a vivid shade of red that matched the first bidder's vest.

"You can't sell that card!" he screamed. "It doesn't belong to you!"

Mary felt a small smile of satisfaction steal across her lips. Just as she had hoped, his extreme reaction confirmed what she had figured out the day she saw Roger's name on the receipt at the car-rental agency.

"No?" She turned back to the clamoring crowd, her gaze still trained on Roger's horrified expression. "Watch me."

Enraged, the landlord barreled toward her, pushed past the people gathered around Mary, snatched the card out of her hand, and raced toward the exit, Bruce hot on his heels.

Caught up in the crush of curious onlookers, Mary found herself swept into the hall, headed toward the exit. Just as curious as the rest, she followed them to the front of the building, where Roger and Bruce had dashed out the double doors.

The group, which had grown during its trek through the hallway, spilled out onto the manicured lawn where Roger sprawled facedown on the ground, with several of Ivy Bay's finest surrounding him. The Ted Williams card lay on the ground, apparently knocked free of his grasp when they had tackled him.

The man in the red plaid vest picked up the coveted card and handed it to Mary, then turned back to watch the unfolding drama as a determined Roger struggled to break free.

Chief McArthur bent over him, planted a knee in the middle of Roger's back, and pulled a pair of handcuffs from his belt. Nearby, a young deputy unsuccessfully tried to corral the nervous Afghan hound that kept circling the ring of officers in an attempt to get to his master.

"Bruce," Mary called. Thinking quickly, she pulled a bit of kitty kibble out of her pocket and held it out to the pacing dog. "Want a treat?"

To her relief, the animal immediately forgot what was happening with Roger and dashed toward her for the unexpected snack. She grabbed his powder-blue collar and fed him the kibble. When he nuzzled her pocket for more, she noticed the deputy had removed his belt to use as a makeshift leash. She kept Bruce preoccupied with the rest of the kitty treat until the deputy secured the belt around the dog's collar.

By this time, Chief McArthur and his officers were putting Roger in the back of a patrol car. The landlord peered over his shoulder, searching the crowd until his gaze landed on Mary. Fury blazed in his eyes, and he loudly and angrily made it perfectly clear he blamed her for his predicament. Chief McArthur pressed his hand to the top of Roger's head as he entered the car, and Roger continued glaring at Mary until the door slammed shut.

Unnerved, Mary shook her shoulders in an effort to rid herself of the negative emotions he had blasted at her.

Chief McArthur stepped away from the car and started interviewing some of the witnesses. He nodded at Mary, letting her know he'd get around to her soon.

The bidder in the red plaid vest fidgeted beside Mary. "Mind if I take another look at that card?"

She obliged and continued watching the officers as they moved through the crowd, collecting statements. The police cruiser rocked slightly. Although Mary couldn't see through the darkened rear window or hear his shouts of protest, it seemed clear that Roger was pitching a fit.

"Well, I'll be a chimpanzee's uncle." The man beside her turned the clear case over in his hands, then held it closer and squinted at the card inside. "After all that fuss over a little bitty card, you won't believe this."

SEVENTEEN

⸻◆◆⸻

Saturday afternoon a week later brought the long-awaited ice-cream-making workshop. Nicole was finishing up her midday waitressing shift and would join them as soon as she could break free.

The lecture and demonstration took place at Bailey's Ice Cream Shop, but when customers surged the shop, Tess had suggested the group finish the question-and-answer session at Mary's Mystery Bookshop across the street.

Tess and Mary had brought over their personal ice-cream makers, and Lucia Azzaro had provided gelato made in her old-fashioned, wood-sided gelato maker. The sweet lady, her words thick with an Italian accent, had refused to refer to it as an ice-cream maker, saying only true gelato like that from her homeland had ever been made in the machine. No mere ice cream for her.

Alongside the ice-cream and gelato makers, sampling spoons and cups sat on a table near the fieldstone hearth at the back of the shop. The coffee table practically groaned under the load of ice-cream recipe books that Mary had ordered at Tess's urging. Some of the books left unsold would go on the shelves for later, and Tess had offered to sell some excess books in her ice-cream shop.

With the Q&A session over, the crowd quickly dispersed. Some attendees disappeared into the stacks to find a mystery to read later while enjoying their own homemade ice cream, and a couple of stragglers clustered around Lucia to ask for travel suggestions for their upcoming trip to Venice.

"That was an amazing turnout." Tess folded one of the chairs and set it against the wall. "Who knew we'd have so many people show up the weekend after Labor Day? I credit you with getting the word out."

"Thank you," Mary said. "This whole learning-annex thing has proven to be quite an adventure."

Tess took the chair from Mary and added it to the growing stack. "You have a knack for it. Will you and Nicole be hosting workshops on a continuing basis?"

Mary stopped in the middle of folding a chair and leaned on the back of it. She contemplated the question that had been nagging at the back of her mind ever since she had agreed to partner with the sweet waitress on her clever idea.

Even without Nicole's frequent changes to the agenda and her lack of organization, the job involved a lot of time and effort—resources Mary couldn't spare while running a bookstore and remaining available to tend to her sister's needs. And, of course, participating in the prayer group. Those were three of her top priorities, and she couldn't allow anything else to interfere with any of them. Betty and the bookshop were how Mary wanted to honor God by serving others. On the other hand, because her heart was not fully in the learning-annex workshops, she couldn't see how such service—no matter how much the attendees enjoyed it— would honor Him. If it were truly her calling, she would push through whatever difficulties presented themselves, but Mary knew her calling lay elsewhere.

She lifted her shoulders in response to Tess's question. "That was the plan, but it's something I've been giving a lot of thought to lately."

They continued cleaning up, leaving only the Fire and Ice Cream for further sampling while they worked. When Tess removed the last book from the coffee table, she stood back and studied the gleaming furniture. Mary smiled, knowing what had caught her friend's attention.

"Something looks different," Tess said.

"It should. Tyson Shepard refinished it for me. He did a beautiful job with it."

"That sweet boy who was working on the rocking chair in your backyard? Wow, I'm impressed."

"*That sweet boy.*" Mary's heart swelled at the positive description of her young friend. Such a different impression than he'd given just a few weeks ago with his surly response to Susan's correction of his ten-dollar mistake. Having seen the real Tyson—the thoughtful, loving Tyson who had previously been hidden under a troubled exterior—it was now hard to believe she'd ever considered him a suspect in the fire at Sweet Susan's Bakery. Best of all, he had accompanied his sister to church last Sunday and had inquired about joining the youth group.

Lucia and the ladies who'd waylaid her wandered past and paused to see what Tess and Mary were looking at.

"Tyson said he enjoyed refinishing the rocker and this table so much that he's thinking of starting his own furniture-restoration business." Mary dipped the remaining ice cream into cups and offered them to Tess and the others. Even Lucia, who claimed mere ice cream couldn't hold a candle to her pistachio gelato recipe from the old country, eagerly dug into the chocolate-and-cayenne concoction. "If he's this good when he's just starting, imagine the kind of craftsman he'll become after more practice?"

One of the ladies, a stylish middle-aged woman who wore her hair in a spiked pixie cut, pointed her spoon at the table. "I have an old marble-topped end table in terrible condition, and I don't know a thing about furniture refinishing," she said to Mary. "I wonder if he could do anything with a piece that has a lot of scrollwork."

Her companion tilted her head as if trying to recall the piece she was talking about. "The one with the curvy legs?"

"Yeah, that's it."

Mary pulled out her cell phone and showed the woman the photo she'd taken of Melody's rocking chair. "The rungs on this rocker are pretty elaborate, but when he was done with it, you couldn't tell it had ever been a different color. He's meticulous."

Excited, the woman asked how to contact Tyson, and Mary directed her to the hardware store three doors down.

After they left, and Tess and Lucia had gone on their way, Mary flopped into one of the overstuffed chairs by the hearth. Limp with exhaustion, she let her hands hang over the arms of the cushioned chair. A moment later, kitty whiskers brushed against her dangling fingers.

Gus bounded up onto the chair and fixed his silver-blue eyes on her as if to ask why she wasn't bustling around the shop in her usual manner.

The bell rang at the front door. Mary considered dragging herself out of the chair to assist the customer, but when she heard Rebecca talking to whomever had just entered, she allowed herself to extend the break for another minute or two.

"Oh, there you are!" Nicole rounded the stacks and stood over her. "You okay? Want me to fix you some tea?"

Mary shook her head and struggled upright in her chair, and Gus jumped off her lap. "No, thank you. I'm fine. Just a little tired."

Nicole sagged her shoulders and frowned. "I'm so sorry I wasn't able to come sooner and help out. If I hadn't been scheduled to work, I would have been here."

"I know you would have," Mary said sincerely. If there was one thing she knew about Nicole, the woman did not shrink away from work.

"*Ooh*, nice coffee table!" Nicole said, easing into the reading chair opposite Mary. Before Mary could tell her about Tyson's new part-time business venture, Nicole started chattering on about her plans for their next learning annex. This time, she wanted to make it "really big!" and include a clown act.

Mary held up a hand and met her friend's gaze. "Nicole, I'm a person of my word, and I believe in following through on all my promises, even when it means putting in long hours of hard work."

"Of course you do. That's one of the reasons I wanted you as my partner in these learning-annex workshops."

Mary nodded her thanks for the validation. "The three workshops we've put on, although wonderful successes"— Nicole beamed her agreement—"required much more work than I ever bargained for."

Nicole's smile drooped. Mary hated to disappoint her, but she forced herself to continue.

"Planning for the workshops frequently involved multiple last-minute changes, and I often didn't know how many attendees to expect," she said, being careful to avoid laying blame on Nicole. "And with speakers being added after the flyers were printed, and buying supplies that I hadn't budgeted for, these workshops have turned into an expensive undertaking."

Nicole looked down at the floor. She seemed to be taking in what Mary said.

"What I'm trying to say," Mary said as gently as she could, "is that I can't continue sacrificing work that needs to be done in my own shop to help organize more of these events."

A long, quiet moment passed. An uneasy moment in which Mary wondered if Nicole might try to talk her into giving it another try. But Mary knew she couldn't give in on this matter. She'd already had a long talk with God about it and felt His leading to return her focus to the priorities that mattered most to her: running the bookshop, spending time with Betty, and participating in the weekly prayer group meetings. The priorities that were her unique calling.

Nicole took a deep breath and let it out in a long sigh. "You're right. I got so caught up in the excitement of coming up with new ideas for workshops that I didn't exactly think everything through." She leaned forward in her chair, her expression earnest. "Y'know, I'm so good at juggling plates and coffee cups and lots of customers all wanting their orders at once that I just assumed I could juggle all the details involved in putting on our learning annexes."

Mary smiled, relieved that Nicole understood where she was coming from. "You *are* good at what you do."

"Yeah," Nicole agreed. "It's like what those people said at church. Serving others is how we honor God." She brightened and sat up straighter as she reveled in her lightbulb moment. "Well, I'm already serving people every day—serving them food! So working at the diner must be my way of honoring God."

Indeed, it was. Every time Mary went into the diner, Nicole always lifted the spirits of her customers, no matter how busy she was. The young woman clearly understood what it meant to serve with a joyful heart.

"If you go by the number of regulars who insist on sitting at your tables," Mary said, rising to her feet, "I'd say you're doing an excellent job of honoring God."

Nicole stood and pushed her purse strap up on her shoulder. "I'm sorry I reached for the moon with your arms."

Mary laughed at the image that perfectly illustrated what had happened between them during their short-lived business arrangement. As a joke, she stretched one arm out and pretended to push it back to a normal length with the other.

"After giving it some thought," Nicole continued, "I've come to the conclusion that I'm much more cut out for event *attending* than event planning."

With that pronouncement, the tiny edge of smoldering tension that had gradually been growing between them finally dissolved.

Mary moved around the newly refinished coffee table and held her arms out to Nicole, who gave her a warm hug.

For a short while, like the coffee table that underwent a renewal process, their friendship had also undergone a minor buffing. But now, like the rich wood tone that gleamed under the light from the wall sconces on either side of the hearth, their relationship had deepened to a warmer hue that shone under the light of love, understanding, and forgiveness.

EIGHTEEN

◆◆◆

A shley, who had been visiting the bakery next door, nearly collided with Nicole who was on her way out.

"Pardon me," she said, then dashed over to Mary, who had joined Rebecca behind the counter. "Guess what? Mr. Crosby just gave Miss Susan a *huuuuuge* anniversary present! A belated one."

She grabbed Mary's hand and tugged.

"He said you would want to see it. C'mon!" Ashley spun around, her blonde pigtails flying, and urged Mary toward the door.

Rebecca smiled at her daughter's antics and motioned for Mary to follow Ashley. "Go ahead. The shop's in good hands."

Mary followed the girl to the bakery, where Clayton Strong and his crew hammered and their drills punctuated the air with occasional shrill whines. To the left, where the tables and display racks used to be, Susan was engaged in a serious conversation with Carol Bates. Neither seemed to notice Mary's arrival, so she left them to their discussion.

In the back, beyond the damaged pass-through window that the construction crew was working to replace, Ryan and a couple of able-bodied men maneuvered an industrial oven into its place in the kitchen. Ryan stopped what he was doing and waved to Mary.

"Yo! Get a load of this," he called, beaming broadly.

Clayton, noticing Mary and the little girl, pushed aside a tangle of electrical cords on the floor. With a hand to his waist, he presented a courtly bow, indicating it was now safe for them to pass. Each of the laborers waited until she and Ashley had picked their way past the construction area before resuming their work.

Back in the kitchen, Ryan awaited her with a proud smile. With an immense sense of relief, Mary realized he held no hard feelings against her for having shared her evidence with the police. In fact, he seemed extraordinarily pleased to see her, and he looked happy, the way he'd always been before he began venting his frustration by kicking Susan's old, malfunctioning oven.

He gestured toward the oven. "It's a beauty, isn't it? It's not brand-new, but it must be at least ten—maybe fifteen—years newer than Susan's old oven."

Mary entered the kitchen, still holding Ashley's hand lest the girl trip over the lumber scraps and paint cans that littered the floor. The men who'd been helping Ryan paused to wipe the sweat from their faces and decided to use the distraction as an opportunity to grab soft drinks.

She moved closer to examine the monster-sized oven. Unlike its very basic predecessor, this one boasted four stainless-steel-and-glass compartments. Precision controls lined a panel to the right. With twice the number of baking racks, Susan would be able to offer an even broader range of delicious desserts and still have room left over to provide sweet fares for special occasions.

"It looks like something from a spaceship," Ashley observed.

Mary squeezed her hand in agreement. "What a fantastic anniversary gift."

"*Belated* anniversary gift," Ashley said, obviously pleased to have learned a new word. Her comment reminded Mary of Susan's fear that her husband's forgetfulness might have been a sign of waning interest in their marriage.

"Yeah, belated," Ryan said, giving a tug to one of her yellow pigtails. "But if all had gone according to plan, I would have given it to Susan before our anniversary cookout."

Instead, that day he'd been hauled away in handcuffs. Mary regretted that they'd all been mistaken about this guy. Sure, he could be impulsive and sometimes a bit hotheaded, but he had a big heart full of love for Susan, the only woman in his life. And, judging by his lack of animosity toward Mary, he had an understanding heart as well.

He broke her reverie with a gentle punch to the shoulder. "Hey, whatever you're thinking, don't worry about it."

Curious, Ashley pulled one of the oven compartments open and peeked inside. "Where did you find this? I didn't even know they made them so big."

Ryan grinned and rubbed his hands together as he recalled the story. "That last time I was out here, trying to fix the piece-of-junk oven, I kind of lost my temper with it."

Ashley's eyes widened. "I remember!"

He nodded sheepishly, apparently realizing for the first time the kind of impression he must have made on the little girl. "If it frustrated me that much when I had to fix a broken part on it every couple of weeks, I knew it must have been

driving Susan right up the wall when she tried to bake in it."
He turned to Mary. "But she never showed any annoyance.
Just kept plugging away, trying to make do." Admiration
tinged his words, and his voice grew soft at the memory. "Well,
she deserves better than that. The day I ended up kicking it,
I knew I had to do something to make things better for both
of us."

He rubbed a hand across the shiny control panel on the
machine.

"I decided right then and there that I was going to buy
her another oven and put it in that same day. Have it ready
for her when she showed up for work the next morning. So I
found one for sale in Chelmsford, rented a pickup truck—"

"A black Ford," Mary interjected.

He pointed an index finger at her. "Not much gets past
you, does it? Yeah, I rented the truck because I knew our old
jalopy might not even make it as far as Plymouth."

Mary smiled and filled in the rest. "You bought the oven
from a widow named Thelma Brodbeck—also known by her
nickname as Tootsie—who used to run the Gingham and Lace
restaurant with her now-deceased husband, Gordy. And this,"
she said, gesturing toward the oven, "is what they used to bake
the dinner rolls their restaurant was famous for."

Ryan's clandestine mission, Mary had soon come to
learn, was the "private matter between Ryan and Susan" that
Chief McArthur had spoken of—the alibi that Ryan had
given the police chief and asked him to keep in confidence.
Unfortunately, that secret had caused Susan additional worry
on top of all her problems that had resulted from the fire.

Ashley sucked in her breath. "Wow, you know everything!"

Ryan nodded and passed Mary a look of admiration. "I had intended to surprise Susan with the new oven. She didn't know it, but I'd been putting a little money aside every week to pay for it. But when I got to Chelmsford, I didn't have exact measurements and didn't know if it would fit in this space," Ryan said, gesturing toward where the oven now sat, snug as cream in an éclair. "Since Tootsie was planning to go on a ten-day Caribbean cruise the next day, she told me to go back to the bakery and check the measurements, then call her after she returned from vacation and let her know if I still wanted to buy the oven."

That explained why the number on the slip of paper that Susan found in the laundry had taken Mary to a voice-mail message that indicated Tootsie was out, "having fun." As it turned out, Tootsie had just returned from her vacation when Mary tried calling that final time, a couple of days before the trading-card show.

"Congratulations on a great deal," Mary said. Personally, she thought Susan had gotten a great deal the day she married this thoughtful man. "I'm sure Susan will enjoy using it to bake her masterpieces, and I'll enjoy tasting more of her delicious treats."

Ashley bounced on her toes. "You don't have to worry. There's plenty of room in there for Miss Susan to make *lots* of cinna-lobsters."

They left Ryan and his helpers to finish installing the oven. On the way out of the kitchen, Clayton Strong offered a hand to assist them past the work-site debris.

From the front of the shop, Susan excitedly waved a sheet of paper and called for Mary to join her and Carol.

Susan swept Mary up in an exuberant hug and squeezed her tightly, the paper crinkling in her grip. "I don't know how to thank you for all you've done," she said once she'd released her.

The haggard expression Susan had worn for the past weeks was replaced by a smile so big her eyes almost disappeared into happy crescents. She turned that smile on Ashley and scooped her up into a big hug and spun her around. Ashley squealed with delight, and Susan set her back on her feet.

Mary glanced back at the construction activity behind her. "It's good to see that repairs are finally getting started."

"If it weren't for your role in exposing Roger for the criminal that he is, I would have lost everything, and he would have set up his trading-card business right here, where he could attract a lot of business from tourists passing by. This is prime real estate, and he wanted it for himself, but I had a lease. The only way he could break our contract was to break me financially." Susan reached a hand up and fluffed her hair in a saucy gesture. "Instead, I'm getting a fresh new start with a new oven. New to me, anyway."

"Roger wasn't too happy about being caught." Mary still remembered the hateful glare and ugly words he'd cast at her when Chief McArthur put him in the police car. "I'm surprised he's being so cooperative about putting the shop back in order for you."

"He didn't have much choice. Chief McArthur told him that if he didn't do the repairs quickly and compensate me for my losses, they would throw the book at him. And since Roger can't afford to pay me all at once, he's going to give me free rent for the next year." She rattled the paper she'd been holding. "And it's all right here, signed by both of us and witnessed by Bea Winslow, the notary public. Sweet Susan's Bakery is going to be here for a long, long time, and I'm even thinking of adding some exciting new additions to our menu board."

Carol beamed broadly and bumped shoulders with Susan in a show of camaraderie.

For the first time since that day Carol had accused Susan of giving her food poisoning, the woman's cheeks were pink instead of a sickly gray. And she no longer had that sour expression that made her look as if she had just smelled something unpleasant.

"Carol and I have worked out our differences," Susan continued, "and she even shared her fabulous frosting recipe with me and said I can use it here at the bakery." She tilted her head toward Carol. "It really *is* better than mine!"

Susan reached for a plastic food carrier that had been set on the windowsill and offered Mary and Ashley a cupcake from the assortment of pink, blue, yellow, and green confections.

"See for yourselves. Tell me what you think."

Mary selected a pink one with a tiny peppermint stick placed in the top at an artful angle. She removed the candy and bit into the cupcake. The fluffy frosting melted on her tongue and the peppermint tang blended perfectly with the sweetness of the cake.

Ashley dug into hers, and green frosting colored her lips. "*Mmm*, yummy!"

Mary licked the pink frosting off her own and savored it a moment longer before sharing her impression. "I didn't think frosting could get any better than yours, but this is truly remarkable."

Susan set the container of cupcakes back on the windowsill. "Carol made the cupcakes. Did you notice anything unique about them?"

Ashley looked up at Mary, a quizzical expression pulling her eyebrows together. Mary returned the look, shrugged, and lifted one hand in a gesture of surrender.

"They're gluten-free!"

"Not a speck of wheat in them," Carol piped in. She fidgeted a moment, then met Mary's gaze. "I want to thank you for calling to suggest I get tested for celiac disease. As you suspected, I had gotten sick from Susan's cupcake, but not because of food poisoning. My body just can't tolerate the gluten in wheat. That's what made me sick."

"What made you think she had celiac disease?" Susan asked.

"Well, the antacids were the first clue."

So was the bloating, but Mary wasn't about to comment on that aspect of Carol's appearance. Now that Carol knew gluten had been causing her to feel so poorly and was able to avoid it, she appeared to have tightened her belt by a notch or two.

"Then the day you had lunch with me at the Black & White Diner," she said to Carol, "you ate a sandwich and some chicken noodle soup, both of which have wheat in them. You became ill shortly after and couldn't finish your meal."

Carol nodded. "Even though I'd only had a few bites, my stomach puffed up so much it felt like I'd eaten a seven-course meal."

"The final hint was the day I saw you leave Pizzeria Rustica and head straight to the pharmacy for a bottle of medicine to calm your stomach."

After that encounter, Mary had browsed through the library's collection of medical articles until she found some entries describing celiac disease. According to recent statistics, for every one person diagnosed with gluten intolerance, eighty sufferers remain undiagnosed. Mary later shared this information with Carol in their telephone conversation. As a result, she learned, it takes an average of eleven years from the onset of symptoms until a diagnosis is made.

Like many people with gluten intolerance, Carol had received excellent care from her doctors, but since the illness frequently presented confusing symptoms, it often took time to rule out other, more serious possibilities before coming to the simple conclusion that a gluten-free diet would resolve all her symptoms.

Mary raised a silent prayer, thanking God that Carol's condition was diagnosed before it did permanent damage.

"Well, I tested positive for celiac," Carol said, confirming what Mary already knew. "Since it runs in families, my teenage nephew got tested, and he has it too."

Ashley looked worried. "Do you have to have an operation?"

Carol laughed. "No, sweetie. All I have to do is make sure I never eat anything with gluten in it, not even a crumb." Her expression darkened. "Can't even bake with flour either."

That last part saddened Mary, but she was glad to have been of help in getting the woman's condition diagnosed. And happy that the only "treatment" Carol needed for it was a strict, gluten-free diet.

Ashley tugged Mary's hand. "I should go back now. Mom might need me."

Mary nodded, and Ashley thanked Carol and Susan for the cupcake before skipping out the door. Mary watched through the bay window until her young friend disappeared into the bookshop.

Carol looked down at the floor and seemed intent on studying the scuffed surface. After a moment, she lifted her head to Susan, who waited through the uncomfortable silence.

"I'm really sorry for all the trouble I caused you," she said, shame deepening the pink hue in her cheeks. "It was stupid of me to be angry with you just because you were living my dream of running a bakery."

"That reminds me," Mary said. She patted her pocket and pulled out the notebook she'd been carrying around on the chance that she might see Carol again. "You left this at the diner the day we had lunch together."

Carol opened it and glanced at the address of the dental office she had inquired about renting for her own cupcake bakery. "I won't need this anymore. It's especially ironic now that I know I'm gluten intolerant and can't even be around flour."

She didn't look angry. Disappointed, perhaps. And maybe resolved, but her sadness seemed directed at herself rather than at Susan.

Susan started to protest, telling her that she should follow her dream—her calling—but Carol stopped her.

"Even if I didn't have this condition," she said, touching a hand to her belly, "I wouldn't have been able to open my own cupcake shop anyway. I simply don't have the finances to start up a business."

Susan helped herself to a blue cupcake, her demeanor thoughtful as she rolled a morsel of it in her mouth and savored the taste. "You can still operate your own cupcake shop," she said at last.

Carol frowned, as it seemed that Susan hadn't heard what she'd just said about her gluten intolerance and the warning to avoid touching flour, which ruled out baking.

Mary smiled, catching on to where this conversation was going, and Susan winked.

"All you have to do," Susan said, "is get a permit for a home bakery, make some more of these delicious cupcakes, and I'll sell them for you, right here at Sweet Susan's Bakery. There must be plenty of people like you and your nephew who would love to have a gluten-free dessert, and I'd like to provide it for them."

Carol's eyes grew round as she considered the possibility.

"It's a win-win proposition for both of you," Mary prompted. "What do you think?"

"I don't need to think. It's a yes!" Carol stooped to throw her arms around the shorter woman's neck.

The bell jangled over the shop door. When Mary saw that it was Chief McArthur walking through the door, she congratulated the two women on their new business deal and left them to their celebrating to join him.

On seeing Mary, Chief McArthur came to a sharp stop, snapped his heels, and saluted her. "Nice job cracking the case," he said, removing his hat. "If the bookstore thing doesn't work out for you, maybe you should consider becoming a police detective."

Mary laughed. "No, thank you. The job wouldn't afford me enough time to read. Besides, Ivy Bay already has a top-notch police chief."

"Well, thanks to your tip, we searched the car at the rental agency that had been rented to Mr. Cline. And just as you had suspected, we discovered blonde hairs in the passenger seat that matched those you found on the gate behind the bakery, as well as the Afghan hound that had been riding shotgun on the night of August 22."

Mary knew that, by themselves, the connections were merely circumstantial evidence and could not be used to convict Roger. But the discovery of the car lease and Bruce's hairs had certainly done a fine job of pointing a finger in the landlord's direction.

"What sealed the deal," he continued, "was when you flushed him out of the trading-card show with that Ted Williams rookie card. Nice call." Chief McArthur chuckled at the memory. "He was so angry with you that he implicated himself by saying you'd ruined his opportunity to set up his own business in place of the bakery. All he could talk about was his prime real estate being tied up in cupcakes and muffins when it could be put to better use as a baseball-card store."

Clayton Strong's crew interrupted with a long round of drilling, and Chief McArthur paused until they finished.

"After a bit of questioning, Cline finally admitted that he tried to make the fire look like an accident so he could run Susan out of business and establish his own shop in this building," he said, confirming what she had figured out the day of Roger's arrest.

Although his tactics were wrong, the concept made good business sense. Main Street saw plenty of automobile and foot traffic, especially during tourist season. Vacationers could impulsively stop in and pick up souvenirs from a shop that catered to their baseball interests. Mary supposed the Internet and trade shows brought in business from die-hard collectors, but a brick-and-mortar store would have targeted new customers who didn't know their way around the other venues.

"I heard you'll be going easy on Roger," she said.

Chief McArthur shook his head. "Easy on the Crosbys. Cline will serve time, but it doesn't help Susan to pile a lot of charges on her landlord, no matter how much he deserves it. So, the more he cooperates to get Susan back on her feet, the better it will look for him at sentencing. And the more strictly he goes by the book after his release, the better it will look to his parole officer."

Mary had known Chief Benjamin McArthur since her childhood summers in Ivy Bay. Even then, as a kid, he had always been good at seeing the big-picture view. And she was grateful that he was as interested in taking care of the victim in a crime as he was in putting away the perpetrator.

"Tell me something," he said, running the back of his knuckles across the midday stubble on his chin. "What made you connect the fire to Roger Cline?"

It was a couple of little things, actually. Things that had almost missed Mary's notice.

"The logos on his stationery," she said. "On his Bingle Property Rentals letterhead, the logo looks like a wooden doorknob. Later, when I received the receipt for his Ribbie Collectibles business, I noticed the tip of the baseball bat in the corner looked familiar. That's because they were both the same artwork."

"Sharp," he said, tapping his temple.

Mary didn't take credit for putting the two together. Just as when she lost something and found it after a moment of prayer, it was by the grace of God that she found the connections she'd been looking for.

"And there were the business names," she said. "Ribbie was pretty easy to figure out. It means 'run batted in.' After I figured out the logos were the same, I looked up *Bingle* and discovered it's a base hit that ends up with the hitter on first base." She laughed. "The man sure seems obsessed with baseball."

And there was one more tidbit.

"The night of the fire, Henry had noticed the burn on Roger's face and assumed he'd been fishing. Roger said he'd gone out on the *Bonnie Sarah*, which was his mispronunciation of *Buona Sera*. But in truth, Gino's boat had been out of the water for repairs during that time."

At the time, Mary hadn't made the connection between the fishing trip on the *"Bonnie Sarah"* Roger claimed to have taken the day of the fire and *Buona Sera*, Gino's fishing boat. But after uncovering the other bits of evidence, she reasoned that Roger had lied to divert attention away from the burn on his face and make them think it was a sunburn.

Chief McArthur held out his hand. "Congratulations. Once again, it was good working with you."

Mary smiled, thinking of the penance Roger had to pay that must surely hurt him far greater than any incarceration or whatever else the judge worked out for him.

"Oh, there's one more thing," she said. "That rare baseball card he dropped in the bakery the night of the fire? It was a fake."

One corner of Chief McArthur's mouth lifted in a smile at the irony.

"It's poetic justice," she said, "that the cheater got cheated."

AFTERWORD

For more information about celiac disease and gluten intolerance, please contact Gluten Intolerance Group, 31214 124th Avenue SE, Auburn, Washington 98092, phone (253) 833-6655, fax (253) 833-6675, or go to www.gluten.net.

ABOUT THE AUTHOR

In addition to her mystery writing, Carolyn Greene is a best-selling romance author. She has been nominated twice for the RITA Award, once for the HOLT Medallion Award, and was presented the Romantic Times WISH Award. Like the main character in this book, Carolyn loves books and welcomes the chance to share her faith through her occupational calling. She and her husband have two children and live in Virginia with their two hyperactive miniature pinschers.

A CONVERSATION WITH
CAROLYN GREENE

———◆◆◆———

Q: *What's your favorite vacation spot?*

A: My husband and I have recently rediscovered the natural beauty and joys of our local state parks. We used to camp out in tents, but more recently have stayed in cabins; they're bigger and more comfortable than motel rooms, cost less, and usually offer a magnificent view of the lake from our cozy little spot nestled in the woods. While on vacation, one of our favorite times is just before bedtime—after a hard day of hiking, boating, swimming, and playing—when we sit out on the screened porch with a cup of tea and listen to the night sounds. We love it so much that we're currently screening in our own porch to recreate the experience at home and provide a calm, relaxing end to our busy days.

Q: *What was something interesting or important that you learned while researching and writing this novel?*

A: It was interesting to learn how susceptible I am to the power of suggestion. Mary's hankerings for Susan's uniquely shaped cinnamon buns had me craving something sweet and cinnamon-flavored almost every day while I wrote. Her outing on the boat with Henry sent me to look at photos of the fun times my family had fishing with my father on his boat in the Chesapeake Bay. And Mary's interactions with Gus and Pumpkin had me wishing I hadn't developed an allergy to cats so I could adopt a feline friend. I'm curious to see what interesting research tidbits and cravings the next book will produce.

Q: *If you could go to Ivy Bay, which place/shop would you visit first?*

A: Definitely Bailey's Ice Cream Shop where I'd choose one of Mary's tasty concoctions. But only for dessert, after filling up on fresh local fish at Sam's Seafood (in which case, Sam's would be first). Then I'd finish everything off with a nice cup of chocolate berry tea at Sophie Mershon's Tea Shoppe. *Hmm*, it looks like the thought of Susan's cinna-lobsters has started my mouth watering for all kinds of goodies from Ivy Bay.

Q: *Do you have any pets? Have they ever helped you solve a mystery like Gus helps Mary?*

A: I have two delightfully naughty, six-pound miniature pinschers—Gracie and Lolly—who keep me company while I write, and they actually helped me find something I thought had been lost. I've always been a happy, playful kind of person, but there came a time when responsibilities and disappointments temporarily gave me a serious-minded perspective. Then I read a study that said, for good health, a person should enjoy at least a dozen belly laughs a day. A day? I couldn't remember the last time I had erupted into spontaneous giggles or dredged up even one soul-stirring belly laugh. Shortly afterward, Gracie and Lolly came into my life, supposedly to keep me company while I trained for 5K and 10K races. They loved running with me and quickly wiggled and cuddled their way into my heart. Now, when Gracie "sings" and Lolly entertains us with silly tricks that she makes up (and my husband talks to them in Scooby-Doo language), I find myself not only giggling, but laughing all the way down to my toes. I'm so grateful for my two pups who, daily, help me find the laughter.

Q: *Mary often goes to the library when sleuthing out a mystery. What's the library like in your hometown?*

A: When I first moved here, our library was so small it could fit in my modest living room. The book offerings were sparse, but the library volunteers were enthusiastic with their help and recommendations. Since then, a large, glorious new library has been built, and its enormous windows overlook a park and wooded trails in our beautiful, rural area of Virginia. Sometimes, when I need to jumpstart my writing, I'll drive over there, take a comfy chair near the window, and open my laptop for an afternoon of fiction bliss. And if I forget to check out a mystery to read before I leave for the day, I can always borrow one from home by downloading it to my e-reader.

Q: *What's your favorite type of book to read?*

A: Mysteries, with romance novels a squeaky-close second. In elementary school, I cleaned the library out of anything and everything written by Phyllis A. Whitney. The characters reminded me a little of myself, but they were smarter and more fearless. And it always amazed me how the author was able to plant a few tiny clues early in the book that helped the young sleuth solve the mystery by the end. Many years later, I was fortunate enough to meet Ms. Whitney at a writers' event and found her to be, at age eighty-eight, a lovely, feminine, classy lady who relished the opportunity to talk to other writers about her favorite passion: creating fascinating stories that readers can't put down. It is my hope and prayer that readers will enjoy the stories I write as much as I enjoy reading mysteries by my fellow authors.

Q: *Mary loves to snuggle up with a cup of tea or a quilt and read at the end of the day. How do you like to spend the quiet hours of an evening at home?*

A: Once our porch is finished, I'll be sitting out there with my honey (and the pups), listening to the cicadas, crickets, and tree toads while we savor the end of another day of God's bountiful blessings.

FIRE AND ICE CREAM

***

2 cups heavy whipping cream
1 cup milk
¼ cup cocoa powder
4 ounces sweet chocolate (bittersweet or semi)
½ cup sugar
2 teaspoons cinnamon
1 pinch salt
1 pinch cayenne
1 pinch espresso powder (instant coffee)
6 egg yolks (lightly beaten)
1 teaspoon vanilla extract

1. Heat one cup of cream in a small saucepan (one quart). Whisk in cocoa powder. Bring to a simmer. Whisk until cocoa powder is well incorporated. Remove pot from heat. Stir in chocolate until completely incorporated.
2. Put mixture into a metal bowl and add the remaining cup of cream. Set that bowl over a larger bowl half filled with ice water to help cool it down. Place a mesh sieve over the bowl with the chocolate mixture.
3. Put one cup of milk, the sugar, cinnamon, salt, cayenne, espresso powder (or instant coffee) into a saucepan and heat until steamy (not boiling), stirring to incorporate the spices and dissolve the sugar. Place egg yolks in a medium-size bowl. Slowly pour the heated milk and mixture into the egg yolks, whisking constantly so that the egg yolks are

tempered by the heated milk, but not cooked by it. Use a rubber spatula to scrape the warmed egg yolks back into the saucepan.

4. Stir the milk-egg mixture constantly over medium heat with a wooden spoon, scraping the bottom as you stir, until the mixture thickens and coats the spoon so that you can run your finger across the coating and have the coating not run. This can take anywhere from three to ten minutes, depending on how hot your burner is.

5. As soon as the mixture coats the spoon, remove it from the heat and immediately pour it over the mesh sieve into the bowl of the chocolate cream mixture. (The sieve is there to catch any curdled bits.) Stir into the cream mixture.

6. Add a teaspoon of vanilla. Let the mixture cool a bit in the ice bath and then chill in the refrigerator until completely chilled, a couple hours or overnight. Right before churning, add two tablespoons of brandy to the mix. This is an optional step, but it will help keep the ice cream from getting too icy if it is stored beyond a day. If you are planning on eating the ice cream the same day you make it, you can skip this step.

7. Churn the mixture in your ice-cream maker according to the manufacturer's instructions.

8. Store ice cream in an airtight container in your freezer for several hours before eating. The ice cream will be quite soft coming out of the ice-cream maker, but will continue to harden in your freezer. If you store it for more than a day, you may need to let it sit for a few minutes to soften before attempting to scoop it.

Yield: Makes one quart.

FROM THE GUIDEPOSTS
ARCHIVES

❖◆◆❖

"See, I have refined you, though not as silver; I have tested you in the furnace of affliction." —Isaiah 48:10 (NIV)

"There's a fire in the Gap!"

The phone call came at about ten o'clock on a Friday evening. Rushing to our porch windows we saw a dull red glow on the east side of Kern Mountain just north of where Route 211 wound up through Virginia's New Market Gap. Unusually high winds were forecast and, indeed, already blowing in from the northwest.

By midnight I was stunned to see a molten red-orange glow on our side of the ridge. By 2:00 AM, it had become a string of fiery pearls laid on the dark velvet of the mountainside. Pockets of fire glowed like suns between the black silhouettes of oak and chestnut trees.

Slowly, the fire burned its way downhill and uphill. By Saturday night it was a glowing red strand looping from north to southeast. Two hundred and fifty acres had been scorched. An old Sikorsky H-34 helicopter hauled buckets of water five miles from a farm pond and dumped them on the leading edges of the flames. From our porch, it looked like a mosquito spitting at a dragon. Yet, after two days, with the help of a Hot Shot team from California and the Park Service firefighters, the fire was contained. By Sunday night only smoldering ash was left. Our friends' homes nestled on both flanks of the mountain were safe.

Upset at the loss of acres of trees and plants, I wondered why the firefighters had not been more aggressive. Then I recalled what I'd heard on a TV program just two days before the fire: A forest fire is not all bad. Deadwood stands of blighted chestnut trees need to be burned out. The sturdier or healthier deciduous trees have thick bark; they may scorch on the outside, but they don't die. Burning pines drop their cones and the seeds nestle into the newly enriched soil. The root systems of many plants are not affected by fire burning off the tops. In a few years, healthy new growth will replace a forest grown too dense. The mountain will be better, healthier, even more beautiful. And the deer and bears and peregrine falcons will have even finer places to roam.

Lord, You burn out the deadwood in my life and plant the seeds of fresh, new growth. Thank You for Your refining fires.
—Roberta Rogers

A NOTE FROM THE EDITORS

◆◆

We hope you enjoy Secrets of Mary's Bookshop, created by the Books and Inspirational Media Division of Guideposts, a nonprofit organization. In all of our books, magazines and outreach efforts, we aim to deliver inspiration and encouragement, help you grow in your faith, and celebrate God's love in every aspect of your daily life.

Thank you for making a difference with your purchase of this book, which helps fund our many outreach programs to the military, prisons, hospitals, nursing homes and schools. To learn more, visit GuidepostsFoundation.org.

We also maintain many useful and uplifting online resources. Visit Guideposts.org to read true stories of hope and inspiration, access OurPrayer network, sign up for free newsletters, download free e-books, join our Facebook community, and follow our stimulating blogs.

To learn about other Guideposts publications, including the best-selling devotional *Daily Guideposts*, go to ShopGuideposts.org, call (800) 932-2145 or write to Guideposts, PO Box 5815, Harlan, Iowa 51593.